# SAVANNAH SECRETS

## VIGILANTES FOR JUSTICE BOOK TWO

## ALAN CHAPUT

## Author Note

While I have frequently used actual Savannah places in this story, Falcon Square, Saint Gregory's Cathedral, The Amber House and the Black Lantern restaurant are entirely fictional places.

# CHAPTER 1

*T*rey Falcon left his law office at three and paused
on the front stoop of the restored nineteenth
century mansion to survey Falcon Square.

A breeze ruffled the Spanish moss hanging like tattered
gray drapes from the ancient oaks. Foraging pigeons took
flight as a young couple settled on a bench. Nearby, two children chased sun shafts filtering through the dense tree
canopy.

As the air was unseasonably warm for September, Trey
loosened his tie. A horse-drawn carriage filled with tourists
clip-clopped on the cobblestone roadway. Another ideal fall
afternoon in historic downtown Savannah, yet his eyes
scanned the entire square looking for anything out of place.
His instincts, which had never betrayed him, warned that
something was wrong.

He massaged the back of his neck, pressing fingertips into
tight muscles. It had been an intense day of depositions and,
as usual, tomorrow would be equally brutal. He again
glanced at his watch. Five minutes after three. A couple of
hours until Father John and his daughter would arrive for

dinner. More than enough time to meet with Trokev before going home to help Patricia get ready. Meeting with Trokev, the mob boss, was more than enough to make anyone jumpy. He released a sigh.

Tonight's dinner was a big step in Patricia's recovery from last year's attack. He swallowed a shudder and the chunk of guilt that erupted whenever her battle came to mind. That was history. Today was a new start for Patricia, for both of them. Everything had to be as perfect as possible.

Trey reached inside his jacket pocket and removed his phone. A little advance support for her big night couldn't hurt.

"Hey," she greeted. "I was just thinking about you." Her voice sounded bright and self-assured. He hadn't heard much of that signature tone in the last year. Her full of life spirit had fallen prey to her trauma. Now her positive attitude appeared to be returning. A smile emerged, topping his reaction.

"I'm leaving my office for my three-thirty appointment and I thought I'd—"

"Check on me?" she inserted.

"Ah, yeah. You know me well; better than my mother. But you did toss and turn all night. Are you okay?"

When Patricia hesitated, Trey figured she might need an escape route. "You know, we don't have to do the dinner tonight. We can always postpone. Father John wouldn't mind."

"You're right, I didn't sleep all that well," Patricia said. "But, don't you know, I woke up feeling darn good. I'm enjoying getting back to cooking for guests, and I'm looking forward to a fun evening with Father John and his daughter. It's time, beyond time, to do this thing."

"I love your positive attitude," he said, glad she was taking the dinner in stride.

"I had a realization in the shower this morning after you left—I've shot people. Our enemies are the ones who should be fearful, not me."

"That's my girl." His skin bristled with pride. He glanced at his watch. "I have to go. I have one brief meeting on the way and should be home by four-thirty. I love you so much, sweetheart."

"I love you too, honey."

With a lingering grin, he stuffed the phone into his coat. Trey slipped on sunglasses and followed the slate sidewalk to the discreet parking lot adjoining his office. His Bentley sat at the back, next to Reva's car. A black SUV was parked closer to the front of the densely landscaped, private lot. Tourists, no doubt. He couldn't fault them. They were an important part of Savannah's economy, an economy his family had successfully cultivated since the eighteenth century.

First one, then three more broad-shouldered bodyguard types in dark suits, day-old beards and aviator sunglasses poured out of the SUV and approached him.

Trey's stomach clenched. He'd seen the tactic before, like a wolf pack on prey. A slug of adrenaline cannonballed into his stomach, jacking his nerves. This was no Welcome-Wagon visit. And sending four meant they weren't here to talk. He should have listened to his earlier intuition; it had never steered him wrong.

He glanced at the thick-necked thugs, opened his jacket and brought his gun hand to his underarm weapon, poised to draw on the slightest provocation. Provocation he knew was coming, he just didn't know which of them would make the first move.

As they spread out surrounding him, Trey jockeyed for position, but had no good alternative other than to back up against Reva's car. The lead tough studied Trey like a coiled cobra deciding when to strike. The man's hesitation was good. He was likely considering his options. Would the man walk? Or would he—

Suddenly, the side of Trey's neck seared with a Taser shock, then another. His torso went rigid. His legs buckled. His mind imploded, then everything went black.

# CHAPTER 2

"*D*o you mind if I bring my phone to the table?" Patricia asked.

"Not at all." Father John held their chairs as Patricia and Connie sat.

Patricia turned to Connie. "So, Connie, what have you been up to?"

Connie, Father John's daughter, glanced at her father, as if seeking permission to reply. Patricia could never get used to seeing them together, a Catholic priest and his adult daughter. But Father John had explained his mistake and redemption long ago. And if the church could forgive him for his sin, then she was obliged to do so as well.

Father John nodded at his daughter.

Connie focused her blue eyes on Patricia. "I'm doing research."

"How nice. What are you looking into?"

Connie eyed her father again.

He nodded ever so slightly.

"I'm researching the relics of Saint Gregory the Illuminator."

"Saint Gregory the Illuminator … wasn't he the one who converted Armenia to Catholicism?" Patricia asked. Thanks to Trey's fascination with Catholic history, she knew about Saint Gregory the Illuminator.

Connie scowled. "I'm actually not that interested in dead saints. I'm doing the research for my dad."

Patricia turned to Father John who was spooning mango coleslaw onto his plate to join the succulent pulled pork Patricia had made from a family recipe. "So you're the historian?"

"Just trying to find some answers for the Church," he said.

Her curiosity notched up. Father John, a papal legate, was always involved in intriguing assignments. "Sounds interesting. Can you discuss it?"

"There's not much to talk about." Father John dabbed his mouth with his napkin and sat back in his chair. "Relics attributed to Saint Gregory the Illuminator have appeared and disappeared for centuries. Some of the relics are repeatedly mentioned in encyclicals as far back as the early twelfth century. The Holy Father asked me to inventory the known relics and to locate the missing ones."

"Relics?"

"Bones. Clothing. They're quite revered."

Patricia took a sip of sweet tea. She couldn't keep her eyes from wandering to the mantel clock. It was so unlike Trey to be late without at least calling. Her voicemail and texts to him had gone unanswered. "Why did the Pope ask you to track down the saint's relics?"

"Because one of the most important of the missing relics was last seen in Savannah."

"When? Where?"

"At the start of the Second World War, a right forearm relic of Saint Gregory was sent to Saint Gregory's Cathedral here in Savannah for safekeeping. It has since disappeared."

"An arm? How bizarre." She shuddered.

"As far as I can tell, it's not a complete arm. Just a forearm and the hand. And not all the bones at that. The relics were encased in a gold box fashioned like a forearm and hand."

"You've seen it?"

"No."

"When did it disappear?"

"Don't know."

"Do you think it's still here?"

"At this point, I have no idea." Father John took a sip of sweet tea. "Patricia, you seem distracted."

"I'm sorry, John, for Trey being late. I don't know where he could possibly be. He's always so punctual."

"I don't think you should worry. Something or someone might have unexpectedly held him up."

She stared down at the Persian rug, seeing nothing, then looked up. "It's not like him. He knows how special this dinner is."

"It is special, Patricia." Father John drew his cheeks in and raised his heavy eyebrows. "I'm sure everything is okay, but if you feel differently, let me contact Chief Patrick for you."

"No. Please don't. I'm sure Trey's okay. I'm just over-reacting because ... well, I want everything to be perfect." Patricia handed Father John the bowl of barbequed pulled-pork.

"Are you sure? It wouldn't take but a moment."

Patricia shook her head. She'd been raised to be emotion-ally stable, to be a proper lady at all times. Though fear had changed her, propriety was still in place. She knew what was expected of her. And she had grown stronger.

"I understand," he said.

"I'm sure he'll be home soon." She felt foolish at being so concerned.

Two hours later, Patricia stood at the front door bidding her guests farewell.

"Do you want us to stay until Trey comes home?" Father John asked.

"I'm okay," she said, though her concern nagged her to take him up on his offer.

"Are you sure you'll be okay?" Father John asked.

"I'll be fine."

"You should call the police. Two hours overdue is really excessively late for a man as punctual and considerate as Trey."

Father John had a good point, and he would likely pester her until she agreed to call. "I'll phone them," she said.

Father John embraced her. "And, if I can be of any assistance, don't hesitate to call. I have access to considerable resources."

She gave him a firm nod. As a representative of the pope, all doors were open to him.

Father John stepped back and gazed into her eyes. "Trust the Lord ... and your weapon." He winked.

"I will." Out of instinct her hand patted her hip where her pistol was during troubled times but not tonight. "Good luck with your relic quest, John." Patricia turned to Connie. "And best of luck with your research, Connie."

Father John and Connie went to their SUV.

A nearly full moon shimmered in the cloudless, ebony sky and a light breeze cooled Patricia's face.

As soon as Father John's vehicle was out of sight, Patricia secured the front entrance and reset the security alarm. She settled at her desk and called Trey's cell. Getting no answer, she left another voicemail, "Where are you, Trey? Please, honey, call and let me know you're okay."

She phoned Trey's secretary, Reva, at home to see if she knew where Trey was. Reva confirmed Trey left at three for a meeting. She didn't know who he was seeing or where.

After speaking with Reva, Patricia considered walking over to Trey's office to see if he'd gone back there for some reason. She used to love to roam the streets of Savannah at night by herself. Back then, being on edge was a turn on, but that was then and this was now. She needed more time to ease fully back into her old self. Plus Trey would be very upset with her if she went searching for him alone at night.

Instead, Patricia phoned Chief Patrick. She'd been friends with Sean Patrick for years, long before he had risen to Chief of Police. In her volunteer activities, she often worked with him. Sure, he went by the book, but she could rely on him to check on Trey's whereabouts and get back to her promptly. Sean knew Trey and wouldn't think she was being paranoid.

"It's late, hours past his commitment, and Trey hasn't come home yet," she told Sean. "You know I wouldn't appeal to you without cause. Could you have someone go by his office and see if he or his car is there?"

"Sure 'nuff, Patricia. Happy to do that for you. But, if you don't mind, may I ask a couple of questions? Just for the record."

"Okay."

"What have you done so far to locate Trey?"

"Called repeatedly for the past three hours. Left voice-mails. Texted."

"Have you checked the hospitals?"

A chill went through her. *An accident, a car accident, how had she overlooked that?* "No, I haven't."

"That's all right. I'm sure you've a lot on your mind. I'll have someone do that as well."

"Thank you."

"Okay. I'll have someone check Trey's office and contact the hospitals. I'll get right back to you."

After the call, Patricia went up to the master bedroom. As she entered, she sensed that something was amiss. Feeling vulnerable, she went to the back of the closet, slid clothes to the side and opened the walk-in safe. She crossed to her side and removed her Kimber 45 pistol from the shelf. Simon, her bodyguard, said she didn't need to have it out as long as she stayed home. And since she only went out occasionally, she had taken to storing it in the safe. But tonight was different.

She checked the pistol to assure it was fully loaded, then hefted it. With her power to protect herself increased, her vulnerability eased. There was no doubt she'd shoot to kill any intruder who dared to invade her home. When forced to, she'd shot people before.

The phone rang.

She placed the gun on the bed and picked up the bedside phone. Caller ID identified Chief Patrick.

"Hi, Patricia. Sean here. Trey's not in any of the local hospitals, and he's not at his office nor is his car there. I alerted my officers to keep an eye out for him tonight.

"I know it's not the answer you were hoping for, but we'll keep on this all night. I want you to let me know the minute he comes home. I'm sure he'll be back by morning. If not, let me know, and I'll send someone right over to get more information."

She knew she wasn't going to get a wink of sleep until Trey came home. Her heart clenched. *Trey, oh Trey. Where are you?* "Patricia?" Sean said, pulling her out of her thoughts.

"Thank you, Sean, for everything."

Patricia called Simon and briefed him on the situation. He kindly offered to come over and stay with her until Trey came home. She didn't want to inconvenience him.

She thought about calling Trey's friend, Lucius. Heck. She could call all Trey's friends. And she could get in her car and go look for him. For what? Sean was the expert. He had plenty of police resources at his disposal. He was her best bet. Besides, Sean and Lucius were close friends. If Lucius could help in any way, Sean wouldn't hesitate to bring him in.

She wondered about calling her friend, Meredith, just to share her worry. Meredith wouldn't mind. Wasn't that what friends were for? No. Sharing worry would assume Trey was in danger, and she didn't *know* that. Not yet.

After folding the bedcover back to the foot of their bed, she put the pistol on her nightstand and sat in the chair next to the bed. Where was he? What could possibly be keeping him?

She called his cell once again, just in case, but the call went straight to voicemail. He would never turn off his phone without a good reason. She checked the *Find My Phone* app, but Trey's phone didn't show up. Then she left another voicemail. "What's going on, Trey? I love you. Call me as soon as you can. Don't worry about waking me up. I can't go to sleep in this ..." she swallowed a lump of anxiety, "empty bed. Love you."

Grabbing his pillow, she leaned back in the chair, and breathed in his distinctive pine scent. Warmth flowed. *I need to be strong. Oh, Trey. I pray you are safe and secure wherever you are tonight.*

\* \* \*

PATRICIA OPENED HER EYES. SLEEP HAD OVERCOME HER. SHE was seated, stiff, and clothed. Where was she? The chair. The pillow. The wisp of air from the ceiling fan. Her bedroom.

She bolted upright to see if Trey had returned. His side of the bed was empty. A tremor went through her. Heart thudding, she glanced at the tableside clock. Four a.m. My God, it was morning, and he still wasn't home.

# CHAPTER 3

*P*atricia, gun in hand, prowled the halls checking the other bedrooms to see if Trey was there, even though she knew he wasn't. Not even when they had the odd disagreement would Trey ever sleep in a guest room. She checked the playroom with the elaborate dollhouse. No reason to do that, but she wanted to be thorough. Disappointment hit her with each empty room. She hurried downstairs to check the sofa and, as a last resort, the garage. Defeated, she trudged back upstairs.

She rummaged her mind for something meaningful she could do right then to find him, but came up empty ... as empty as her bed. She flopped down in the chair. It promised to be a long day of concern until Trey came home. She'd wait until seven, still three hours away, then she'd call friends to see if they knew anything. She decided not to call her daughter until she had more information. No point in worrying Hayley unnecessarily. She needed to keep her inquisitive mind on her college courses.

Patricia grabbed her phone from the nightstand and punched in Meredith's number. It was early for Meredith, but not that early. Meredith, an insomniac, had never kept banker's hours. The call rolled right into voicemail. She wasn't ready to compose an elaborate message, so she simply said, "I'm up. Call me when you can."

She put the phone on the nightstand and put the gun in the drawer. She was considering calling Sean for an update when she came to her senses and realized it was way too early to call him. Five or six would be much more suitable than four. She dispensed with calling Lucius for the same reason. He'd been ill from the recent round of chemo he'd undergone to fight his lung cancer and needed his sleep. She could call Father John, but what would he know? No. Sean was the key player here. She'd call him at his office after six. She knew his routine. He'd be there.

She stood, ventured into the bathroom, and turned on the shower. While the shower warmed, she shuffled back to the bedroom. The bed was disheveled.

A cold chill skittered up her spine. *What? Why hadn't I noticed that five minutes ago?*

Patricia recalled turning the bedcovers down last night, but now the sheets were rumpled . . . and she hadn't used the bed. In all her fidgeting and phoning had she sat on the bed? She couldn't recall.

Her sense of order disturbed by the disarray, she stepped to the bedside and pulled back the top sheet to straighten it.

A huge, brown, diamond-patterned snake filled her vision.

"Eeck!" escaped her lips as both shock and surprise caused her to jump back from the bed.

The snake coiled, rattling ominously, and arched its head in defense.

Instinctively, her hand dropped to her pocket. Her gun was gone ... she'd put it in the nightstand next to the bed. Too close to the damned snake to retrieve. She bolted from the room and stumbled down the stairs, taking two at a time.

Once in the foyer, she scrambled to the wall switch, flicked on the lights, and looked up the stairs. No snake. She fumbled the front door open. Lingering night sounds of birds and insects filled the foyer.

The cool pre-dawn air sent a sobering chill through her. Her teeth chattered. A poisonous snake. In her bed. What if she'd gone to bed, rather than wait up for Trey? She cringed.

She grabbed the phone and punched in 911. Once the dispatcher, a woman with a gentle voice, came on, Patricia said, "There's a snake in the house. A rattler. Send someone. Now. Please. I'm by myself."

"A rattlesnake?"

A lump formed in her throat. "Yes. Send someone. Please."

"I'll connect you with animal control."

"I want someone to come to my home and remove the damn thing."

"Animal control will remove the snake. Please stay on the line."

"Stay on the line? There's a snake up there." The foyer suddenly seemed small and stuffy. She was caged with a deadly snake. She glanced upstairs. There was still no sign of the rattler. "I'm alone. I—"

"This is animal control," said another soft-spoken woman. "How can I help you?"

"There's a rattlesnake in my bed."

"Are you positive it's a rattlesnake?"

"I think I would know a six-foot diamondback rattler if I saw one," she said through gritted teeth.

"Six foot?"

"Look, lady, just send someone over here right now."

"Is this snake six feet long?"

14

A loud thump sounded from upstairs. She swallowed hard. "Yes, damn it. Send someone here. Now!"

"Here being 111 Falcon Square?"

"Yes."

"We'll have someone there within an hour."

"An hour? What am I supposed to do for an hour with a poisonous snake slithering around my house?"

"You could go to a neighbor's home. However, if you do go, be sure to watch for our truck to arrive."

She caught sight of her disheveled image in the foyer mirror. "I'm not going to the neighbor's at this time of the morning."

"That's your choice."

"Let me talk to your supervisor."

"She doesn't come in until eight."

"So what do I have to do to get y'all to come over right away?"

"You have to wait your turn."

Well, hell. This was going nowhere. "Thank you."

She slammed the phone on its cradle and shot another glance up the stairs.

She took the floral arrangement from the antique foyer table and opened the hinged top, revealing a Benelli 12-gauge tactical shotgun and a box of super magnum shells. She hadn't fired the shotgun in a couple of years, but that didn't mean she didn't know how to use it. If that thing even appeared at the top of the stairs, she'd stand her ground and kill it on the spot. Down here. Not up there. There was no way she was going up there to hunt it down.

After loading the gun, she closed the table lid, laid the matte black shotgun on the polished oak top, barrel pointing toward the stairs. The gun reminded her of Simon, who owned one as well. He'd know what to do. She called him.

"Snake? I'll be right there," Simon said.

She shut the front door and, with her back pressed to the cold steel, fixed her eyes on the top of the well-lit stairs. The loaded shotgun was an easy reach away.

How long had that snake been in the house with her? She was asleep in the chair in that room–had it been in the room with her all night long? *Hurry, Simon. Please hurry.*

Ten minutes later the foyer phone rang.

"You're not answering your cell," Simon said.

"It's upstairs, with the snake."

"I just wanted to let you know I'm here and coming in the back door. I didn't want to startle you."

His thoughtfulness made her want to hug him.

A click sounded from the back of the house and Simon came into the hallway dressed in fatigue cargo pants and a white T-shirt that accentuated his muscular frame. His long, scruffy hair looked like he'd just gotten up. He wore a pistol and had a black garbage bag and a pair of leather work gloves shoved in his waistband.

"Are you okay?" he asked as he walked into the foyer.

"No."

He looked around. "Where's Trey?"

"He didn't come home last night."

"Out of town?"

"No. And he didn't call. I'm concerned."

"I'm sure he's okay." He solemnly stared at her. "I see you've armed yourself."

"You too."

He patted the pistol. "I hope I don't have to use this."

"You're planning to take the snake alive?"

He gave her one of his rare smiles. "If I can. Then I'll relocate your intruder far from Falcon Square. Snakes have their place. They're good for natural balance."

He produced a flashlight and went up the stairs.

Patricia inched closer to the shotgun. Who knew what the snake's reaction would be to Simon's attempts to capture it?

Five long minutes later, Simon appeared at the top of the stairs, somber and empty-handed.

"What's worse than a snake in your bed?" he asked.

"What?" she said in a shaky voice.

"A missing snake. Call Critter-Gitters and ask them to come right over. Use my name. The snake is somewhere in the house, and it's best we find it fast." Simon headed back into the coarse darkness toward the bedroom.

She did as Simon asked and was pleasantly surprised at how helpful the Critter-Gitters' dispatcher became when she used Simon's name.

Her chest tightened as she returned the phone to the cradle. Where had the snake disappeared to? Had it left the house? There was only one set of stairs, and she hadn't seen it come down.

It hadn't left. The snake had to be hiding upstairs. A cold shiver spiraled down her spine. What if the creature had slithered into one of the return air ducts or a laundry chute? Had she left any of the chutes open? She balled her hands into fists. How did it get in?

The doorbell rang, startling her. Checking the video monitor, she saw three stone-faced, middle-aged men in black coveralls and military style buzz cuts. There was no evidence of whom they worked for. "I'll need to see identification," she said over the intercom.

One man put a photo identification card from Critter-Gitters up to the external camera.

She released the deadbolts and opened the door.

"You have a snake you want removed?" the closest man asked.

"A rattlesnake."

"Where?"

"Second floor." She pointed to the stairs. "On the left. Simon's up there."

The guy doing all the talking eyed her shotgun. "Nice weapon. Yours?"

She nodded.

"I had one just like that when I was in Special Ops. Absolutely lethal. I haven't seen one since I left the military. Didn't realize they were available to civilians." He gestured toward the Benelli. "Do you mind?"

She questioned giving a stranger her gun, but he was obviously an acquaintance of Simon's. "Not at all. It's loaded."

He picked up the shotgun. She noted he didn't check the chamber. He brought the butt to his shoulder, sighted down the hallway, and then returned the gun to the tabletop. "You can put that away. We'll take care of the rattler."

"You're pretty sure of yourself."

He smiled, then scampered up the stairs with his two buddies, shouting Simon's name.

Five minutes later, one of the varmint rustlers appeared at the top of the stairs with a writhing garbage bag that obviously contained the snake.

Her neck prickled. "Do you think there's any chance there's more?"

"Couldn't fine none but dis un," he said, descending the stairs with Simon, the other two right behind him. At the bottom of the stairs, Simon came over and handed her a red ribbon with a simple gold ring tied on it.

A chill ran up her arm as she took the ribbon. She recognized the ring, but just to make sure she read the inscription. Her eyes welled.

"Trey's?" Simon asked.

Too choked up to speak, she nodded.

She saw the confirmation on Simon's face that someone

had taken Trey. "That snake was intentionally put in your bed, probably while you were asleep."

She slipped Trey's ring on her thumb, brought her hand to her mouth, and kissed the ring. "How could that happen? I have security. The best. They'd have to know the override code to get in, wouldn't they?"

His eyes bore into hers. "There's a number of ways to get through the system, but each would require a knowledgeable person."

Her heart pounded. She looked at the ring. Her head swirled. She opened the front door. "I ... I need some air."

She stepped out and inhaled.

The varmint rustlers went out with her and put the bag into the back of their truck.

She watched the truck pull away until the taillights disappeared. If only she could make all of her problems disappear so easily.

*I will not be broken.* Not by a damn kidnapper's snake. Daddy used to say, "If someone knocks you down, get up. Get stronger. Face your enemy without fear. Protect. Defend." She returned to the foyer. "Okay, Simon," she rasped. "What do we do about this?"

"First, I'll check all possible points of entry for physical evidence, including the old tunnel in the basement. Then I'll change your security codes. Once the new codes are in, you can relax. Then I'm going home to get my gear. I'll come back and hang out here for a few days to provide you additional security. Fair enough?"

She nodded. "What about Trey?"

"We'll call the police."

"I've already done that. What else can I do?"

"You just go about your household activity as normally as possible, considering the circumstances, and let me start handling it."

"I'd like to do something. Oh God, this can't be happening. I just can't believe Trey would be kidnapped."

"I hate to say this, Patricia, but that," Simon nodded at Trey's ring, "seals the deal. Your husband has been kidnapped, and his abductors are sending you a message."

# CHAPTER 4

*H*alf an hour later, Simon returned from his home inspection and handed her a card with numbers. "Your new security code."

"How'd they get in?"

"No sign of forced entry," he said. "By the way, did you know there's a walled-in space under the basement stairs?"

"Yeah. There's nothing but an old safe in there."

"Okay. Well the house is locked up tight and you have new codes. Until things settle down you should keep your pistol with you."

"Armored vest?"

"Not yet."

Patricia nodded her understanding.

"I'm going to get my gear. I shouldn't be gone long."

"Thank you, Simon."

"That's what the Coalition pays me for."

Once he was gone, she unloaded the shotgun, returned it to its hiding place and went upstairs to remove the tainted bedcovers. She remade the bed with fresh bedding, limped to the bathroom and turned on the tub faucet. Without the comforting sight of Trey in his sleep shorts shaving at the sink, the bathroom was a desolate room of white marble and glass.

After placing the floating thermometer in the water, she adjusted the flow until the proper temperature was achieved. As the water filled, she settled into the warm tub.

Following the bath, she watched the local news while she dressed. The sensationalized stories had little relevance to her cloistered life and even less meaning to her.

So many times Trey would listen to a news story and then, using inside information, explain to her what was actually going on. She twisted the ring on her thumb, wishing she had his experience and analytical ability. She could use those skills today.

Although, whenever she would question him, he'd always told her there were things she may think she needed to know, but really didn't want to know.

By his own admission, it had taken Trey years to learn how to cope with evil. It was not something he enjoyed, nor his choice. He'd inherited the responsibilities of confronting the dark side. What little she knew about his world compounded her worries for his safety.

*Trey, honey. Where are you?*

The shocking image of Trey, bound and gagged, again took form in her mind as if it were some kind of telepathic message. She shook the image away. Where was that reassuring breeze from last night when she needed it? If she kept her mind riveted on finding Trey she wouldn't have time to dwell on the horrible alternatives.

Right at five, she called Chief Patrick on his private line. "Anything new?" she asked.

"Let me check." Moments later, he said, "I see you made a 911 call an hour ago."

"Someone left a snake in my bed with Trey's ring attached."

"Are you okay?"

"I wasn't in bed at the time. Simon came over and took the snake."

"I'm glad you're okay. Let's see, other than your 911 call, we've made no progress overnight."

"What's taking so long?"

"These situations progress at their own pace," he said in a gentle voice. "Sometimes fast. Sometimes slow."

Unshed tears welled. She dabbed her eyes. "It's maddening."

"I know, Patricia. Believe me, I know."

"I want it over. I want Trey home. Here. With me."

"We all want him home. We're doing everything we can to find him and return him to you. But the reality is that we're not having much success."

A chill of trepidation went down her spine. "What's that supposed to mean?"

"It means the case could take some time."

Her face heated. "Do more."

"We're doing everything necessary." The gentleness was gone from his voice. It was as though he was scolding her.

She caught herself holding her breath and let it out. "The FBI. Did you call in the FBI?"

"This is not a Federal case. The FBI wouldn't get involved at this time."

"I know people. People who could make it happen."

"I know the same people, Patricia, and I guarantee they wouldn't be able to bring the FBI into this case," he said in the same scolding tone.

"For Christ's sake, Sean, what the hell do I have to do to get my husband back?"

"You're doing everything you can." The gentleness had

returned, but now it felt like he was talking down to her. "Leave the rest to us. Try to calm down. And, Patricia?"

"Yes?"

"Be patient. Pushing us isn't going to bring Trey home any sooner."

"I suppose so. Do you have any clues at all?"

"None. But we're just starting to investigate."

"You'll call as soon as you get anything—night or day?"

"Of course."

She felt empty. Her best hope for finding Trey had found nothing.

She called a reporter friend, Willy Maye, at the newspaper and asked if there were any unidentified crime victims last night. He checked, said there were none, and asked why she wanted to know. She said she was calling for a friend. He was polite enough not to ask whom.

When she tried Meredith again, the call went straight to voicemail. Meredith was probably still sleeping. Patricia left another message and called her lead attorney, Isabel.

Isabel, bless her heart, offered to come over.

Patricia politely declined. It wasn't a time for company. She had too much to do.

She considered contacting a private investigator, but realized she had no idea who was good and who wasn't.

She called Trey's friend Lucius to find out if Trey was doing Coalition business, but the call rolled into voicemail. She left a message. All through this, she thought of calling Hayley, but couldn't bring herself to burden her daughter unnecessarily.

Precisely at eight, she called Trey's secretary. Anticipation mounted as the phone rang. Reva knew everything.

"Falcon Law," Reva said.

Patricia gathered herself, picturing Reva in a dark business suit with her gray hair pulled up in a bun. "Hi, Reva. Is Trey in?"

"He hasn't arrived yet, Miss Patricia. Is there a message?"

"He never came home last night."

"Oh, my. I'm shocked. Are you okay, Miss Patricia? I hope he's okay. Have you checked the hospitals?" she said with a quiver in her voice. "Perhaps——"

"I called the police last night." The hair on the back of her neck rose. "They contacted the hospitals. He wasn't there." Patricia's hand shook so much she was having trouble keeping the phone next to her ear. "It's so strange that he didn't call."

"He has a meeting later this morning. I suppose I should reschedule it."

"I suppose," Patricia said, though she didn't like the sound of that. It seemed like giving up on Trey returning any time soon, and she hadn't arrived at that point yet.

"I'm sure everything will turn out well, Miss Patricia. Oh, the police are here. Is there anything else you need?"

"No."

"If Mr. Falcon comes in or contacts me, I'll tell him to call you immediately."

After an hour of more unproductive phone calls, a detective named Jackson showed up at her door in jeans and a wrinkled white shirt. He was a couple inches taller than her, middle-aged, and average looking. The kind of guy you'd pass on the street and never notice, which probably served him well.

She led him to the kitchen.

"Would you care for coffee?"

He nodded.

"Milk? Sugar?"

"Black." He settled his thin frame at the dinette table and took out his notebook and recorder.

She handed him a mug of freshly-brewed coffee and sat across from him.

He pressed the record button. Though his head was bald, the back of his hand was in need of a shave. "September twelfth. Ten a.m. Interview with Mrs. Patricia Falcon."

Her pulse quickened. She wasn't sure what to expect, but whatever transpired was certain to be unpleasant.

"When was the last time you saw your husband?"

"Do you know something?" Patricia asked, her voice quivering. "Is he okay?"

"I don't know where you husband is, but I intend to find him. Now, when was the last time you saw your husband?"

"Yesterday morning."

The overhead light lit his face. His hard eyes fixed on hers. "Did you notice anything unusual about his behavior yesterday?"

*Unusual? Trey was anything but usual.* "Nothing at all."

"Did you contact him during the day?"

"No."

"Did he contact you?"

"He called me at three to tell me he was going to a meeting and would be home at four thirty."

"Would you say that was normal?"

"Yes indeed. Very normal. He's an extremely busy man. A hard worker. We do all our personal business before or after work. Never during."

"Has your husband received any threats lately?"

"None that I know of, but he may not have wanted to worry me, and might have kept something like that private." She clenched her jaw. Uncertainty spiked her concern.

"He routinely keeps secrets from you?"

She nodded.

The interview continued for half an hour. Trey's habits.

Identifying marks. People closest to Trey. Names of family members. When she mentioned Hayley, he asked where she was and if she had security.

"Just one final question, Mrs. Falcon."

She nodded.

"Both you and your husband have concealed carry permits. Why is that?"

She hated airing dirty laundry, but Trey's safety was at stake. "We have enemies."

"Specific people who might harm your husband?"

His question hit her like a bolt of lightning. She felt vulnerable. Her gaze traveled to the kitchen window, the yard beyond, and the church steeple above the trees. Their church. God the Father. Their protector. "I suppose."

He gestured, palms up. "Suppose?"

She pushed back a sleeve, exposing the horrific scarring on her forearm. "I know so," she mumbled.

"I'm familiar with that tragic situation, Mrs. Falcon. You acted bravely."

She pushed the sleeve down. "Thank you."

"I'd like a list of those who are potential threats to your husband."

She gave him five names: Geoff Ruby, Preston Somerset, Judy Simpson, Lee Anderson, and Tony Mercer. "I suppose there are more. But these are the ones who immediately come to mind."

Patricia thought about mentioning Trey's involvement with The Cotton Coalition. She quickly decided to honor Trey's insistence that she never, under any circumstances, reveal he was involved with the secret group. He operated in two different worlds that could never be permitted to intersect. The separation protected her from even more enemies, the hard-core criminals he was sworn to defeat.

"Do you mind if we tap your phones?" Jackson asked.

His words sucked energy from her. She closed her eyes and shook her head. What was he saying? This couldn't be happening. Tap the phone? Why? Pulse pounding in her ears, she looked up at him. "I don't understand. Why would you want to tap my phones?"

"It's just a precaution."

She shivered at the implication. "For what?"

"Someone with knowledge of your husband's where-abouts might call. If they do, I highly recommend we have a tap in place to document everything said, and possibly trace the call."

"Sure. Whatever gets Trey back safe."

"I'll need that permission to tap your phones in writing." He pushed a form across the table to her.

She signed it.

He shoved the form in a manila folder. "You know, every-thing is probably fine, but it certainly never hurts to take all the security precautions you can. Until this matter is resolved, I suggest you increase security precautions for yourself and family, lockdown your house, and stay inside."

Patricia had anticipated a wrap-up, and instead she got a warning. She thought Trey had trained the paranoia out of her, but apparently not. "Please spell out just what you're saying, Detective. What kind of danger do you believe my family is in? Have you found any clues?"

"Nothing specific, Mrs. Falcon, but until we know exactly what is going on it would be prudent to take precautions."

Jackson had included 'family.' Hayley had no security at all. Hayley was vulnerable. Hayley might be—

"This can't be happening."

"At this stage, I'm afraid we have to consider all possi-bilities."

Trey. Hayley. Danger. Whole family. People trying to do who knew what to us. *I want my family back.* Why us? Why now? She turned away, concealing her tears. "My daughter is—"

"Get your daughter to safety. Right away."

# CHAPTER 5

*H*er stomach churning with worry, Patricia paced the kitchen. She didn't know what to do with herself. Television held no interest, and she was too riled up to read. It had been a half hour since she left the urgent messages for Hayley to call. Jackson said to take precautions immediately.

Of course, there could be a perfectly acceptable explanation for Hayley's failure to answer. She might not have received the messages yet. She might be in a class or on some sort of field assignment; Hayley had mentioned attending court as part of her Criminal Justice course.

Patricia poured a cup of coffee, inhaling its aroma. Just the smell of the bitter brew made her more awake. She took the china cup to her desk, a roll-up antique she inherited from her mother, and opened her email folder. Her heart sank on finding nothing at all from Trey or Hayley.

She checked Hayley's Facebook profile and found no posts for the day. That was quite unusual for Hayley, who used Facebook like an hour-by-hour diary. A knot formed in Patricia's throat. Each minute that Hayley was unaccounted for and vulnerable pained worse than the previous one. She left additional messages on Hayley's phone, Facebook and Twitter to call home immediately. Then she sent her daughter an email with the same message. Considering the urgency, message overload seemed appropriate.

What else? None of her daughter's boarding school friends had gone to Emerald University with Hayley, but they might know how to reach her. Patricia called two of the girls without success.

Having Hayley leave Savannah to attend college in Atlanta had seemed like a good idea at the time. Patricia pressed her hand against her chest. Now, with trouble brewing, having Hayley out on her own and so far away seemed like a big mistake. If only Patricia knew someone who lived in Atlanta. Wait. The guy Hayley was seeing last summer. Shawn. Hayley said they were still friends, and that he didn't live far from campus. Patricia grabbed her purse. She had his cell phone number in her contact list.

As she paged down to Shawn's listing, her phone started playing Meredith Stanwick's distinctive ringtone, *The 1812 Overture*. So appropriate for Meredith, who had fought like a warrior to return to normal after being shot in the head last year. As a fellow *Vigilante for Justice* and her best friend, Patricia always made time for Meredith, but not today. Not with danger threatening and Hayley unaccounted for.

"Hi, Meredith," Patricia said, trying to rein in her emotions. "I need to talk with you, but could I call you back?"

"Are you okay?"

"I'll call you back in an hour or so."

"Sure, honey. Just checking in with an idea for reconstituting the *Vigilantes for Justice*. It can wait. Get back to me when you can."

Patricia loved Meredith's dedication to their now decimated group and agreed it should be rebuilt, perhaps with a broader mandate than assisting abused women. "It could be a day or two."

"No problem."

Patricia called Shawn's number. The phone rang seemingly forever, then bounced into voicemail. Her shoulders slumped. She left a message.

Moments later, Shawn called back, startling her. *Why does everyone screen their calls? What was wrong with just picking up on the first or second ring?*

"Hi, Shawn. This is Hayley Falcon's mother. I need to speak with Hayley. It's an emergency, and she's not responding to cell or text. Do you know where she might be or how else to contact her?"

"I had coffee with her this morning. She's probably studying in the library. Cell phone reception in the stacks is bad. I'd be happy to go over there and check. It won't take more than a half hour. Is everything okay?"

"We have a family emergency. I don't want to upset her, but she needs to call me immediately. And if she's not in the library, please let me know."

"No problem. I'll get right on it, Mrs. Falcon."

After disconnecting the call, she leaned back and closed her eyes. First Trey. Then Hayley. Thank God for Shawn. Well, thanking God might be premature if Hayley wasn't at the library. Patricia opened her eyes and stared at her cell phone, willing it to ring.

While she waited, Patricia called Isabel, who had the good manners to answer on the second ring. "Do you know if Trey's doing something for the enterprise?" With the phones being tapped, she couldn't mention the Cotton Coalition, but Isabel would know which enterprise.

"Honey, he's always doing something for them. Why?"

She stood and paced the library, stopping at the hall doorway. "He didn't come home last night, and he didn't call or message me. That's not like him. And someone left a snake and his wedding ring in my bed. I thought—"

"Oh dear, that's not right. Are you okay?"

Patricia put a hand on the wall to steady herself. "I'm worried sick."

"I can imagine. Have you contacted the police?"

"Yes. Last night. They haven't found anything. That's why I thought whatever is going on might have to do with enterprise business."

"Good thinking. I'll look into it and get right back to you. Oh, by the way, the state just approved the Certificate of Need for the new burn center. Your mother, bless her soul, would be proud of the work you're doing."

Patricia brushed aside a tear that hung on her cheek. She knew that old cliché: 'fate wasn't always kind' but, to her, it was a brute. It had been over a year since Mama, her bedrock of stability, had been murdered and Patricia still missed her and her loving ways very much.

"Thanks from the bottom of my heart for all you do for us, Isabel."

"My pleasure. I'll get right on this and call you back as soon as I know something."

Patricia started making a contact list of people who might know what Trey was up to. Isabel Alton was checking on Trey's activities with the Cotton Coalition. Father John seemed in the dark. Bishop Reilly would know if Trey was involved in some church business. Meredith could use her banking connections to check recent activity on Trey's credit cards. Unfortunately, Trey kept everything, even their cell phone plans, separate. Patricia put her pen down and looked out the window, wondering if Detective Jackson had checked Trey's recent cell phone activity. She sure hoped her—

Patricia's phone sounded. It was Isabel. "Hi, Patricia. I spoke with my father. He said Trey has been working on some sensitive enterprise business. Too sensitive to discuss on the phone. Could you meet us at my office to go over what Father knows?"

"Does he know where Trey is?" Her head whirled. "Is Trey okay?"

"Daddy doesn't know where Trey is or his condition, but he has some suspicions—"

Her heart raced. "Suspicions? What suspicions?"

"Patricia, honey. I know you're upset. But I can't discuss this on the phone. Can you come to my office?"

"Sure. When?"

"Right now."

"Is Trey safe?"

"We'll discuss that here."

She's barely hung up when the phone rang again. Simon's rugged face filled the display. She couldn't believe how settled she became on seeing his face. "I'm outside in the garage," he said. "I'm coming in the back with the command center gear. I didn't want to startle you."

Simon, dressed in a white polo shirt and gray slacks, entered carrying two enormous black duffels. His upper arms bulged under the load. His stony face showed no worry. As usual, he was all business.

The phone erupted with Hayley's ringtone. *Finally.* Relief washed over Patricia. "It's Hayley. I need to talk with her."

He removed his laptop and put it on the table. "I'd like to talk with her as soon as you're done."

"Hi, Hayley."

"Hi, Mom. What's up?"

"We have a problem here that could affect you. I haven't heard from Daddy since he left for work yesterday morning." Her eyes welled. "We think he's been taken. The police suggested that we ... you need to take precautions. Immediately."

"What do you mean? What's going on, Mama?"

"It's just precautionary until we know more. I want you to pack up some things, go to a hotel and don't open the door until I—"

"No," Simon said. "Let me talk to her." He held out his hand for the phone. The light from the monitor accented the scar that crossed his face.

She gave him the cell.

"Hi, Hayley. This is Simon. I'm going to call you back on my phone."

"What?" Patricia said.

"I'm not sure, but your phone may have been compromised," Simon said.

Simon rang Hayley.

"I'm sorry we have to go through this again," he said. "I guess it's the price of fame."

"I'm not famous."

"You'd be surprised," he said. Patricia watched as Simon scrolled down the digital address list on his monitor and stopped on those in Atlanta. He clicked an icon and the addresses displayed on a map. "You're at Emerald now?" he asked.

"Yes. I'm right outside the library."

"Is anyone with you?"

"Just my boyfriend, Shawn."

"Ask him to leave and to not contact you for a few days. If he asks you why, tell him your mother needs you in Savannah for some family business. Understand?"

"Why can't he contact me?"

"Hayley, we don't have time for this. Tell him to leave. Now."

"Yes, sir."

Moments later, Hayley said, "Okay. He's gone."

"How much money are you carrying?"

"About fifty dollars."

"Take it from your purse and put it in a pocket. Don't remove anything else from your purse."

"What's going on, Simon?"

"I'm going to make you disappear. But first I want to give you an address that is about a mile from where you are. Do you think you can memorize it?"

"Of course I can."

Simon told Hayley the address and asked her to repeat it back. Not surprisingly, Hayley repeated it verbatim without hesitation.

"Hayley, go to the nearest main road. One with heavy traffic. As soon as you come across a trash can, toss your purse, your books, your book bag, your laptop and your cell phone. Everything. Then hail a taxi. Take it to the south entrance to Piedmont Park. Cross to the east side of the park and get another cab. Take that cab to the address I gave you. They'll be expecting you."

"Simon, I need my things."

"Don't worry. We'll get you everything you require after you're safely tucked away."

"My classes?"

"We'll take care of those, too. I'll put your mother back on."

Patricia took the phone from Simon. "I love you, Hayley. I'm sorry you have to go through this again."

"It's a bit easier the second time, but it's just as scary. I wish Daddy had a normal job."

"He wouldn't be happy with a normal job."

"But I worry about his safety."

"We all do. That's why we take precautions. Now, make sure you do exactly what Simon told you."

"Don't worry, Mom. I understand. And Mom ... I love you."

"Love you, too." Patricia disconnected the call, then, recalling her promise to call Meredith, began to tap in her phone number.

"What are you doing?" Simon asked.

"Calling Meredith."

He shook his head. "I want you off the grid too. At least for a day or two until I get this situation figured out."

"She's expecting me to phone. She'll panic if I don't call her back. You don't know Meredith like I do."

"A call like that could compromise you. You can contact her, but don't tell her about Trey or Hayley. Just innocent chitchat. Understand?"

"You know, you're right. I'll call her back later. Right now I have to leave for a meeting."

He looked up. "You're *not* going anywhere today."

She flinched. His directness shook her. How dare he speak to her in that tone? You would have thought someone would have taught the man some manners. Still, his lack of manners didn't give her reason to respond in kind. She didn't like his rudeness, but, as a proper Southern woman, she rolled her eyes and plastered on a smile. Though totally artificial, it felt good. After all the crying and fear and worry over Trey, it felt good to have even a tad bit of control over her reactions. "Simon, I'm meeting with one of my attorneys."

He shrugged. "I don't care if it's with the Pope. No meetings today. Reschedule your attorney for next week."

"Can't do that. It's urgent."

"Who is it?"

"Isabel Alton."

"If it's so urgent, meet her here. I can clear her for visits in a couple of minutes. Call her and ask her to come over."

Patricia realized she didn't have Isabel's phone number. "Could I have my phone?"

"No. You can't make outbound calls on your phone. It's unsecure. Your calls can be compromised. Use mine. It's secured and encrypted."

"I need Isabel's phone number."

"Look it up."

She glared at him. "Simon."

He sighed, then handed her the phone.

Patricia keyed Isabel's number into Simon's phone and made arrangements for Isabel and her father to come right over.

She returned the phones to Simon, feeling imprisoned and hoping Isabel's father Lucius would bring good news— or at least good enough news that her nerves would settle.

Patricia tensed, recalling how imprisoned she had felt the last time, even with Trey around. Now she was going into solitary confinement. Well, she did have Simon, but experience told her not to expect much company from him. He was certain to have a mountain of security details to keep him busy. She grabbed her purse and headed for the front door.

"Is your gardener working today?" Simon asked before she could get out of the kitchen.

She angled her body to him. "Rhett works most days. There's always something outside that needs his attention."

Simon went to the window. "Have you seen him yet this morning?"

"I've been so busy I haven't noticed."

"So Rhett doesn't know about Trey?"

"As far as I know, he doesn't."

"Let's keep it that way for as long as we can. If Rhett asks, just tell him the increased security is an annual shake down to test everything. Oh. I'll need a list of who you expect to visit so I can check them out before they come by. Will it be the same folks as before?"

"Yes, plus a Detective Jackson."

"Did he leave a card?"

Patricia retrieved Jackson's card from her purse and gave it to Simon.

He laid it next to his laptop. "Okay. First off, I'm going to set up a tap on your house phone in case Trey's been kidnapped and the kidnapper calls you. Mind you, I'm not suggesting Trey has been kidnapped. I just want to be thorough."

"Detective Jackson is doing that, too."

Simon waved his hand dismissively. "Don't worry. My taps won't interfere with his. Totally different software than the Savannah Police. Mine uses artificial intelligence and voice recognition to accelerate the traces." He paused. "As a matter of fact, it would be a good idea if you didn't mention my taps to the good detective."

*Bureaucratic infighting.* "Why can't y'all cooperate?"

"Cooperation gains us nothing, compromises our methods, and magnifies the probability of a leak." He walked over to a duffel and unloaded electronic equipment on her dining room table.

"How long is this going to take?" Patricia asked.

"Not long."

"How long?"

As soon as he put her phone on the table, it started to ring. Simon's face went sour as he reached for the cell. He answered it, made a grimace, then handed the phone to her.

"We have a breakthrough of sorts," Chief Patrick told her. "We found blood in Trey's parking lot."

Her skin went cold. Nausea followed.

"We're running DNA tests on it."

Pressure built behind her eyes. Fear of what the blood might mean held her captive. "Blood? DNA?"

"Blood that might be Trey's or might be the blood of someone who knows where Trey is."

Patricia let out a raw wail that sounded like a wounded animal. "Trey's blood?"

"Not necessarily."

"When will you know?"

"Preliminary results within the hour."

When the call was over, Patricia turned to Simon. "There's too much going on. I can't go without a phone."

"Use your landline."

"I need my cell phone."

"I told you it may be compromised."

"Then I need a secure cell phone."

Simon let out a breath of resignation, dug through his duffle, pulled out a cell phone still in bubble wrap and handed the phone to her.

"How will people know to call this number?"

"I'll register it to your existing number."

She held up the new phone. "This is secure."

He shook his head.

"Then why—"

"Just use this phone, and don't forget to charge it."

# CHAPTER 6

*D*etective Jackson enjoyed visiting the GBI Medical Examiner's Office. Dr. Prissy Tseung was a single woman roughly his age, an exceptional examiner, easy on his eyes, and a pleasure to work with. They'd been out a few times. She was preparing to do an autopsy on his Jane Doe when he walked in.

"You doing anything after work?" he asked, pulling his stomach in.

"I'm likely to be working late."

"How late?" He ogled her beautiful face, knowing better than to drop his eyes to what he would have preferred to stare at.

"Hard to say. Could be six or seven."

"Dinner afterwards?"

"Maybe some other time."

He didn't like that she'd dodged his last few invitations, but took that as his cue to move on. He stepped closer to the autopsy table.

Jackson twitched as he studied the corpse Prissy had just positioned on the table. If he ignored the entry wound centered in the deceased woman's temple, the matted hair, and water-shriveled skin, he might say she was attractive.

The designer clothes Prissy had removed from the body suggested wealth. The emerald ring had to be worth five figures. No wedding ring. Since he'd found no identification on the woman nor anything around where she washed up, he had to wait for dental impressions, fingerprints or implants to identify her.

His fingers played with his shirt cuff as he went through his mental checklist. What had prompted her death? Theft? Not likely. The killer had left the emerald ring. Suicide? Possibly. Prissy would check for powder residue. Accident? Possibly. She might have been a bystander to a violent crime. But why would a bystander victim end up in the Savannah River with no identification. Murder? Quite likely. A professional-looking job. One shot, precisely over the central cortex, then toss the body in the river so it would be discovered well away from the crime scene, if it was found at all. From where the body came aground in Savannah, the river quickly flowed twenty miles or so into the Atlantic Ocean.

"Any other injuries?" he asked.

"Nothing significant. Just some contusions that would be consistent with banging against river pilings."

"Rocks?"

"No rocks upstream."

"Time of death?"

"Not long ago."

"Hours? Days?"

"Hours."

Jackson nodded. "I don't have any missing persons' reports that match up with her." Jackson took a closer look at the entry wound. "Large caliber?"

"Appears so."

"Plastic surgery?"

"Extensive." A smile flickered, then faded. "The very best."

"Implants?"

Prissy nodded and picked up a scalpel.

There would be ID numbers to run against the manufacturer's patient registry. The good news brought him relief. Jackson didn't need to witness the autopsy. He headed for the exit. "Text me when you get an ID."

* * *

PATRICIA REMAINED SEATED IN THE LIBRARY WHEN THE DOOR chimes pealed. Simon's lockdown procedures dictated he'd answer the door and scan the visitors for weapons before bringing them into the library.

Anticipation rose when she heard approaching footsteps in the hall. She stood, straightening her black slacks, just as Isabel Alton, tall and manly, and her father Lucius, heavily jowled and hunched over with extreme scoliosis, entered the room. Lucius, a pillar of Savannah society and one of Trey's closest friends, flashed her a smile.

Her jaw clenched. Not having seen anyone but Trey and Simon in over a year, she was shocked by Lucius' deterioration. The cancer was winning.

Patricia greeted both and ushered them to the circle of chairs where she had placed a carafe of coffee and a plate of benne wafers. She poured coffee for them and waited while Lucius sugared his. Finally, cup in hand, he settled as far back in a chair as his scoliosis would allow.

"How have you been, Lucius?" Patricia asked as nonchalantly as possible.

"I've had better days. Those infernal cancer treatments do me in. I wonder—" He took a sip. "I wonder if it's worth it."

Isabel, seated to his side, gave him a look of disbelief and then patted his hand. "Of course it's worth it, Daddy. The

43

treatments give us more time together. Time I wouldn't swap for anything."

"I suppose so." He took another sip of coffee, then put his cup down. "About this Trey business and this ...," he nodded at the door, "this tightened security. Isabel says Trey hasn't been home since yesterday morning, and that someone put a snake and Trey's wedding ring in your bed after Trey went missing."

A lump formed in her throat. Though she swallowed, the obstruction remained. She thought she had prepared for this conversation, but she wasn't ready to put Trey's absence into words. Tears welled, stinging her eyes. Too choked up to speak, she nodded.

"He went to work yesterday?" Lucius asked in a gentle voice.

"Yes," she croaked out. "Reva said he was there nearly all day."

"What time did he leave?"

"Three."

Isabel keyed a note into her smartphone.

"Have y'all been arguing?"

Patricia's head jerked up in surprise. Nerves prickled. How many times was she going to have to answer that ridiculous question? "No."

"Any threats?"

"None that I know of. But with the attorney-client privilege there's much Trey never discusses with me."

He gave her a knowing but tense smile. "Finances okay?"

"I guess. He would've ... yes."

Staring at the coffee table, he rubbed his chin. "Another woman?"

Her face burned. "No!"

Lucius took a benne wafer and nibbled on it, then swiveled his bowling ball head to her and placed his hand over his heart. "I'm truly shocked by Trey's disappearance. Lawless barbarianism like this is precisely the reason the Coalition was founded centuries ago. Rest assured we will do everything possible to find Trey, return him to you, and punish the perpetrators."

Barbarianism? What did he know ... or suspect? When she ran a hand over her face, it came back damp. She was coated in sweat. It was going to take iron resolve to get through this, and she worried she might not succeed.

"I have to be honest with you," he said in a tender voice. "At present, I'm perplexed as to his whereabouts."

Patricia flinched. She appreciated his honesty, but she was expecting more insight from him. Much more. He was as well connected as anyone in Savannah. "Isabel said you wanted to talk about Trey's recent work with the Coalition."

"You know we never discuss our activities with outsiders. We do that to protect others as much as to protect ourselves."

Since Trey's disappearance, she'd become an outsider to virtually everyone who mattered. No one trusted her. She didn't like it, but what choice did she have? "Yes. Trey has been quite clear about that."

"I've decided to make an exception today, but I'm only going to provide a minimum amount of information. Understand?"

Fearing bad news, she stiffened. "I understand ... and I appreciate your thoughtfulness."

"As you know, the Coalition does everything within its power to keep organized crime out of Savannah." His gaze flicked around the room, as if seeking assurance nobody else was listening in, then he eyed her carefully. Even though he was slumped with scoliosis and fighting cancer, his voice was firm. "We recently determined a newly arrived crime organization was setting up shop in our city. As is our customary practice, we dispatched Trey to speak with the crime boss and make him an offer to relocate."

Her heart sped up. "What kind of crime?"

"I'm not going to say. The less you know, the better. And, to tell you the truth, the nature of the criminal enterprise is probably irrelevant to Trey's disappearance."

Why was he dancing around the issue? What was he hiding? She felt like screaming at him, but showing negativity was unbecoming and certainly not courteous. As a proper lady, manners were all important.

His eyes searched her face.

Could he tell she was agitated? Goodness gracious, she hoped she wasn't that transparent.

"Are you okay?" he asked.

She wasn't about to admit to fuming. "I'm fine as I can be, considering the circumstances." She exhaled. "So ... you think the crime boss may have done something to Trey?"

He shook his head slowly. "I don't know if Trey ever made contact with him, but if Trey did, it's entirely possible the guy reacted negatively."

She knew Trey had dealt with hard-core criminals before and that some of the encounters had turned violent, but Trey had always come home promptly, and his injuries had always healed. Such was the price of peace, he'd said. She didn't like that he got hurt, but she respected his willingness to engage in the important, but dangerous, work to keep Savannah secure. "In view of Trey's possible involvement with this person, what's the next step?"

"I'll have someone else speak with the crime boss."

"And if they disappear?"

He brought the tip of his finger to his lip, his mouth a thin, granite line, and stared past her with hollow eyes. "Trust me, the next negotiator won't disappear."

"What about Trey?"

"I'll put someone from the Coalition on his case immediately. We'll find him. Meanwhile, if you need anything, anything at all, just ask Simon. He's one of our best. You can trust him completely."

"Thank you." Trey needed finding and there was no one in Savannah better equipped to find him than the Cotton Coalition. Of that she was sure.

"I'm afraid I must cut this short. We've got a lot to do." Lucius' eyes seemed far off as he pushed himself out of the chair.

She stood. "I feel much better knowing you're on this."

"You leave the worrying to me." He smiled. "You just focus on staying safe."

There was a distance in his voice that puzzled her. Concern rose. Was all the kindness he'd shown earlier an act? Had he already moved on? Or was this somehow meant to get her to stand on her own? She stiffened. Had Trey told Lucius about her paranoia and related dependency issues? Plenty of questions. No answers. She was, after all, an outsider.

After Lucius left, Patricia went upstairs, checked the windows to make sure they were still locked, and checked the bathroom and closet to make sure no one had snuck in. Assured she was safe, she closed the bedroom door and slid to the floor. Despair wrapped around her like a boa constrictor, and needful tears erupted until she was bawling uncontrollably.

* * *

AUGUSTA PAYNE ENTERED THE GRYPHON RESTAURANT feeling out of sorts. It wasn't exactly the kind of establishment a college journalism intern on a Hope Grant frequented, but her boss at the *Savannah Post* approved her using the trendy restaurant in order to set the right tone for the interview.

It wasn't hard spotting the most impressive female in the room. Plus, the woman had provided a photo. Ksenia Torva sat at a discreet table in the back. The VIP table Augusta reserved.

As Augusta approached, she could easily appreciate why some man might contribute $1,000 or more to take the beautiful, twenty-year-old Russian woman to dinner. It was a high visibility, Society section story Augusta was eager to write.

There were some aspects about the auction that bothered Augusta, but the proceeds would benefit an important, underfunded charity, the local homeless. And, if stunning Ksenia was any indication, the event was certain to raise an immense amount of money.

Ksenia, as tall, slender, and composed as a model, stood. She was taller than Augusta by at least six inches. A new experience for her as someone who had played center for Ohio University basketball. A gracious smile filled Ksenia's heart-shaped face. Perfectly aligned, snow-white teeth contrasted sharply with her glistening tan. She wore a well-tailored white silk suit.

Augusta, feeling shabby in khakis and a wrinkled blue L.L.Bean blouse, extended her hand. "Thank you for agreeing to this interview, Miss Torva."

"My pleasure." She flipped her long, blond hair behind her shoulders. "Please, call me Ksenia."

"Ksenia it is. I go by Augusta."

Ksenia's brown eyes sparkled. "Augusta. What a beautiful name. Do you mind if I ask what it means?"

"It's derived from a Latin word that translates to 'great.'"

Ksenia's eyes widened. "Well then, it's *great* to meet you, Augusta."

Augusta gestured to the chairs and they sat. After a moment of silence while the reporter removed her notebook and digital recorder, Ksenia fluttered her false eyelashes. "How can I assist you?"

Augusta wondered what the fluttering eyelids meant, but not enough to interrupt the preliminaries. "Would you mind if I record this? I wouldn't want to misrepresent you."

When the woman nodded, her hair bounced on her shoulders. "Not at all. I appreciate your thoroughness. It's a nice trait." She smiled again. "I like thoroughness in people."

Augusta turned on the recorder and picked up her pen. "How long have you been in Savannah?"

The woman fixed her doe eyes on Augusta's. "I arrived a month ago to set up the auction. I've really enjoyed my time in your beautiful city. Everyone I've met is so very charming and thoughtful."

"You're from Russia?"

She nodded.

"What do you do there?"

"Student. Majoring in History of Religion. I plan to do graduate work in early Christianity, specifically relic cults."

"Graduate work in Christianity in a Russian university?"

"Oh yes. We're quite progressive."

Augusta didn't buy Ksenia's answer, but decided to circumnavigate the issue. "What exactly do you mean by relic cults?"

"People who venerate bones and personal effects of religiously important dead people. The Shroud of Turin is a well-known relic that many people venerate."

"How did you become interested in that subject?"

"Curiosity. It seemed unusual to me when I first heard of it. I wondered why it was accepted in modern society. One thing led to another."

49

"They have a course on religious relics at your university?"

"No. I used the internet."

"What drew you to study Christianity?"

Ksenia frowned. "I don't understand what this has to do with the gala."

"Just background information." Augusta fiddled with her pen. "Our readers want to get to know the person behind the story. By the way, you speak English very well."

The corners of Ksenia's heart-shaped mouth turned up, as if happy for the change of subject. "My parents made sure I attended American schools in Russia."

"Where in Russia?" There was something odd about this too-perfect woman. Something out of reach, hidden in the shadows. A look. A tone. Something not perfect.

"I've lived all my life in Saint Petersburg."

"Ah. The Amber Room," Augusta said, pleased she'd remembered. "A room made completely of amber."

Ksenia tilted her head to the side. "You've been to the Catherine Palace?"

"No. I'm a fan of Steve Berry, an American author who wrote a novel about the disappearance of the Amber Room during the Second World War. I interviewed him a couple of times."

"I've read the book. It was excellent." She gave an impish grin. "I would like to meet Mr. Berry someday."

"He lives in Saint Augustine, Florida. Just a couple of hours south of here. I'll see if I can arrange a meeting for you."

Ksenia straightened her shoulders and lifted her chin. Her eyes shone with new respect. "I'd be most grateful if you could do that."

"Was the idea of this charity auction yours?"

"No. I and the other girls were approached in Russia by an organizer."

"Someone from here?"

Ksenia covered her mouth with her fingertips and glanced at the ceiling for a moment. "I think he was Russian. It was all done by mail. An address in Moscow. I signed a contract and received instructions."

"Why did you agree to do this?"

"The pay is good and the climate is ideal. Winter is coming to Saint Petersburg."

"The auction started last week and will conclude a week from today at the gala. How is the bidding going so far?"

"I'm not permitted to say."

"I've heard that bids on one woman have already exceeded $5,000. Can you confirm that?"

"No."

"That's a lot of money. It would have to be a very special date."

Ksenia lowered her eyes and nodded.

"Sex?" Augusta asked.

Ksenia's smile dropped. Her gaze flitted to the recorder, then back. "Oh no. Nothing like that."

"I didn't mean to—"

Ksenia waved her hand. "Not to worry. It's a common misunderstanding."

"Will you be leaving Savannah once the auction is over?"

She looked up, her face serious. "I've made many friends here, and I've grown fond of the city and, of course, the climate. I'm making arrangements to extend my visa."

"Really? Will you be pursuing your graduate studies here?"

"Um. I don't think so. Not immediately."

"What exactly would you do?"

"I'd like to set up an import/export business."

"Retail?"

"I think wholesale to start."

"What kind of goods?"

"Religious antiques. I've heard Savannah is a good market for antiques."

"Sounds fascinating." Augusta consulted her watch. "I want to thank you, Ksenia, for being so helpful. I'll definitely get back in touch with you, minimally to set up the meeting with Mr. Berry." Augusta offered her business card.

Ksenia studied the card, then put it in her handbag. "I'm all out of cards, but don't hesitate to call me if you need additional information about our auction. The more people who participate and attend the gala, the more money will go to the homeless. And I can't wait to meet Mr. Berry."

Augusta left, relishing the idea of writing the auction story. Her first story for a big city paper. She hoped the first of many. And the relic angle fascinated her, though she had a hunch all was not as it seemed. Why would a student who seemed so driven suddenly put her education on hold?

# CHAPTER 7

*W*hen Detective Jackson's phone vibrated with a new text message, he put down the hot coffee and read: *Jane Doe is Allison Hope. Details on your desk. Prissy.*

Like a bass fisherman who'd just hooked a trophy fish, excitement built. A name was a big step forward. He threw a tip on the table, paid the check and headed outside. Though it was unseasonably hot for September, a breeze and dense shade provided some relief. He slipped on sunglasses and walked purposely down the block toward his vehicle.

Allison Hope? Why was her name familiar? Hope? He didn't know any Hopes.

Once in his car, he used his dash-mounted computer to log into the criminal records database and found nothing on Miss Hope. He'd do a more thorough check once he got to the office.

He keyed the engine and, preoccupied with questions about Ms. Hope, nearly sideswiped an Escalade while pulling into traffic. He jammed on the brakes to let the SUV pass.

What kind of car did Miss Hope drive? Based on her clothing, she could have driven any car she wished. So, why was her name so familiar? He didn't travel in those circles, not that he wanted to.

He parked in the lot next to the Justice Center. The dead lady was high cotton. No doubt about that. So, how did a hot-looking, rich woman end up on a slab without anyone missing her?

Could Miss Hope have been a local business executive? Yeah, that worked, too. And it would explain the familiarity of her name. When he'd worked a commercial fraud unit a while back, he came into contact with a lot of business-women. A few seemed hungry for a man, but came across as fearful about entering into a relationship, apparently fearing that some men wanted to fondle their bank account not their breasts.

He learned more about fearful women after spending a few wild weekends with Shelby Georgia, a hard-nosed exec-utive who coordinated private investor relations for Coe Somerset. He wondered if he should call her. His cell phone would melt in his hand once he heard her sultry voice. No. Not today.

Jackson stepped from his car and made his way toward the Justice Center. A mother and daughter in matching yellow sundresses approached. The little girl skipped with the energy only a child could possess. He gave them a broad smile as they passed, feeling proud he was able to help make their part of the world safer. He went up the Justice Center steps, passed through security and headed to the elevators.

His phone vibrated. He glanced at the display and read the text message from Chief Patrick: *How's my Falcon case going?*

Jackson's nerves prickled. The Falcon case was going nowhere. In his book, murder trumped a missing person case, but not in the chief's book. Not when the missing person was one of the chief's fat cat supporters. The old man had made it crystal clear from the beginning; the Falcon case was *the* top priority. Miss Hope wasn't in a position to complain if Mr. Falcon got Jackson's attention, and apparently no one missed her either.

Jackson sat at his desk and, out of curiosity, pulled Prissy's report on Ms. Hope over to scan. It would only take a moment and wouldn't distract him from the Falcon case. Just a bit of temporary closure on the Hope case.

Oh hell. The DMV photo. Full makeup. A sexy hairdo. Not a dead, shriveled face with matted hair. Like a bloodhound on a fresh trail, his senses alerted and his pulse sped. He knew this woman. She was a high-priced escort, so well connected that no one in the prosecutor's office was ever able to initiate a case against her. Rumor was that she had slept with everyone in Savannah's Justice Department who could afford her. At $2,500 a night that wasn't many, but it would certainly include the chosen few at the top. He'd seen Bobby Gilbert, the DA, with her several times.

Shaking his head, he closed the folder. No one important in the Justice Department was going to want Allison Hope's murder investigated, though they probably wanted her client list found and destroyed.

He dug through the towering pile of his pending cases and found the Falcon file. He called the legal department and asked a staff law clerk to draw up papers to subpoena Trey Falcon's cell phone, office phone and credit card records. Then he contacted the interagency guy at TSA and asked to see if Trey's name was listed on any outbound flights. He made the same request from passport control at Immigration and included sailings. If all went smoothly, in twenty-four hours he'd be buried in reports.

\* \* \*

Augusta turned the auction story over to her mentor at the _Savannah Post_, Willy Maye, who spent a half hour showing her how to energize her story with stronger verbs. Vivid writing was something her Ohio University professors told her she excelled at, but apparently not enough for Willy.

After she made the changes, he accepted the story. He'd said there was no guarantee the story would run, but it was likely.

When he asked her if she had any other story ideas, specifically subjects truly unique and broadly interesting, she replied, "Relic cults."

His jaw muscle clenched as he studied her, stretching the silence.

The urge to say something pressed hard. Anxiety crept over her.

"I don't like the sound of cults," he said, pointedly. "Too dark. People still remember the Jonestown Massacre."

Feeling like a rebuked child, she drew back. Too dark? What the hell was he talking about? A spark of defiance ignited. She wasn't going to let his ignorance get in the way of a good story. But how did a lowly intern correct her mentor? Should she even try? Maybe he was testing her. No question he was wrong. No question she should speak up.

Her mouth was bone-dry, and she feared her voice would come out weak. "It's not that kind of cult," she said in a strangled voice. "I'm talking about _relic_ cults."

He looked at her hard. "Enlighten me."

"They're people who venerate bones of dead religious icons. It's an accepted practice in the Catholic Church."

"If the veneration of bones is an accepted practice, where's the news story?"

"Voodoo." She paused for effect. "Local voodoo."

"Forget it." He folded his hands. "That's just rumor. Ever since that damn movie, _Midnight in the Garden of Good and_

*Evil,* everyone in Savannah thinks there are witch doctors holed up in their neighborhood. The tourists love it, that and the ghost stories. But I tell you this, ain't a word of truth in any of 'em."

"If I can find a local relic cult practicing voodoo and prove it, would you be interested?" she said, trying to keep the edge from her voice.

"Of course, but you're wasting your time. And good reporters don't have time to waste."

"Well, I could always write about booty clubs." She made quote marks with her fingers. "Sin and Sex in Savannah."

"Not in this city, Missy." He gave her a big smile. "Don't even think about it."

* * *

JACKSON LEANED BACK IN HIS OFFICE CHAIR AND REMOVED THE enemies list Mrs. Falcon had provided from his pocket. Five names. He recognized two: socialite Judy Simpson, an escaped felon, and attorney Preston Somerset, the brother of Coe Somerset, the prominent developer.

He wondered why Preston was on the list. Both Somerset and Falcon were successful attorneys and were, no doubt, members of the same private clubs. Even if they had faced off in a contentious case, becoming enemies was a stretch. Any attorney with ambition knew how to move on after defeat. He'd talk to Mr. Somerset and get his side of the story tomorrow.

Jackson ran the remaining three names through the criminal records database. Two names, Anderson and Mercer, came back dirty. Both were felons with weapons charges. Both had been represented by Falcon, and both had been convicted and served their jail terms.

Mercer had served ten years and lost his family.

Anderson had killed another inmate when several prisoners had tried to gang rape him for the second time. He was found not guilty on the grounds of self-defense. Anderson was a wounded, changed man.

These two felons had motive, means, and probably had opportunity to do great bodily harm to Falcon. He'd visit each of them.

He ran the third name, Geoff Ruby, through the newspaper archives and pulled several hits. Ruby was a real estate developer. One story about Falcon suing Ruby drew Jackson's attention. The story was light on facts, so Jackson checked online court records.

A few clicks revealed several civil suits against Ruby initiated by Falcon, and some high six-figure judgments for Falcon that could have put Ruby in bankruptcy. Another click and there it was on the screen - Ruby filed for bankruptcy last year.

The man had motive and probably had opportunity, but there was nothing in the records to indicate that he was violent. Not even a parking ticket. Jackson would work Ruby into tomorrow's bulging schedule.

Next on Jackson's 'to do' list was Falcon's vehicle, a late model Bentley. The drive-by on the night Mr. Falcon was reported missing indicated Falcon's car wasn't at his office. Someone moved the Bentley from the office parking lot.

Though the plates had been on the BOLO alert list since the call to the chief, the vehicle was still missing. It was time to scour parking lots, starting with the airport. A Bentley would be easy to spot.

Did Falcon have surveillance cameras in his office parking lot? Unfortunately most downtown businesses found them necessary. He'd ask Falcon's secretary when he met with her again.

And so it went for what little remained of the afternoon;

sorting through crap, making decisions, and booking interviews. Shortly before five, Jackson sent the chief an update.

* * *

CHIEF PATRICK CALLED PATRICIA AT SIX AND FILLED HER IN ON what Detective Jackson was doing. Patricia was impressed. Jackson seemed to be doing everything possible, though what did she know about police work? Still, if Sean had faith in the man, she did as well. But faith could only do so much, and fear for Trey's safety still consumed her. Time was the enemy.

After picking at dinner, Patricia sat at her desk trying to figure out names for the enemies list.

Frustration crept into every part of her being, seizing control. She'd had it. There was too much negativity. All the focusing on people who hated her husband, on home invaders and potential kidnappers, was about to push her back into all-encompassing paranoia. Every name she came up with was like a kick in the gut, pushing her closer and closer to the edge. She shivered, unsure of how much additional negativity she could take. She added a few names to the list, then gave up.

She supposed Simon and the authorities had to focus on the possibility of something horrible happening to Trey. That was how they did their work and it was where their expertise lay. But she didn't have to think negatively. There was always a positive aspect. And, right now, focusing on the positive would be far better for her mental state.

Hayley was safely tucked away, far from harm. Patricia tried to imagine Trey on a beach in Tahiti, negotiating with the Russian crime boss over pina coladas. It was ridiculous, but it made her laugh and laughing felt good.

The Coalition hounds were on the hunt. It was only a

matter of time before they'd pick up a trail that would lead to Trey. Everything that could be done was being done. *Thank you, Lord.*

Patricia's phone erupted. Not a familiar ringtone. She glanced at the display as the phone went off again. Detective Jackson.

"Hi, Patricia," he said. "I just want to give you an update. That blood we found in the parking lot—"

Her phone beeped, then died. Damn battery. Aghh.

CHAPTER 8

*P*atricia sat at the kitchen table, desperately thumbing through the *Savannah Post* looking for clues about Trey's disappearance. Something someone may have missed. A clue. A connection. The leads she had given to Jackson had gone nowhere, and the blood in the parking lot had proven useless.

Morning sun bled through the plantation shutters, highlighting a headline on page three, sending a violent shiver through her, shaking her to her core. Her friend Allison Hope had been murdered. Murdered? Patricia closed her eyes against the news.

She'd just seen Allison last week at the Historical Society gala. They'd spoken at length about plans for the holidays. Dear, gracious Allison. A ready smile for everyone. Kind to a fault. Land's sake, why would anyone want to hurt her?

Allison was sweet and kind to her. But Allison had fallen into the wrong business, and Patricia couldn't condone that.

Patricia racked her mind trying to recall what she knew of Allison's family and came up empty. As much as she dreaded seeing the details of Allison's murder, she scanned the article looking for funeral and next-of-kin information. Finding none, she checked the obits. Nothing there either. Had Allison died without family? Patricia made a digital note to check further, intending to handle Allison's burial if there was no family to do so.

Paging in the newspaper, her eye was drawn to a photo of five Russian women who were auctioning dates to benefit the homeless. Her initial reaction was positive. The auction benefited charity. How could *that* be bad?

But the more she thought about the auction, the more indignant she became. Was sex involved? Prostitution? In Savannah? According to the reporter, the young lady interviewed for the article said no. Allison had repeatedly told her the same thing. But, short of going along on the date, how would anyone really know? How weird that Allison was murdered and, shortly after, a new bevy of beauties arrived.

There were photos and names for each of the women. They were all gorgeous. Certainly worth the thousands of dollars men were reportedly bidding for dates with them. But still, transporting Russian women to Savannah and selling dates for a charitable contribution seemed alarmingly close to prostitution.

She'd call Willy Maye and ask him what was up with his newspaper promoting prostitution. She chuckled. *That* would set him off. She liked Willy a lot. Rather than calling him, they could have lunch and talk about the story. Besides, as an investigative reporter he might have some ideas on what Trey might have been doing lately. Lunch with Willy. Yeah. She needed to do something proactive. She swallowed. No. That was impossible. Simon had her on lockdown. Damn.

Speaking of the devil, Simon came into the kitchen. He was dressed in a pale blue polo shirt and jeans. A flat-black, holstered pistol hung at his side. His long, dark hair was disheveled. He'd stayed on duty all night, which she appreciated immensely.

"Did you get any sleep?" she asked.

He massaged his neck. "Enough, but I'll have someone else take the night shift from now on. By the way, do you have shells chambered in your shotgun?"

A chill went through her. "No."

"Do it."

"Okay." She returned her attention to the newspaper.

"Now!"

"I won't have you talking to me in that tone." The sledgehammer words were as measured and as acidic as she could make them. "Do you understand?"

"I'm sorry," he whispered. His face seemed sincere. His unbelievably sad eyes, fixed on hers, held no deceit.

In all the time he'd been her bodyguard, he'd never apologized. Wondering why now, she nodded. "I 'ppreciate that. I truly do."

"It won't happen again."

"I know." She gave him a smile. "Let's go load up that shotgun."

In the foyer, Patricia removed the flowers from the table, lifted the lid, and took out the 12-gauge shotgun. She opened a box of shells, placed two in the chamber, and returned the shotgun to its hiding place. "Happy?" she asked.

"Yeah. Have you ever used a shotgun?"

"Sure have."

"Recently?"

"A couple of years ago."

"Skeet?"

"Yes. By the way, when are you going to let me go out?" she asked as they returned to the kitchen.

"Soon." He crossed to the fridge and filled his glass with

water. Simon drank coffee, not water. She glanced at the half-filled pot simmering on the coffee maker.

"How soon?"

He turned toward her, his face expressionless. "Today, depending on where you want to go."

"I'd like to go out for lunch. I'm getting tired of take-out."

He popped a handful of pills in to his mouth and took a long gulp of water. "Dining alone, or were you planning on joining someone?"

Willy's name came to mind, but she'd rather spend time with her closest friend. "Meredith."

"Stanwick?" He put the glass in the dishwasher and took a mug from the cabinet.

She nodded.

"You won't discuss Trey with her, not a peep?"

"She's my best friend."

"Discussing Trey's situation with anyone beyond the authorities and the Coalition could create problems for us and possibly for Trey."

"What kind of problems?"

He shook his head. "Just find something else to discuss with Meredith. Okay?"

"All right. Can I borrow your phone?"

"Where's yours?"

"It's charging."

He handed her his phone.

Patricia made the arrangements and returned the phone.

"So, Simon. Why the change in letting me go out?"

He filled his mug, then shoveled in three spoons of sugar. Simon took his coffee black. "Since we haven't heard from the abductors, I'm beginning to think this might not be a kidnapping."

"What do you mean? Do you think Trey's dead?" She shivered. "Killed?"

He took a sip of the coffee, then added two more spoons of sugar. Was he making coffee or dessert? "I really don't know, but if this were a kidnapping we'd be hearing from the kidnappers ... and we haven't."

"If not kidnapping, then what?"

He shook his head. "I wish I knew."

She wished he shared more information, but understood that he wouldn't. "What do we do?"

"Me, I have the easy job. I keep digging. You have the hard job. You keep waiting."

"I have to do something." She crossed to the coffee maker and poured herself a cup. "Anything."

He frowned. "I don't mean to be harsh, but there's nothing for you to do."

"There's got to be—"

"No," he said sharply. "Believe me, there's absolutely nothing for you to do but wait."

\* \* \*

DETECTIVE JACKSON ENTERED THE FALCON LAW OFFICE. A receptionist with auburn-colored hair and curves that should be illegal showed him to a luxurious conference room. Reva Williams, Trey Falcon's secretary, was already there. Though attractive, she was older, thicker, and dressed much more conservatively than the receptionist. Her curly hair was the same color as the receptionist's. Did they use the same hairdresser?

After they exchanged greetings, Reva stepped to the credenza, poured coffee for them, and handed a cup to him. While she added milk and sugar to hers, he looked out the picture window over the public square. It had rained overnight and though there were still a few puddles on the street, the morning sun had dried the sidewalks. The shrubs looked more vivid, the grass darker, the magnolia leaves sparkled. "Falcon Square looks nice this time of year."

"Yes, indeed," she said.

"Have the Falcons always had a law office here?"

"I'm told they moved the business to Broughton Street when the historic district went into decline, but they were among the first to come back when redevelopment began in the late fifties."

He gestured for her to sit. "Have they always lived on Falcon Square?"

"Oh yes. The Falcons have lived here continually since their home was built in the early nineteenth century."

He sat across from her and placed a digital recorder on the table. "You seem to know a lot about them."

"I've worked for Mr. Falcon since he went into private practice here." She looked into space as tears welled. "Let's see. That would be twenty-five years next June."

Jackson reached out and turned the recorder on. "I'll be recording this interview."

She nodded and flipped open her jacket, revealing a small black box. "Me too. Mr. Falcon taught me self-preservation."

He should have anticipated that. It wasn't a disaster, but he'd have to watch himself. "Fair enough. So, you've worked for Mr. Falcon for twenty-five years. Have you had any problems with him?"

She straightened. "Nothing significant. Uh, in the beginning we had to get used to each other's work habits. That was a bit rough. But. No. We get along fine."

"Did he have any odd habits?"

"No, he's just intense."

"Do you socialize with Mr. Falcon?"

"No. Not at all. Well, I go to his annual Christmas party, but it's mostly big clients who I've known for years."

"Do you admire him?"

Reva folded her hands and looked down. "I respect Mr. Falcon greatly. I think you'd find most people do."

"Does he pay you well?"

She looked up, glaring at him. "Very well, but I don't see what that has to do with his disappearance."

"When did you last see Mr. Falcon?"

"Quarter of three on the day of his disappearance."

"What was his state of mind?"

"Focused. Rushed. Typical for him."

Jackson sat back. "I heard the law business can be contentious."

"It's supposed to be. Presenting the strongest possible arguments is how justice is approached. Though the strongest argument doesn't necessarily serve justice ... just the client."

"So, Mr. Falcon is always feuding with other lawyers?"

"In court, most certainly. But when the court adjourns, he and his opponent will often go to lunch or dinner together."

"They're able to set aside the legal wrangling that easily?"

"For the most part."

"Most part?"

She looked him square in the eye, apparently a straight shooter. "They're human. They have pride. They don't like to lose."

"Preston Somerset?"

"Oh. I see you've heard." She straightened, glanced at his recorder, then back to him. "Definitely bad blood there, but it has nothing to do with lawyering."

"What then?"

"Some organization Mr. Somerset wants to join. He feels Mr. Falcon is preventing him from gaining membership."

"Sounds important."

"It is to Mr. Somerset." Mrs. Williams took a drink of coffee.

"What's the name of the organization?"

"I don't rightly know. Mr. Falcon keeps his personal business to himself. Though, come to think of it, it might be a men's organization of some sort."

"I'll need a list of Mr. Falcon's clubs."

She gestured to a thick folder. "I figured as much."

"Is a copy of his calendar in there as well?"

She shook her head. "Attorney-client privilege."

"I'm sorry. I don't recall. What time did he leave work on the day he went missing?"

"Quarter of three."

"Are you sure?"

She rolled her eyes. "Of course."

"Why?"

"He had a meeting at three thirty and he asked me to let him know around two forty-five. I put a reminder in my digital calendar."

"Who was he meeting?"

"He didn't say."

"Was that normal?"

She nodded. "From time to time. He didn't bill for those meetings, so I assume they were personal."

"How frequently?"

"The personal meetings?" She consulted her laptop. "Three or four times a week."

"How long would Mr. Falcon be away for these personal activities?"

"At least an hour. Sometimes for as much as half a day. Mostly an hour."

"And you have no idea what those activities involved?"

She shook her head.

"Do y'all have video surveillance of your parking lot?"

"Oh, yes. But the service called last week to say it wasn't working."

*How convenient.* "Has that happened before?"

"All the time. It's an old system."

"I'll need the name of the company."

"ADT." She wrote the name and phone number on a piece of paper and handed it to him.

He put the note in the folder she provided. "Has Mr. Falcon received any threats recently?"

She nodded. "'Fraid so. Happens all the time. Never lets up. No one likes to lose a dispute, and they always blame their lawyer."

"Recently?"

"All the time."

"Names?"

"Attorney-client privilege."

He had hoped for more cooperation, but he understood. "One final question, Mrs. Williams. Who, in your opinion, would want to harm Mr. Falcon?"

"Several clients come to mind."

"Who?"

"Attorney-client privilege."

He exhaled. "What about non-clients?"

She massaged her temple. "Hmm. I suppose Mr. Somerset. He's the only person I can think of right now."

"If any others come to mind, I'd appreciate knowing."

"Most certainly."

Jackson wrapped up the interview and left, considering how to subpoena those attorney-client privileged answers.

* * *

IN A GUARDED, BUNKER-LIKE BASEMENT OF A HISTORIC HOME just off Reynolds Square, Lucius Alton and three other men met to deal with their latest challenge - the disappearance of Trey Falcon, one of their own. Lucius, as the senior member of The Cotton Coalition, presided. Joining him were Benjamin Hempfield, Roland Potter, Beau Simpson, and their aides.

Roland, a wiry structural engineer who'd restored several of Savannah's historic homes, produced a bottle of port along with five tulip glasses. With practiced preciseness, he filled the glasses halfway and presented one to each director. He placed the fifth glass where Trey Falcon would have been seated.

Roland hoisted his glass. "To secrets."

The other three repeated, "To secrets," and took a token drink.

Beau, a lean, six-eight cardiologist, rose and brought his glass up chest high. "To unity."

The members responded and drank.

After Beau sat, Benjamin, a beefy, former UGA fullback, stood and raised his glass. "To renewal." As soon as the members repeated his toast, he returned to his seat.

Lucius booted up his laptop, as did the others. When his system asked for a password, he removed a token from his neck chain and placed it in a USB port.

"Gentlemen," Lucius said, even though his daughter Isabel stood behind him. She was, like the other aides, there to observe and learn, and she was never addressed. "As you may know, Trey Falcon is missing and, if he's still alive, he may be in grave danger."

Murmuring erupted from around him.

Lucius rapped on the table. "Gentlemen, let's have order. At this moment it is our highest priority to find Trey and return him to safety. To do so, it's imperative we quickly sort out this situation." Lucius cleared his throat. "I've spoken with Patricia who, as you might imagine, is taking this hard. I've assured her we are focused on Trey's return. Let's not disappoint her.

"Simon reports he didn't have any problem immediately locking down the Falcon home and activating a tap on the phone. He's also keeping an eye on all the newspapers for hostage communications and 'proof of life' photos. He'll be our go-to man if this is a kidnapping. He says Patricia is bearing up as well as might be expected."

Benjamin leaned forward, locking his beefy hands together on the table. His University of Georgia class ring lit up from the overhead fluorescent lights. "Trey was dealing with the new Russian mob boss. It's possible the Russian could be involved."

Lucius nodded. "Agreed. I'd like you, Benjamin, to step in and pick up the dialogue with Trokev. Find out what he knows about Trey's disappearance."

Benjamin smiled, exposing the gap between his front uppers.

"Since we don't know this new fellow very well, and because he may be implicated in Trey's disappearance, let's change our procedures for approaching him. I want you wired and to have a fast response team within seconds of you at all times that you're dealing with Trokev."

The other two nodded their assent.

Roland spun his cell phone, encased in Georgia Tech's school colors, and engaged Lucius' eyes. "According to Trey, Trokev is willing to negotiate with us and work out a beneficial solution for all concerned. Trokev has to know that abducting Trey wouldn't achieve that end. Perhaps someone else is behind Trey's disappearance."

"I agree," Lucius said. "Chief Patrick has a detective working a list Patricia provided of five of Trey's most aggressive enemies, none of which are related to Trey's Coalition work. We need to draw up our own list of people who might have reason to harm Trey, people reflective of Trey's Coalition work. And once we have that list, we'll have to quickly determine if any of them have recently taken any overt action against our good friend. We need to contact Reva, Trey's secretary, and get his client list. I'm sure she won't give that to the police, but we can get it. I'd like you to handle that aspect, Roland."

"Of course," Roland said.

"Beau, track down Falcon Square videos from the day Trey disappeared and get them over to Fort Stewart for facial recognition. Chief Patrick's detective has already subpoenaed Trey's phone and credit card records. We'll get a copy as soon as the chief receives them."

Roland glanced at his computer monitor. "What about Allison Hope?"

Lucius took a deep breath. In the reflection on his monitor, he caught a grimace on Isabel's face. She seemed to tense up at the question. He wished she would learn to control her physical reactions in Coalition meetings.

"Chief Patrick told me the murder of Miss Hope was a professional hit," Lucius said. "I think it's highly possible her murder is part of Trokev's plan for setting up his high-end prostitution business. You know, make a show of eliminating the competition. Kill a top independent 'escort' and the others will flee rather than risk being the next victim, thus leaving their clients high and dry.

"Of course, we can't tolerate murder so I've arranged for Trokev's Savannah assets to be frozen and for one of his five women to be sent on an extended vacation. That'll get his attention. Benjamin, when you meet with him, make sure he understands that murder is unacceptable to us."

"Trokev has a history." The concern in Benjamin's usually calm voice was unmistakable.

"And?"

"He's prideful. He may lose a battle or two, but he won't lose the war."

"Oh, no."

"Oh, yes. He and Trey are cut from the same cloth."

# CHAPTER 9

*P*atricia straightened when Simon turned the Mercedes into the alley behind The Olde Pink House restaurant, a former bank building on one of Savannah's many historic squares. As the car stopped at the back door, a young woman in black stepped out to greet them.

"Wait here," he said. "I want to verify the security arrangements."

Patricia's peace of mind depended on Simon being close and, though she understood his need to double-check, she didn't like being a sitting duck in the stationary car. The thought of being an easy target echoed repeatedly like a shout in a canyon, diminishing each time but still painfully present.

She pulled down the visor mirror and was surprised at her reflection. The harsh daylight made her face look pale and sickly. She'd lost weigh during the past year and her hollow face showed it. She frowned at the image and shoved the visor back up.

Still nervous, she checked her surroundings. The narrow

alley, front and back. The rusted dumpster. The wrought iron balconies above the alley. All barren. Though she was alone, she couldn't shake the feeling she was being watched.

To her relief, Simon returned a few moments later to escort her into the kitchen, down the worn concrete stairs, and through the wrought iron, gated entrance to the elegant basement dining room far away from the lunch crowd. Sterling flatware was set on linen tablecloths. Graceful antique chairs were pushed against the well-spaced tables.

At the back of the room was an old walk-in vault furnished with one table and two chairs. Once Patricia was seated inside the safe, Simon placed a wireless camera on the polished-steel doorframe and left.

A waitress delivered cheese straws and filled the crystal water glasses. Patricia wondered what the somber-faced, middle-aged woman thought of Simon's security precautions.

Five minutes later, Meredith, dressed in a black silk suit, clumped into the vault. Meredith looked at her expectantly.

Patricia's heart leapt at seeing her best friend.

At six-two, Meredith was five inches taller than her, and fifty pounds stockier. Where Patricia was eternally slim, Meredith was big. Thick bones. Broad shoulders. Athletic build. And, until the shooting a year ago, a large laugh. The kind of business executive who demanded attention.

Though Meredith's long black hair covered the gaping scar in her scalp, Patricia knew exactly where the plate and scar were, and couldn't help but admire how well they were hidden. If only the scars on Patricia's arms could be hidden so easily.

There were no scars in her friend's sparkling black eyes, eyes that had been blank for months while she had labored in the coma. Now her entire face shone again with the vibrancy that had been there before the shooting. Each time Patricia saw Meredith, she was in awe of how thoroughly Meredith had recovered. Recovered? Hell, she was even more formidable now than she'd been before the shooting.

They greeted each other with cheek kisses then sat. The waitress appeared out of the shadows and took their beverage orders. Frogtown Chardonnay for both.

"I see Simon is still being hyper-vigilant." Meredith waved at the security camera.

"It's his job."

Meredith widened her black eyes. "I do declare, Patricia, it's been a year since your accident. Don't you think it's 'bout time for you to get on with your life? Nothin' is going to happen."

"It's a dangerous world." She considered telling Meredith how exactly dangerous it had recently become, but Simon had been adamant about remaining silent.

"Honey, there's always going to be dangers." Meredith patted her purse. "That's why we carry our little guns."

"I'd prefer not to be put in the position of using mine again."

Meredith gestured to their surroundings. "Are you going to dine in vaults for the rest of your life?"

"It's reassuring."

"I'll tell you what is reassuring, a walk on the beach."

"You know very well, I'm not up to that."

Meredith shrugged, pushed back her dark hair and looked the menu over. "The fried flounder is too much for me. I think I'll just have a crab cake."

"Quiche for me."

The waitress arrived with their beverages and, now chattier, took their orders.

Once the server was gone, Meredith laid a flash drive on the table in front of Patricia.

"What's that about?"

"I put a copy of your husband's credit card records on the device."

Did Meredith know Trey was missing? No. If Meredith knew about Trey, she'd be offering condolences, not a flash drive. "Why are you giving me his credit records?"

"I received a subpoena this morning. Apparently the police are investigating your husband. I was going to phone you right away, but then you called for lunch. I thought it would be better to deliver this information to you personally. Is everything all right?"

"Have you responded to the subpoena?"

"Not yet. I wanted to alert you first. If you don't want to talk about this, just know that I'm here for you." Meredith gestured to the memory stick. "So, do you want this information or not?"

Patricia grabbed Meredith's hand and squeezed, then placed the device in her purse, eager to see if the transactions held any clue to where Trey might be. A hotel deposit. An airline ticket purchase. A recent transaction in a different city. Something. Anything.

She had an odd thought. Maybe Simon and the others weren't going to find Trey. Maybe they weren't the right people for this task. Maybe, just maybe, she and Meredith were better suited. Maybe their kind of creative thinking was what it would take to crack this case.

The idea scared her. What did they know of such things? Sure, they'd helped countless women escape abusive situations and solved a few high society crimes, but they'd never tried to track down a kidnap victim. They'd worked the underground before, but not this avenue. Not this close to home. And not this deep, considering the difficulties the authorities were having.

"You'll give the records to the police this afternoon?" Patricia asked.

"I have no choice."

Patricia nodded.

Meredith took a cheese straw. Between polite bites, she asked, "Why do you suppose the police would want Trey's credit card data?"

Patricia hung her head and closed her eyes. She and Meredith had survived by being frank with each other. Injecting half-truths and outright lies into their relationship was point-blank wrong. Meredith had been shot trying to track down the killer of Patricia's mother. She'd suffered brain trauma and a lengthy coma trying to help. Meredith could be trusted. She'd demonstrated that over and over again during the past twenty years. She had a right to know.

Patricia looked up into Meredith's puzzled face.

"What's up, girl?" Meredith asked.

"Trey's missing. He hasn't been home or at work for two days."

Meredith's mouth dropped open. "Oh my gosh. What happened?"

Patricia quickly filled her in on the details.

"Lordy."

"I'm so sorry I didn't tell you sooner."

"How can I help?"

"You're helping plenty by being here." Patricia dabbed her eyes with her napkin. "Simon told me not to tell anyone, but I just couldn't keep it from you any longer." Patricia's shoulders slumped with relief at finally sharing. She'd been too tightly wound trying to keep a stiff upper lip.

"If there's anything you need, just let me know."

"I need you to keep the situation under wraps."

"I understand. Have you contacted the police?"

"Oh yes. I called Chief Patrick the night Trey didn't come home."

"Now I understand the subpoena I received for Trey's financial records," Meredith said in a whisper.

Still feeling guilty for not telling Meredith earlier, Patricia nodded.

"What have the police discovered so far?"

"Just some unidentified blood in Trey's parking lot," she shuddered, "and a snake in my bed with Trey's wedding ring tied around its neck."

Meredith slumped and covered her mouth. "I don't think I could handle that."

"I didn't." Patricia dabbed her eyes.

"I can imagine." Meredith straightened. "Do the police have any clues? Any theories?"

"Nothing."

Meredith gestured toward the thumb drive. "Those records should prove helpful."

"I certainly hope so." Patricia sniffled, then touched her napkin to her nose.

"Do you need me to come over for a few days?"

Patricia shook her head. "No. I'll be fine. Simon's set up camp in the dining room again."

"He's not much company."

Patricia chuckled. "I prefer it that way."

"Are you sure there's nothing I can do?"

"Yes."

Her irreplaceable friend reached across the table and patted Patricia's hand. "You change your mind, you call. Anytime. Meanwhile, I'll look through those records too. I might catch something useful."

"Thank you. By the way, have you seen the story of the five women who've come to town to auction themselves off as dates?"

"Yes. Why?"

Patricia tsked. "I don't believe it's right."

"It's a date." Meredith reached for her wine glass.

"At that price, it's a date with a lot of potential benefits. Besides, those women aren't from around here. Doesn't that seem strange to you?"

Meredith took a sip of wine. "Honey, you have an overactive imagination. What those women are doing is just a creative way to get rich guys to part with big bucks and, in the process, provide a great deal of help to the homeless. Nothing more."

"What do you think about Allison's murder?" Patricia asked.

"That was so sad. She was such a gracious woman. You know, in all the times I've been with her, I've never seen her drunk, catty, or cruel. Sure she got around, which we don't condone, but she was out in the open about what she did. The wives of the married guys she escorted to our galas didn't seem to mind. Helen said Allison was the sister Brad never had."

"I've heard tell, Brad has so-called sisters salted away all over the Southeast."

"I wouldn't doubt that. And, if Allison is any indication, he's got excellent taste in women."

Patricia chuckled. "And a big hole in his wallet."

"There's a lot more where that came from."

"You would know."

Meredith smiled broadly. "One of the privileges of being his banker."

Their entrees arrived. While the waitress went about her chores, Patricia studied the bottled wine stacked to the ceiling in the vault.

Once the waitress had left, Meredith said, "By the way, Willy called me this morning."

"Willy Maye?"

Meredith nodded. "He's doing a story on Allison."

"An obit?"

"I don't think so." Meredith dabbed her lips with her napkin. "The questions he asked were focused on her social life."

"He'll have plenty to write about; she was out every night, but I doubt her clients are going to like that." Patricia frowned. "I mean, we know what she did, but why should all of Savannah?"

"I didn't tell him anything he couldn't find out for himself."

"I'm sure of that."

"He hasn't called you?" Meredith raised her eyebrows.

"We talked this morning."

"About Allison?"

"No."

"Honey, you talk with Willy, and he's likely to turn anything you tell him into a story."

"That's right," Patricia said. "That's what I had in mind."

Meredith's eyes widened. "You're going to give that man a story? I hope it's not about any of us."

Patricia waved her hand dismissively. "I'd never do that."

"Then what was it about?"

"We discussed that bachelorette auction."

"Are you back to that?" Meredith chuckled. "I told you, there's nothing wrong with what those women are doing."

"Then Willy, bless his heart, won't have a story. But Allison's death occurred just after those girls arrived. If there's anything seedy going on, I do believe Willy would be the one to find out." And with Willy on it, she could clear her mind of concern.

"Wait a minute." Meredith's eyes darted back and forth like balls on a rolling deck. "Are you implying that Allison's death has anything to do with those Russian women? Hmm ... like maybe the Russians are establishing an escort business here in Savannah. And they're doing it by scaring off the competition."

Patricia nodded.

## CHAPTER 10

*N*o one answered when Augusta called the Russian student, Ksenia, hoping to get background information for her article on relics. Augusta tried the number three more times without success.

When she was setting up the first interview with Ksenia, the woman was responsive, usually answering her phone immediately, or calling right back. Now she was unavailable. Well, Ksenia was obviously a busy woman and the relic story could be developed without her.

Augusta, who grew up in the Lowcountry, where voodoo and witch doctoring were common, continued her online search for root doctors in Georgia. Along the way, she learned that root doctoring was illegal in Georgia because courts considered it to be practicing medicine without a license. For this reason, root doctors operated in the shadows, restricting their practice to friends and neighbors. To pull back that veil, she would have to go deeper than the internet.

There was much written online about Dr. Buzzard up in South Carolina, and she read every word of it. He got his name when buzzards appeared while he was casting a spell. He'd practiced root doctoring in Beaufort County in the early part of the Twentieth Century and had died long ago in 1947.

By the end of the day, she had identified several living root doctors, and, by checking their references, had eliminated them as charlatans one-by-one. But one name couldn't be eliminated - Doctor Snake. The name Doctor Snake came to him early on after he performed healings using snakes. And he had, apparently, healed many over the years. She'd spoken to several of his 'patients'. Snake had emigrated from a remote mountain region of Cuba twenty years ago and had quickly established a community of devoted followers in Savannah, truly a cult. He claimed his mantle, his source of power, came from a relic he possessed. A forearm. Though, according to reports, only a few insiders had ever seen the bones.

Dr. Snake proved to be an elusive target for Augusta, but a man called Eustis Zuma blogged about the root doctor weekly. Eustis's blog was heavily focused on healings accomplished by Dr. Snake, but offered little insight into Dr. Snake himself. Augusta contacted Eustis through his blog and set up a meeting with him early that afternoon at a barbeque joint just off Abercorn Street.

Augusta had second thoughts about the meet-up when she saw the place: a biker bar. Harleys. A dozen or so. Smoke billowed from a large mobile grill to one side of the small brick building. Rusted ironwork protected the blacked-out storefront windows. She parked between a couple of beat-up old choppers, went to the open door and paused. The stench of stale beer engulfed her. Every survival instinct told her not to go inside.

Augusta remained in the doorway as her eyes adjusted. Directly in front of her was a bar with a few big gents in black leather jackets slumped over it. It was hot and humid. She wondered why they hadn't removed their jackets. The place smelled of gasoline, grease, and unwashed bodies. No TV. No pool table. The wrong place to wear a little L.L.Bean shirt. Just as she stepped further in, boisterous laughter erupted from her right, startling her.

She turned to the sound and could make out five or six men sitting around a circular table playing cards of some sorts. From the looks of the money piled up in the center of the table she'd guess it was a high stakes game.

To her left, across the damaged wooden floor, were four booths with partially illuminated hanging lights. The vinyl booths were all occupied by men and manly-looking women dressed in black leather. Not a mini-skirt in sight. Most of the tables scattered around her were occupied by one or two men.

The bartender, who had been cleaning a glass, looked up, eyebrows raised, as she crossed the dim room.

She held his gaze.

Curly gray hair accented his dark face. "Are ya here fa Eustis?"

Did she have a sign on her forehead? "Yes. How'd you know?"

"Doctor Snake dun said you'd be comin' by. Eustis be over dere." The man pointed to a corner table in the shadows. An overweight African-American gent with a pudgy nose sat facing the door. He watched her, his big frog eyes steady.

Augusta headed to the table.

Eustis stood and gave her a sparkling grin. He wore a gray T-shirt and black sweatpants. Dreadlocks framed his round face. Not what she'd expected from his brilliant blog.

They exchanged greetings.

"Do ya care for a drink?" he asked in a deep Barry White voice.

"Sweet tea?"

"Sonny," Eustis shouted toward the bar. "Bring da lady sum sweet tea." Then he turned to her. "So what can Eustis do for ya, Miss Augusta?"

"I'd like to meet Doctor Snake."

He gave her a suspicious look. "Are ya a cop?"

"No."

"What would ya be wanting with Doctor Snake?"

Her tea arrived, along with another bottle of beer for Eustis. "I'm a reporter. I'd like to do a story on him."

Eustis shook his head. "I write all his stories."

"I've read your blog."

"Have you now?"

"Yes. Doctor Snake is doing fascinating work. And you convey it so well."

He beamed. "Thank you kindly, Miss Augusta."

"More people should be aware of the Doctor's work," she said.

"If they be interested, they can read all 'bout him in my blog. It all be there."

"How many people are reading your blog?"

"Um. I suppose der be close to seventy or so."

"How would you like to get Doctor Snake's story to seventy thousand?"

His eyebrows shot up. "You could do that?"

She nodded. "Possibly."

"What kind of story?"

"Same as you're writing, but with more details."

"What kind of details you be talking 'bout?"

"Nothing that would get Doctor Snake in trouble with the law or invade his privacy."

"Ya sure?"

She nodded.

"I imagine that might work, but I best discuss dat with the

man hisself."

"I understand." She handed him her business card. "If he's willing, call me."

Eustis took the card and gave her another sparkling grin. "I like ya ... and I do believe Doctor Snake will too. You got good vibes."

Eustis called her an hour later, and said he'd meet her at the Carnegie Library at dusk and take her to see Doctor Snake that evening.

After picking her up, he drove her through Savannah to a dirt road close to Bonaventure Cemetery, and told her to go to the house at the very end of the unlit road.

Old oaks lined the dirt lane, creating a thick, dark canopy. As far as she could see, there were no homes on the lane apart from those on the corner. Not a good situation. But she had mace, a cell phone, and a burning desire for the story.

"You'll wait here?" she asked.

"Oh, yes. Don't ya worry none. You be okay. Doctor Snake, he be waiting on ya. On ya way now, Missy."

It was a short, silent walk through the darkness to the log cabin. No frog chirps, owl hoots, nor cicada hums. Just the sound of blood rushing in her ears and the clomp of her shoes on the dirt road. And humid air filled with the musty smell of decay and fertility.

Light spilled from the curtained windows.

She knocked.

The door opened slowly to reveal a tall, Hispanic man in a loose, ankle-length black tunic and black dreadlocks similar to Eustis's. No trace of gray. No wrinkles. Not a young man, nor an old one. Ageless. From the look of his forearms and face, he was probably lean as well as tall. His chin and nose were sharp and well defined, like a Spanish conquistador. Snake's shoeless feet were dirty.

Though it was night, he wore sunglasses. Her research

had informed her that wearing sunglasses was a common practice intended to prevent others from looking into the root doctor's eyes and stealing his power.

A three or four-foot live serpent dangled from Doctor Snake's right hand.

She quickly stepped back.

The doctor smiled at her. He curled his fingers around the green snake's head, raised it, and kissed the reptile. He lifted the serpent toward her and puckered his lips.

He had to be kidding.

His expression said otherwise.

She turned her head away. She had no interest in playing with snakes.

"Kiss it," he said, like a teenage boy wanting a girl to go further in the front seat of his car.

She realized it was a test, but she didn't think she could pass it. Snakes were slimy, ate mice, had fangs, and germs and ... well, they were just plain vile.

He moved the snake closer to her mouth.

The serpent's black tongue flicked out, seeking her.

She tensed. Oh my. Creeping out, she shivered at the idea of that tongue touching her. This whole idea was a big mistake.

But he'd kissed the snake and nothing bad happened. What could happen to her? A little snake tongue? She looked at the snake's mouth. She didn't see any fangs, just that damned tongue. If she kept her lips sealed and did it quickly, what could happen? She wasn't sure she wanted to find out, but—

He moved the snake closer. It loomed just inches from her face. "Bertha be waiting on ya, child."

Bertha? What the hell kind of name was that for a snake?

The snake, apparently startled, moved back an inch. Fear? Welcome to the party.

Was she going to let fear control her? She shook her head. The story was more important than her fear. She needed to do this. Quickly. Before she changed her mind. She leaned forward, lightly pressed her lips on the snake's mouth and pulled back. As kisses went, it wasn't bad. The snake's mouth was hard, boney. She wiped her lips.

Apparently satisfied with her sincerity, Dr. Snake curled the snake around his neck and ushered her into his cabin, which was, other than a pile of boxes in the back, surprisingly Spartan. There were no other doors save the one she had entered, which was now closed.

There was neither bed nor table. Did he sleep and eat on the floor? Or was this some sort of meeting place, and he lived elsewhere? There were no chairs. Worn carpets were scattered on the floor. He gestured for her to sit on a carpet in the middle of the room under a dangling light bulb.

The doctor went to the pile of boxes and placed the snake in a glass container with several serpents, then opened a cage filled with white mice and tossed three of them in with the snakes. With too few mice for the snakes, would they fight each other to eat? She couldn't watch.

Doctor Snake slowly crossed to a corner of the dimly-lit room and returned with a clay pot and two cups. He poured a brown liquid and offered her a cup.

"What do you do with all those snakes?"

"I use dem for healings. I sell de nasty ones. Just sold me one a few days back to a Russian fella."

She cradled the cup, wondering what was coming next - perhaps a vampire bat.

He signaled that she drink.

"What's this?"

He just repeated his silence.

Poison? Drug? Or just tea? Trust or distrust? Drink or leave? If she left, there'd be no story. She placed the lip of the cup to her mouth, grimaced, and took a sip. The lukewarm brew was bitter, but not unpleasant.

"All of it," he said, and drank his with one gulp. He set the cup down and waited on her.

She gave him a forced smile and poured the rest in her mouth, praying she wouldn't vomit, get sick later that evening, or, in a couple of weeks, have her doctor tell her she'd contracted parasites from bad food.

"You wish to write about my magic. Yes?" His voice had become a deep whisper. More a rumble than a voice, but she understood every word.

She looked around half expecting a physical reaction to the tea, but her hearing and balance seemed fine. "I would like to write about your mantle ... the arm. I want to share the inspiring story of its miraculous power."

"Why do you wish to do this, child?" He offered her a clay plate of roots. According to her research, an accepted practice.

She chewed on a root that tasted like licorice.

"Why, my child, do you seek the source of my magic?"

"I'm a reporter. I want to share knowledge."

He chewed on a root as well, apparently satisfied with her reply. "My disciple Zuma said you were not like the others." Doctor Snake nodded. "He was correct. You are special."

She looked down.

"No, child. You must look at me, so I can see de truth in your soul."

She brought her chin up to discover he'd removed his sunglasses. He had one green eye and one yellow eye. How does that happen? The reporter in her was drawn to his eyes.

"Your eyes are—"

"Dey be dat way since birth. Dey be special. I see everything. I see you have a good soul."

"Thank you."

"You got de gift. Have you conjured?"

She shivered at the depth of his insight. Her interest in the occult had gone well beyond curiosity. "Yes."

"What do you know of the arm, my mantle?"

"Nothing."

"I shall tell you, and you shall write."

She took out her pen and notebook.

"Do you know of Doctor Buzzard?" he asked.

She nodded. "As much as anyone else."

"What most people don't know is dat on his death in forty-seben, portions of his body were distributed to his four greatest disciples. His son, Buzzy, retained the rest of his relics, including de right arm."

"How did you obtain his arm?"

"In time, my child. You must be patient. First I must give you dis charm." He held out a small leather pouch on a braided leather necklace. "You must wear dis charm whenever you be in the presence of de arm."

Her heart raced. Was he going to show her Doctor Buzzard's arm? Would he permit a photo? Her hand found her phone in her pocket and her fingers toyed with it. Then, as if commanded by someone else, her hand left the phone and her pocket.

She placed the necklace over her head. The bag smelled of lavender.

Doctor Snake shuffled to the back of the room where crates were neatly stacked to the ceiling. He shifted some of the boxes around and removed a long, dark container. He returned with the weathered wooden box and placed it between them.

Her head swirled with dizziness. Her eyelids drooped. Suddenly her energy seeped from her toward the box. No. It couldn't be. But the fact was, she'd felt fine until the box was produced. The box. The arm. Could it be what she drank?

Doctor Snake lifted the lid on the box. A horrible sulfuric odor permeated the room.

Her dizziness intensified, then everything went blank.

Augusta awoke to the thumping of reggae music. She tried to stand, but she was restrained. What the hell? She should have never gone down that lane. Adrenaline shot through her. Now fully alert, she struggled against the strap that held her and blinked her eyelids open. She was in a car with a seatbelt across her chest. Eustis was driving. Thank God.

"Wha ... what happened?" she asked.

"You done have too much of Doctor Snake's magic."

Oh, yes. She remembered the stench and blacking out. The interview had gone well until then. Panic rose. She checked her purse. All was in order. She felt her back pocket. Her notebook was there. She checked her blouse. Everything was buttoned and tucked as before. "Where are we going?"

"Ya haus."

She'd been careful to meet up with him at a public location. "You know where I live?"

"It be on ya license."

Duh. Of course. "Thank you for doing all this, Eustis."

"Weren't nothin', ma'am. De doctor, he took a shining to ya. He wants ya to come back Saturday night. It be full moon. Big time party. He think ya like that. Right?"

She closed her eyes and leaned her head back. What would she learn about his magic at his 'big time' meeting? Would there be more tea? Would he bring out the arm again? Would people pass out? Would she? He was the real thing. No doubt about that. And she had a story to write.

"You be coming Saturday?"

"Yes indeed." She felt for the necklace Doctor Snake had given her. It was gone.

# CHAPTER 11

*A*s soon as Patricia got home from lunch with Meredith, she retrieved the flash drive from her purse and shoved the device into a USB port on her desktop computer. Card transactions appeared in reverse chronological order, most recent purchases first. She concentrated on the records for the week before Trey's disappearance.

Simon, coffee cup in hand and face devoid of emotion, walked by her. "Doing some accounting?"

"You might say." Her cheeks heated at the lie. She hoped her foundation hid the telltale flush. Caution required vagueness. She didn't want him interfering with her sleuthing.

"Have fun." He disappeared into the kitchen.

She returned her attention to the screen and, searching for something out of place, one by one eliminated familiar transactions. Within five minutes, she had a dozen restaurant transactions she didn't recognize, including four from the same place. And the charges were well beyond what Trey would spend just for himself.

Trey, not a creature of habit, went out of his way to incorporate variety in his daily life. Going to the same restaurant four times in one week meant someone else was selecting the place. It wasn't likely he was repeatedly meeting a client. Not four times in a week. Trey was too efficient for that. It was more likely these were social meetings. A lump formed in her throat. A woman? No. Not Trey. Something else was going on.

The other eight transactions were no less intriguing. She could visit each place tomorrow; they were all in the historic district within walking distance of each other. She'd take a picture of Trey and ask if anyone remembered seeing her husband. As for the place he visited four times, she'd have lunch there tomorrow ... provided she could convince Simon to let her go out again. She tensed. There shouldn't be any problem getting his approval, but if he resisted this was important enough she was prepared to fight him.

She removed the flash drive, shut down the computer, and went into the electronics-strewn dining room. A rifle with a large magazine leaned into a corner.

Simon, dressed in black and wearing a shoulder-holstered weapon, sat in front of a screen, keying in something. When she entered his field of view, his head snapped up like a cat catching sight of a mouse.

"Got a moment?" she asked.

Though he nodded, his somber face gave no clue as to whether or not he minded. It would be more pleasant if the man would smile occasionally, but she knew from past experience a smile was asking for too much. He wasn't sour, just hyper-vigilant, and there was no humor in that condition. Did he ever relax? Was his sourpuss permanent? She hoped not and suppressed a grin.

"You want something?" he said pleasantly.

"Yes. I'd like to go to *The Black Lantern* for lunch tomorrow."

He consulted his watch, a chronograph in flat black. No

doubt military issue. Joint Ops she recalled he'd once said. "Sure. I'll do a risk assessment this afternoon to see how secure it is. Determine if any of the staff are armed. Check the police call records for the place. That kind of stuff. What time?"

"Noon."

He keyed a note into his computer. "Who will you be lunching with?"

"Probably Lucius." If he was available, he might be able to shed some light on why Trey used that restaurant.

"Have you made arrangements with him?"

"No."

"I can do that for you. What do I tell him is the reason?"

"Just social."

For a moment, Simon's expressionless eyes widened, then returned to normal. "Assuming the place is reasonably secure, we'll leave here at eleven forty-five. Standard procedure once we arrive."

She nodded, surprised at how easy he'd agreed to the excursion.

"And take your pistol," he said.

The pistol. She knew the drill, but that didn't mean she liked it. Simon, Lucius and Lucius' security detail would be there between her and any danger. Anyone who overcame Simon probably wasn't going to be intimidated by her holding a pistol. She turned to go.

"By the way." Simon cocked an eyebrow. "Do you mind if I bring Father John along? I have a couple of things I want to go over with him."

She knew better than to ask what Father John had to do with this. When, and if, Simon was ready, he'd tell her. "No problem."

* * *

PATRICIA SAT ON THE EDGE OF THE BED, BOUNCING HER LEG and staring at the blank television screen across the room, a gaping black hole on the wall. A void as empty as the gaping hole in her heart.

She felt adrift at sea with no anchor, swept here and there by waves and tides she didn't understand, much less control. Her head ached and aspirin had been ineffective. She had prescription painkillers and sleeping pills available, but she wouldn't take them. They dulled her, and with the possibility Trey could call at any time of day she didn't want to be foggy.

The bedroom loomed dead silent and almost still. Just a continuous ripple of air from the overhead fan, a raw breeze that chilled her. If she was going to remain there, she should switch off the fan.

She didn't feel like getting under the covers just yet. Not with Trey unaccounted for ... and the latent image of the snake still fresh in her mind. She shuddered. But lethargy, and perhaps defiance, kept her from turning the fan off.

What was so wrong with a bit of physical discomfort? The fears, unanswered questions, and harsh images that filled her mind were much more painful - and they couldn't be switched off. Not until Trey returned.

* * *

THOUGH THE BEDROOM WAS COMPLETELY DARK, SLEEP wouldn't come to Patricia. The bed was cold, then hot. The sheets too tight, then too loose. She turned to one side, then the other. Nothing settled her.

For the past hour she had heard an urgent voice telling her to find Trey. She was a woman of faith and didn't believe in spirits. She wasn't crazy. The whisper in her mind was her intuition. Unfortunately, the message didn't include how to go about it. And, as much as she wanted him home and was willing to do whatever it took to bring him back, she wasn't about to go rushing off without a finite plan. After all, the police and the Cotton Coalition were already hunting for her husband.

Unfortunately, though, that was all their work was - a hunt. They were the best, so why should she try? Lucius had told her they'd find Trey, but never called back. The thought of what that could mean made her shiver. Concern as thick as smoke burned her eyes, bringing tears. She brushed them away.

She couldn't just sit there. Trey wouldn't. But what could she do besides spending probably wasted time at some restaurant?

Emotional waves spilled over her like an incoming tide on a foggy coastal marsh. Helplessness? Maybe. Self-doubt? Probably. She prayed for God's help, and for dawn. The days since he vanished were terrible, but these lonely, angst-filled nights were impossible.

If she could just figure out what was keeping Trey from coming home, the answer could point to where he was. Once she knew where, she'd hire some of Simon's ex-Ranger friends to get him and bring him back.

One thing was for sure, Trey hadn't disappeared voluntarily. Chief Patrick said Jackson quickly tracked down all the leads she had given him and came up empty. The chief also said there had been no recent activity on Trey's cell phone or credit cards, and that, though Jackson was developing additional leads, the police were stumped. Jackson's expertise was only turning up dead ends. Of course Jackson didn't know about Trey's involvement with the Coalition.

So the most promising answers had to be within the Cotton Coalition. What had Trey been doing for them recently? Though Trey never talked about his Coalition activities, she racked her mind for some idle comment he might have made that would provide a hint. Lucius knew what Trey was doing, but he wasn't going to tell her. Their mantra was that secrecy protected the Cotton Coalition. A lot of good that did for Trey.

What evidence could Trey have left that might help?

His credit card activity. While the records didn't indicate whom he was with, they certainly showed where he had been in the days immediately before his disappearance. It wasn't much, but at least it was something tangible to start with. Visiting those restaurants tomorrow seemed the best she could do.

Accepting her plan worked like a sedative, as sleep quickly took her.

\* \* \*

BENJAMIN HEMPFIELD PULLED UNDER THE BRIGHTLY LIT *PORTE cochere* that fronted the Amber House, Savannah's newest and most exclusive bed and breakfast - and Trokev's latest acquisition. His first objective in this meeting with Trokev was to keep Trey alive, without showing weakness. His second objective was to negotiate Trey's return, and that would require showing strength. Restrained strength.

A young, attractive female valet in full livery held the door for him as he stepped confidently from his Bentley. A similarly dressed female doorkeeper, and equally as enticing, held one of the etched-glass entrance doors as he went into the ... what would he call it?

He looked around. It wasn't a foyer or a lobby. And it certainly wasn't Southern. He decided it was a sitting room. An ornate, European sitting room with high-backed, upholstered chairs arranged in discreet conversation circles, cut-crystal chandeliers grander than any he'd ever seen in Savannah, and dark mahogany walls. Sandalwood scented the air.

Maybe some aftertones of musk and old leather. Red oriental rugs complimented the black marble floor. But what distinguished the room was that the tables were made of amber, as well as the picture frames. Amber, as in Amber House. Effective branding, he thought.

A mature brunette with exquisite features approached. Her tailoring was impeccable. When she offered her hand, he noticed a Faberge bracelet and a regal emerald ring. "Mr. Hempfield, I presume," she said.

He nodded and, eyes on hers, delicately shook her hand in a show of formality. This was a business meeting after all, though with Trokev in charge he had no question what kind of business actually went on here.

"I'm Maria, Mr. Trokev's personal assistant. If you'll follow me." With musky perfume trailing her, she led Benjamin into a small, barren anteroom and produced a scanner. He raised his eyebrows and backed off in feigned surprise. Before he could get very far she had swiped it over his body, smiled as though satisfied, and returned it to wherever it had come from.

He assumed there were other scanning devices hidden in the ceiling and walls, taking an inventory as well. He wasn't worried. The wire he wore was completely biological and transmitted in microbursts in extreme frequencies used only by the National Security Agency.

A beep sounded; apparently someone outside the chamber was satisfied. Maria showed Benjamin into a cigar-scented, austere office. Grigory Trokev, dressed in a black suit, white shirt, and black silk tie, was seated. To his right, a picture window overlooked an illuminated swimming pool. The filmy sheers were drawn. All in all, a stark step down from the inn's ornate lobby.

As Maria departed, Trokev, a handsome man with piercing pale blue eyes and combed-back dark hair, stood and approached. His trim suit jacket was buttoned and his pale hand outstretched. A Rolex watch. Diamond cufflinks. Manicured nails.

His look and manner suggested he was a European diplomat, a privileged man seemingly unfamiliar with human suffering. Of course, Benjamin knew him for who he really was - a cunning Russian mobster looking to set up a high-end escort service in Savannah. An enterprise the Cotton Coalition wanted shut down.

Benjamin took Trokev's hand in his. The man's grip was firm; a bit too firm to be cordial. No doubt intended to convey superiority.

"Good evening, Mr. Hempfield," Trokev said in a stiff voice that gave no hint of his Russian citizenship.

"Thank you for agreeing to meet me on such short notice, Mr. Trokev." Benjamin released Trokev's hand.

Trokev gestured to the pair of high-backed leather chairs by the fireplace. They sat across from each other. The cigar smell was stronger around the chairs. Benjamin noticed a clean ashtray, a cigar cutter and a humidor on the table. No beverages were offered, nor expected. Plus, Benjamin wouldn't put it past Trokev to drug any drink provided.

"It is a pleasure to finally meet you, Mr. Hempfield. How is Mr. Falcon these days?" Grigory's cold eyes glinted behind gold-framed glasses.

Benjamin kept his face expressionless, echoing his calm interior. "I might ask you the same question."

"I might be inclined to answer that question," Grigory put his hand on his chest, "if my lost property were to be returned."

"You've lost something?" Benjamin, knowing very well the Coalition had detained one of Grigory's prized escorts, widened his eyes for dramatic effect.

Grigory nodded. "And I should like to have it returned."

"The woman for Mr. Falcon?"

Grigory set his mouth in a thin line. "The woman has no great value to me. I have many more available."

"Your money for Mr. Falcon?" The Coalition had frozen Grigory's Savannah assets. For a wealthy man like Grigory it was certainly a minor matter, but apparently there was a principle at stake here.

"Yes." Grigory took out a cigar case with three cigars. He offered the selection to Benjamin, who took one and cut the tip off with the cutter next to the ashtray. Grigory followed suit, then offered a light to Benjamin.

"Okay. So now we know what is on the table." As the Russian puffed his cigar to life, Benjamin said, "There is other business as well."

Grigory puffed out a smoke cloud. His gaze drifted up with the ascending cloud as he watched it break up. "What business would that be?"

"That would be your Savannah venture."

"That discussion is irrelevant to the return of Mr. Falcon." Despite his tone, Grigory's face reddened.

Benjamin snuffed out his cigar in the ashtray and stood. "In that case—"

"Not so fast, Mr. Hempfield. We have already established the price of Mr. Falcon's return. When Mr. Falcon last spoke with me, I told him his offer on the matter of my business venture was inadequate and he, unfortunately, resorted to intimidation. Now you insult me by leaving before we have our business settled."

"I'm fully aware of Mr. Falcon's negotiation limit regarding your venture." Benjamin sat. "I have the same limit. If the amount is inadequate ... then it is inadequate. I'm sure Mr. Falcon made you fully aware of the next steps."

Grigory gave a smug smile. "And I'm sure you're fully

aware of how we handled Mr. Falcon. Knowing that, how can you come to me with the same offer?"

Benjamin gestured palm up. "Well, it's not exactly the same offer. This time, if you do not agree to return Mr. Falcon immediately and leave Savannah within the week, we're prepared to implement action against you and your business."

Grigory removed his glasses and placed them on the end table. "Really, Mr. Hempfield, you're in no position to dictate to me."

"I'm not?" So far everything had gone according to plan. The Coalition hadn't really expected Grigory to cave easily. "You've doubtlessly misinterpreted our Southern politeness and good manners as a sign of weakness. A common mistake made by outsiders."

Grigory, his face showing no sign of offense, shrugged.

"I suppose a demonstration of the true power behind our gentle words is in order." Benjamin gestured toward the picture window. "Understand this is just a demonstration. That's your hotel swimming pool out there, isn't it?"

Just as Grigory nodded, the pool erupted in a watery explosion. Concrete debris peppered the window, shattering it. Grigory dove under the table.

Maria rushed in, gun in hand.

Grigory, red-faced, stood and waved her away.

Eyes darting right and left, she hesitated.

Grigory, now scowling, waved again. "Get out. Now."

She left.

"Your assistant will be back in a moment," Benjamin said in an intentionally flat tone.

Grigory jerked his head. "Why?"

"The swimming pool in your Thailand brothel at Chang Mai also exploded."

Grigory broke his cigar. "Impressive coordination."

"I have more demonstrations prepared. Shall I continue? Or do you wish to reconsider our demands?"

"Your little pyrotechnics demonstration makes an undeniable point, which I'll respect for the moment. We have guests in the hotel. Important guests who value their privacy and safety. Guests who should not be disturbed."

"No guests were injured. And I expect Mr. Falcon will likewise remain unharmed."

"I'll speak with my superiors. The amount Mr. Falcon spoke of is your maximum?"

Superiors? Damn. It was Benjamin's turn to nod. "You have twenty-four hours."

Grigory was no longer the kingpin Benjamin had thought when he'd entered, the opulence now all window dressing for an underling. "Thank you for coming, Mr. Hempfield. I'll get back to you."

\* \* \*

AN EXPLOSION ROCKED PATRICIA'S BED, AWAKENING HER. A sonic boom from one of those Army jets from Hunter? Why couldn't they limit flying to daylight? A wailing siren penetrated her thoughts. Now what? She kicked the sheet off, rushed to the front window and watched a fire truck race by.

She went back to bed and turned on the TV just in time to see a News Alert scroll by: *An explosion of undetermined origin at a bed and breakfast in the historic district. Police investigating. Stay tuned for updates.*

She grabbed her tablet and logged on to Twitter. Tweets about the incident began trickling in. WTOC 11 tweeted that the site of the explosion was a bed and breakfast named The Amber House. Savannah Fire and Emergency Services tweeted that there was a minor fire and some property damage. The fire was extinguished and no injuries were reported. Savannah Metro Police indicated a bomb squad was on the scene.

* * *

ON THE OTHER SIDE OF THE WORLD, TREY AWOKE, DESPERATE to escape. He'd been told he was in Siberia - literally, not figuratively. Where the hell could he go? From what he'd seen during his daily exercise in the guarded compound, the location was surrounded by snow-capped, treeless mountains. No one ever walked out of Siberia.

He wondered how Patricia and Hayley were holding up, and prayed out loud in a low deep voice, "Dear Lord, keep them safe."

# CHAPTER 12

*P*atricia awoke the following morning surprised and grateful she'd slept so long. Guilt surged at being so rested when Trey was still unaccounted for. But he was strong and resourceful, and he had Savannah's finest searching for him. A potent combination.

Sitting up, she studied the drawn bedroom curtains. Her lethargy had kept them closed for the past two days. Lethargy that fed on itself ... until today. She grabbed the remote and opened the curtains. Sun poured in, filling her with hope.

Invigorated and eager to get answers on Trey's where-abouts, she called Lucius.

"To what do I owe this call, Patricia?" he said in a remark-ably calm voice. No sense of urgency there. No doubt an old man's refuge from an insane world. Her upside down world.

Glaring at the phone, she exhaled slowly, trying to vent her agitation at his mellowness before speaking. "You promised you'd call back, and I haven't heard from you."

"Well, to tell you the truth, I haven't had anything to report. I wish I could give you better news."

"I thought you said you have your best people working on finding Trey."

"True. But unfortunately they're not meeting with success in locating him."

Her head throbbed. She grasped the phone tighter. If the Cotton Coalition couldn't find him, who could? Though she wanted to scream, she forced herself to keep her composure. "What's going on, Lucius?"

"I wish I knew, Patricia."

She tried to swallow over the sudden lump in her throat. "Are you telling me all you know?"

There was a long pause before he muttered, "No."

Anger surged. Anger at him for being so secretive. Anger at herself for being so trusting. "Damn it, Lucius. He's my husband."

"I realize this situation is impossibly hard for you. And I know asking you to calm down is pointless. But being impatient with me isn't going to bring Trey home any sooner. The people I have working on this are world-class experts, and they'll find and recover Trey—"

"What do you mean by recover?"

"We'll rescue Trey. It's going to take time, but in the end it's going to be okay. Fretting won't help. Do your best to relax as much as you can. Your physician can—"

"I'm not taking any tranquilizers!"

He let out an audible sigh. "As you wish."

"Have you heard of The Black Lantern restaurant?"

"The name sounds familiar. Oh yes. Simon called and asked if I'd join you for lunch. I told him I had a conflict."

"Sorry to hear that, Lucius. Do you know of any reason Trey might lunch there regularly in the past week?"

"No. Not at all."

"Okay. Please keep me informed on your progress on

finding Trey. Call me. Daily. I want to hear from you regularly, even if you have nothing to report."

"I understand," he said in an unconvincing voice.

She wanted to shout at him and tell him how disappointed she was in the all-powerful Cotton Coalition, a bunch of impotent good old boys being outmaneuvered by a kidnapper. But she didn't. She simply said goodbye.

She went into the bathroom, closed the door, and slid down it to the floor, shaking with anger and wanting to cry. A lot of good crying would do. She had to find a way to settle her personal situation while the Coalition and the police went about their work. She had to refocus, and get her mind off Trey and the Coalition. She could go for a run in Forsyth Park. No, not while in lock down. Run on the treadmill. Yeah. Intense exercise might help divert her mind.

She changed into workout gear and headed down the hall to the exercise room, where she set the air conditioner to fifty-five, put the ceiling fan on high and stepped on the treadmill.

She punched in her normal warm-up pace and began a slow, easy jog. After a minute, she cranked the machine up to a seven-minute-per-mile pace and started her daily half hour run. A rehab routine that had become habit. At least until Trey went missing. Damn it. She couldn't escape the reality of his absence. Increasing the intensity would force her mind on running. When she raised the incline a couple of degrees, her heart rate elevated even more, and her mind returned to the run.

Following the treadmill, she took on four sets of inclined sit-ups and some weight work. By the time she finished, her workout clothes were drenched.

A half hour later, she got out of the tub and gently toweled off. Over a breakfast of dry toast and strong black coffee, she read the *Savannah Post's* report of last night's bombing.

One new tidbit that caught her attention was the Russian surname, Trokev, the current owner of The Amber House. Beyond Vladimir, she knew of no other local Russians. But then, she had a narrow circle of acquaintances - a circle that had, sadly, grown smaller due to neglect in the past year. She missed being busy with friends. She hadn't seen Vladimir for a while and wondered how his export business was going. She'd phone him later and see what he knew about Trokev.

Patricia took her coffee cup to her desk and called Willy. He picked up on the third ring. After exchanging greetings, he said, "It's your nickel. What can I do for you?"

She couldn't believe he used that old saying about nickels, but that was Willy. She wanted to tell him about Trey and ask him for his help, but didn't. As good a friend as he was, he was also a dedicated reporter and Simon had said it was best to seek Trey in secrecy. So far secrecy wasn't getting them much, but she'd respect Simon's request and keep Willy in the dark about Trey.

"Are you familiar with the gala for the homeless next week?" she asked.

"I don't do galas."

"It's the event auctioning off bachelorette dates."

"Oh, yeah. We have an office pool on how much the top date will go for."

"You men will bet on anything."

"Our women are participating in the pool, too. And I'll tell you, putting ten bucks into the office pool is a heck of a lot cheaper than dating one of those babes. I've heard they're likely to get five, maybe ten thousand dollars for a date."

"Do you think there's anything more to those dates?"

"Could be. Why?"

"It smells rotten to me. Who pays five to ten thousand dollars for a date and doesn't expect more?"

"I understand your thinking, Patricia, but when you have enough money and a high pressure job, a couple of hours of decompression might easily be worth ten grand."

"No sex?"

"Yeah. No sex."

"But there might be sex."

Willy chuckled. "There's always a 'might be.' For some, that's the point of dating."

"Men! Do y'all ever think of anything besides sex?"

"We're wired that way. Besides, you brought up this subject."

"So, are you going to look into the 'sex for hire' aspect of the auction?"

"No."

Surprise swept through her. Willy was a good, upright fellow who repeatedly fought local crime with journalism. "Why?"

"Too busy. Besides, where's the story? Man goes on date and has sex. That's not going to sell newspapers."

"Sex for money?"

"Unsubstantiated. Sorry."

"Umm. Okay." She wasn't upset with him. She understood his thinking.

"Do you have time for a question, Patricia?"

She looked at the clock. There was still plenty of time to get ready to visit the restaurants. "Sure."

"Did you ever see Bobby Gilbert, you know, the DA, with Allison Hope?"

She twitched at the mention of Allison's name. "Why?"

"I'm curious why Miss Hope never got herself busted. It's no secret what she did for a living."

"No, it wasn't a secret," she said, disappointed by Willy's

muckraking. "But why would you want to look into that now? She's dead."

"Bobby's alive and running for reelection. He's a public figure. He's accountable. I know he's not a nice guy, but if I can tie him to Miss Hope, that might explain why she could operate so openly and never be prosecuted."

Oh my. A shudder slid down her back. She could see why Willy was interested. Her stomach clenched. She knew Bobby, but did Willy? "If you try to take Bobby down, you're gonna have a mountain of hurt."

"I'm good with that."

She couldn't wrap her mind around his naiveté. "You're good with hurt?"

"Yeah."

"You're crazy, Willy."

"And a damn good reporter. If I have to take some heat to get important news, so what. And, really, what can the man do?"

"Bobby ... he has connections." She recalled the night Bobby and Trey, after a few too many Mint Juleps, went head-to-head over a bribery issue and the ensuing death threats that had Trey in lockdown for a month. Lucius and the Cotton Coalition ultimately resolved the problem, but the rift between Bobby and Trey never fully healed. "He knows the right people. Trust me."

"You know that for a fact?"

She paused, then said, "Yes."

"Who?"

She clenched her jaw. It had been a mistake to have this conversation. "Can't say."

"Why?"

"I value my life. Apparently more than you do."

"Okay. Forget about me. I'll make it simple. Bobby and Allison. Were they lovers? Yes or no?"

"Yes. But it's totally off the record. And before you ask, I'm not going to say another word on this subject."

"I understand, Patricia. And, tell you what I'm going to do; I'll take a closer look at that auction. I owe you."

"Thanks, Willy." She gave a fist pump. Give a little. Get a little.

# CHAPTER 13

*J*ust before the noon rush, Simon, Father John, and Patricia met a burly man in a dark suit at the alley door of The Black Lantern.

The greeter showed them through the restaurant to the foyer, then departed into a small bar immediately off the entrance. The abstract paintings and stylish furniture gave the restaurant a contemporary European feel, and the patrons seated in the bar were dressed too formally to be locals. Soft, foreign-language music added to the ambience. The menu posted just inside the dining room doorway included Armenian, Polish and Hungarian dishes. A distinguished, middle-aged gentleman in a black tux came out of the bar and inquired if they desired to be seated.

"The lady will be dining alone, as I have business to discuss with my colleague here," Simon said.

The maitre d' quirked an eyebrow. "This way, Madame." He inclined his head and seated Patricia at a window table overlooking the square.

Then he led Simon and Father John to a corner table.

Simon sat so he could keep an eye on Patricia and Father John at the same time.

"How are you coming on locating Trey?" Father John asked.

"Not well."

Father John frowned, then nodded ever so slightly toward Patricia. "How's Mrs. Falcon doing?"

"As well as might be expected."

"She's a strong woman." Father John lowered his chin and leaned forward. "I appreciate you meeting with me on such short notice. I know you're focused on finding Trey and protecting Mrs. Falcon, so I'll be brief."

Simon, his head too full of caring for Patricia's safety to pay full attention, nodded.

"My daughter Connie has received several threatening emails in the past forty-eight hours. I thought you might be able to help track down the source."

"What kind of threats?"

"Injury. Possibly death. Though nothing was said directly about death."

"What did the emails say?"

"Several variations of 'stop nosing around or else.'"

"Do you have any suspicions about where these threats might be coming from? Or why they're being made?"

"Not a clue on the source. The 'why' seems to have something to do with some research she's doing for me."

"What kind of research?"

"She's looking for some missing antiques that might be located in Savannah."

"Why would someone care what she was researching?"

"I don't know," Father John said.

"Has Connie been threatened before?"

"No."

"Can you think of anyone who would want to hurt your daughter?"

"Hundreds."

"Hundreds?"

"I've made a lot of enemies."

"And they know you have a daughter?"

"Apparently. What do you say, Simon, can you help me out?"

"Of course I'd be happy to help. But why not use your Vatican security people?"

"Since Connie's computer and email service are in the United States, they feel you'd have a better chance of success."

"Did you bring her computer?" Simon asked.

Father John placed the laptop on the table and handed Simon an envelope. "Her email address and password."

"How soon do you need an answer?"

"What do you think is realistic?" Father John said.

Simon stared at the computer for a moment. "It won't take long. The National Security Agency database will immediately kick out full details on every message sent to her email address at the time the harassing emails were received. The harder part will be identifying and locating what computer sent the original messages. If it's a prankster or known hacker, identifying them won't be a problem. Maybe an hour or two, maximum. I could get back to you with a name and location by mid-afternoon."

"Good."

AFTER ORDERING SWEET TEA, PATRICIA ASKED TO SPEAK TO THE manager. According to the credit card report, Trey visited The Black Lantern four times the week before his disappearance. It was hard to imagine a restaurant that important to

Trey. Repetition wasn't in his nature. Not in the least. Had he been coerced to meet there? Her stomach went queasy.

She reached into her purse and pulled out an antacid. Could she be wrong about the significance of his visits? Could this be just another dead end? She hoped not. It was the only lead she had.

An attractive, middle-aged woman came to the table. "I'm Petrina, the manager. How may I help you?"

Patricia stood and took in the woman's appearance. She wore a tailored black suit and a black silk blouse that would be more at home in New York City than in Savannah. Her black hair was pulled up into a topknot. Her somber expression matched her couture. Patricia extended her hand. "I'm Patricia Falcon."

The lady took her hand. "Pleased to meet you, Miss Falcon."

"Mrs."

"You asked to speak with me?"

"Would I be correct to assume you visit with your guests?"

Petrina's previously indifferent mouth curled into a smile. "Most assuredly. I speak with every guest shortly after their meal is served. If I might inquire, why are you asking?"

Patricia produced a four-by-six headshot of Trey. "My husband's credit card was used four times in this restaurant last week. Do you recall seeing him here?"

Petrina briefly studied the photo, then returned it to Patricia. "Yes. Your husband regularly lunches with us. Our goulash is his favorite."

Her mouth went dry. She slid Trey's picture into her purse, freeing her hand so she could turn Trey's ring on her thumb. Could this be the start of the trail to Trey? Ask the easy questions first. Get her talking. "How long has he been coming here?"

"Hmmm. Perhaps a month."

Patricia scanned the strange restaurant. Trey never mentioned liking goulash or Eastern European food. Never mentioned the restaurant. "How often did he visit your restaurant?"

"A couple of times a week. More lately."

"He dines alone?"

"Oh no. Always with the same gentleman."

Patricia's heart surged. "Do you know the gentleman?"

"I do. He recently renovated and reopened a bed and breakfast just down the street. Very exclusive. I visited him shortly after it opened and asked him to send us his guests. It's unfortunate ... the bombing ... you know."

"His name is?"

Petrina's face morphed into puzzlement. Her hand went to her mouth. "I'm so embarrassed. I don't recall his name offhand, but I have his card in my office." She stepped back. "I won't be a moment."

Patricia checked her emails on her phone while she waited for Petrina to return. One message was from Willy. It read: *You were right.*

Her adrenaline spiked.

A bright flash lit up the interior. Flames? No. Not flames. Not again. Her heart leapt to her throat.

Patricia spun to see a chef stirring a flaming copper frying pan atop a small burner. She eased out her gasped air.

The couple at the table, an elderly man and an immaculately dressed younger woman, seemed mesmerized by the show.

Patricia returned her attention to her emails, sipping tea as she read.

"Mrs. Falcon?"

Patricia looked up.

Petrina stood alongside a tall, trim man in gold-rimmed glasses.

"This is Grigory Trokev, the gentleman who dines with your husband. He just arrived for lunch."

Patricia tensed. This man could possibly unlock the mystery of Trey's absence.

A fleeting smile passed over his face. His sparkling brown eyes surveyed her.

She swallowed hard and stood.

"Trokev. Interesting name. What's its origin?"

"Russian."

"You don't have an accent."

"Swiss boarding school."

"My husband is Trey Falcon."

His gaze turned stone cold for just a moment, then went blank, as though his concern was neutralized.

She wondered at his reaction to her husband's name. Negative? Had they fought? Yet they dined together four times in a week. "You had lunch with him?"

He nodded.

"Regularly?"

He nodded again and gave a slight smile, as if remembering something pleasant.

"Have you had lunch yet?"

Hesitating, he looked at her with a question on his face. "No. I have not."

"Would you care to join me?" She gestured to a chair next to hers. "I have some questions for you."

He stiffened and looked at her intently. "About what?"

She gave him her best Southern belle smile. "My husband."

"I'm afraid I can't discuss our business."

The harsh look on his face concerned her, but she rallied. "I understand. Actually, I'm just interested in my husband's activity last week. He's gone missing, and I'm trying to assemble a map of who he saw and when."

"The police do that."

"They may or may not. I don't want to chance it."

Trokev put his hand on the back of the chair.

Her heart sped. "Please."

"I can give you a few minutes," he said as he sat. "And you are certainly entitled to know. I wouldn't want to impede your investigation."

"Thank you."

"Let's make an agreement," Trokev said.

"What kind of agreement?" She spun Trey's ring.

He looked around. His pale blue eyes flicked back to hers.

Butterflies fluttered in her stomach.

"Let's not tell the police about this conversation," he whispered.

"Why?"

"They might not approve of some aspects of my business."

"Are you doing something illegal?" She hesitated, ready to gage his reaction.

He smiled and nodded. "Isn't everyone?"

"Is my husband involved?"

"No. In fact, he disapproves."

"What kind of business?"

"I won't discuss my business," he said in a clipped tone.

Well, dirty or not, he had involvement with her husband, and she needed Trokev to be open with her. "I don't know if I can lie to the police."

"Then this conversation is over." He placed his napkin on the table. But he didn't stand. He was negotiating. Why? For what? There was only one way to find out.

"Let's say I agree to not volunteer this information, but I'm free to answer a direct question from the police."

He shook his head and stood. "I don't want the police in

my business."

Her mouth went dry. She had known it was going down this way as soon as he'd mentioned an agreement. She looked away. Cleared her throat. She didn't know this man. Could she trust him? Trey had. Four times. Could she ignore the warning signs? Could she ignore her respect for the law? She shivered. Did she have a choice? She couldn't blow this opportunity. "Okay," she finally said.

Trokev sat and ordered wine. The waiter returned promptly with his beverage.

After the waiter left, she directed an inquisitive expression at him. "How do you know my husband?"

He rested his hands on the arms of the chair. Diamond cuff links. A Rolex watch. A signet ring of some sort. Manicured nails. "Shortly after my arrival in your beautiful city, he came to visit me about a complex business matter." His calm voice was confident.

"How long ago was that?"

He paused for a moment. "A month ago. More or less."

"And you've met him several times since?"

"Yes. Always for lunch." He took his sterling silver wine goblet and swirled the wine.

"Always here?"

He sipped the wine, glanced around, and then returned the goblet to the table. "Mostly. But occasionally elsewhere."

Patricia interlaced her fingers, then she studied his face, poised for a reaction to her next words. "Did you know my husband is missing?"

His eyebrows arched. "No, I did not until you mentioned it. I am sorry to hear that, Mrs. Falcon." Grigory leaned forward, resting his forearms on the table. "How might I help you?"

"Based on your conversations with my husband, do you have any idea where he might be?"

Grigory, his face a picture of bewilderment, stared into space for a moment, then said, "No, I am sorry to say, I do not. We only spoke of business."

"Hotel business?"

"It was more than the bed and breakfast." His cheeks drew in. "As I mentioned, very complex."

"What kind of business?"

"I would prefer not to say."

"And you were able to conclude that business with my husband to both your and Trey's satisfaction?"

"I would say so."

Petrina returned and whispered something to Grigory, then left.

"I am afraid I have to wrap this up. I am meeting a client. She just arrived. I am sure you understand."

"Do you mind if I contact you in the future?"

"Not at all." He reached into his jacket pocket.

She noticed Simon, seated across the room from them, stiffen.

Grigory produced a sterling case and handed her a card from it.

She took the card and examined it approvingly before placing it in her purse. "Thank you, Mr. Trokev."

"Call me any time." He stood and offered his hand. She again noticed his gold signet ring. A cross with a forearm superimposed. A curious image.

When she took his hand, he brought her hand up and kissed the back of it. "It is a great pleasure to have made your acquaintance, Mrs. Falcon. I do hope your husband returns promptly."

As he stepped away from the table, Petrina entered the room with a young woman who could have passed as a model. Grigory introduced her as Ksenia. Then Petrina showed Grigory and Ksenia to another table.

SIMON PUT HIS FORK DOWN AND DABBED HIS MOUTH. "IT looks like Mrs. Falcon is finished eating and preparing to leave. Would you mind keeping an eye on her while I bring the car around front?"

"Not at all," Father John said. "Text me as soon as you're in place, and I'll escort her out."

"Thanks." Simon paid the check and made his way through the kitchen to the back door. Before stepping out, he got his bearings. The Mercedes was parked across from a rusted dumpster. Two men in white cook's uniforms stood next to the dumpster smoking. The men were surprisingly fit, and their uniforms were spotless. An uncomfortable lump rose in Simon's throat.

He slipped the safety off his concealed pistol as he scanned the rest of the alley. No one else was visible. He could go back inside and pick up the car later, but if those thugs meant to harm Patricia there was nothing to prevent them from coming inside. The thought sharpened him. It was better to deal with the threat in the alley, far away from Patricia and innocent bystanders. Two on one seemed manageable, though there were plenty of nooks and crannies where reinforcements could be lurking.

Simon took out his smartphone and punched the 'assist' icon that would summon any nearby mercenaries to his aid. When no one responded promptly, he stepped out into the alley and headed toward the Mercedes.

The two grim-faced men crushed out their cigarettes and spread apart. The situation screamed danger.

Simon yanked his pistol out as he advanced on the two thugs.

Both raised their hands, straining their chef's coats over their massive chests. Neither looked at all fearful.

"Excellent idea, boys." Simon's heart hammered. "I don't want any trouble. I'm going to get in my car and leave. I don't want you to follow me ... and I don't want to see either of you again."

"Just one thing, sir," the one closest to the car said in a deep, rumbling, Sylvester Stallone voice. "I have a message for you in my coat pocket."

"Which pocket?"

"The right one, sir."

Simon pointed the gun toward the other man. "You. Go beside your buddy, take the note out of his pocket with your left hand, and lay it on the ground. Then the two of you back off."

The second thug did as instructed.

Once they had backed off, Simon shifted his grip on his pistol, stooped, and, knowing he was vulnerable, picked up the message. Time slowed as he stood. If they were going to attack him, this was their best opportunity.

They remained in place.

Getting out of the situation without a scuffle was imperative. Reading the note could wait. "I'll go over this later. Now turn toward the dumpster and press your palms on it. Stay that way until you hear my horn. Understand?"

"Yes, sir," the one nearest the car said.

Keeping an eye on the two, Simon got in the Mercedes, started the engine, and, gun still at the ready, drove away, scattering a foraging flock of seagulls. At the end of the alley, he let out a breath of relief, put the gun away, and hit his horn.

On the way to the front of the restaurant, Simon read the note: *Stop nosing around.* The very same words Father John had used to describe the threatening emails. Too much coincidence. Simon shoved the note in his pocket. He'd bet a bundle that both messages came from the same person, and that the person was local. So, what did Connie's research and his detective work to find Trey have in common? He'd bet his military-honed instinct they were up against the same adversary.

When the Mercedes pulled up in front of the restaurant, Father John hustled Patricia to the car and left. Once inside the car with Simon, she asked about going to the next restaurant on her list.

"What? That's crazy," he said. "What are you thinking? We can't just walk into a restaurant. It takes time to set up a secure entrance and exit."

"It's important I visit these restaurants as soon as possible. Certainly in the next day or two. We can work as a team. I can go in while you arrange the next—"

"What are you up to, Patricia?" The uncharacteristic frost in his voice chilled her.

"I'm looking for my husband." She forced a smile.

"That's what the police are for," he snapped.

She shook her head. "So far they haven't come up with anything. And I can't just sit and wait. I need to do something to help find him."

He rolled his eyes. "In a restaurant?"

"No," she said, trying to control the anger in her voice. "I want to speak with people he was with the week before he disappeared to find out if they might lead me to Trey. His credit card receipts reveal where he ate that week." She held up the head shot of Trey. "I intend to show them this photo and see if they remember him." Her cheeks burned. "I have to do this, Simon. For my sanity, I must do this."

He grimaced. "Okay. Here's what we're going to do. We'll go to the restaurants. You stay in the car while I go in and see if anyone remembers Trey."

"It's my job, Simon, and because I'm less intimidating than you I'm more likely to get cooperation."

"You're also more vulnerable in an unsecured restaurant. We do it my way or not at all."

"I'm vulnerable sitting in the car."

"Not in an armored vehicle with bullet-proof windows."

"Do I have to remind you that my state-of-the-art home security system was breached?"

"Apples and oranges. Irrelevant comparison. If you want me on this, you stay in the car."

"If you insist."

"I absolutely insist. Okay?"

She nodded.

He started up the Mercedes. "What's the first stop?"

Patricia directed him to a pub on a side street just off Falcon Square.

After driving around the block twice to make sure they weren't being followed, Simon took the picture and went in. Five minutes later, he came out.

As soon as he entered the car, Patricia asked, "Well?"

He waved his hand toward the historic brick building and shook his head. "No one there remembers him."

Hope wilted. And so it went for the next four leads.

When Simon returned from the sixth establishment, he was smiling.

"How'd it go?" she asked, full of anticipation.

"The manager remembers Trey having lunch with a frail, old man severely bent with scoliosis. The date on this credit card transaction is the day before Trey disappeared. The manager said the two had an extended, animated conversation, but they seemed to end their discussion on agreeable terms. From the description, I'd guess this was Lucius Alton."

The seventh and eighth restaurants were dead ends.

So Trey spoke with Lucius the day before he disappeared

and Grigory on the day of his disappearance. Now she had to find out what business they discussed. Could she get Lucius to talk? No way. Lucius was iron-willed on Coalition secrecy. Frustration mounted. Lucius wouldn't talk, but Grigory might. She glanced at the dash clock. It was too late to contact Grigory today. Or was it? He ran a hotel. He might keep late hours. She called the number on his card without success.

Patricia rang Willy immediately on her return home. "I got your text. What did you find out about the bachelorette auction?"

"You were right, Patricia." Willy's voice was vibrant. "There's something fishy going on."

She scuffed the carpet with the toe of her shoe. "Prostitution?"

"Yes. More than your average pimp-controlled independents. Possibly organized crime."

So, her intuition had been right. "Drugs?"

"Not at this point."

"What exactly did you find out?"

"Snooping around, I found one of the young women, who claims to be a student, lives in a luxury condo on Jones Street and drives a 7 Series BMW."

"That's some high-class living for a student. She must be a sugar baby with a sugar daddy."

"She's not a student here. She's the PR Manager for The Amber House, the bed and breakfast that was bombed last night."

Patricia nodded. "Amber House? I just met the owner."

"Grigory Trokev?"

"Yeah. Do you know him?"

"No. But get this - he's also the owner of the condo complex the bachelorette lives in."

Patricia shivered. "That job couldn't possibly cover her

rent, much less her car lease. Unless he's losing money, which I doubt by the way he dresses."

"Exactly."

"And she's not getting any money from selling a date for charity."

"True," he said. "But she's getting a lot of exposure to the right people in Savannah. Those gala tickets cost $500 per person."

Patricia switched her phone to the other ear. "What makes you think it's organized crime?"

"Five girls doing the same thing has to be organized. But what clinches it is Allison Hope's murder."

She gritted her teeth. "Allison's murder?"

"Two things. Cops say the murder was a professional hit. Do you have any idea how many *professional* hits we have in Savannah? Almost none. So I'm reasoning that organized crime takes out one of our most visible independent 'escorts' and the rest, fearing for their lives, leave. When the independents leave, the five now well-known women fill the void."

"Clever."

"The missing element for me is how these new women are going to avoid prosecution," Willy said. "To make this kind of enterprise work, you have to have dirt on the upper echelon of the local justice system. As far as I know, this operation is too new to have that kind of influence."

"So the women get arrested. Get convicted. Go to jail."

"Organized crime wouldn't go into a venture like that," Willy said. "I'm missing something here."

She prickled. "What are you going to do with what you have so far?"

"Sit on it until I figure out the missing element."

"I'm glad you got this far so fast."

"Thank you for the tip. I should have known better than to doubt you."

* * *

Around three, Simon came into the study carrying Trokev's business card like an Olympic torch. As he crossed the room toward Patricia, she wondered what was up. The smile he wore suggested good news. Good news for whom?

"This guy Trokev is a big operator," Simon said. "Too big to be in Savannah. He appears to have international connections with major players on both sides of the law. A guy like him doesn't just come to town and open a small bed and breakfast. There's got to be more going on."

"Like organized crime?" Patricia stared at him.

He shrugged. "Well, he's providing employment and housing for one of the bachelorettes. Other than that, I haven't the slightest idea. Father John is my international go-to guy. I've asked him to have his Vatican people check out the man. Meanwhile, I think it would be an excellent idea for you to have lunch with Mr. Trokev again."

She forced a smile. "Why?"

"Because you said you wanted to talk with him."

"But why are *you* so interested?"

"Just curious. Call it intuition."

"And you want me to help you?"

"Yep. Sometimes a woman, even a fine Southern woman like you, has to get her hands dirty."

* * *

Chief Patrick called that evening with his customary report that Jackson was getting nowhere.

She bit her tongue and squashed the toxic urge to scream at his incompetency. She had managed to find Trey's link to an organized crime boss in less time than it took the chief to pick a Krispy Kreme doughnut.

## CHAPTER 14

*P*atricia dropped the morning newspaper in the recycle bin and, with the television playing in the background, brewed another cup of coffee. Willy's incendiary story of Allison Hope's murder and relationship with District Attorney Bobby Gilbert filled the front page. What's more, the story had caught the attention of the local television stations, and every morning show host editorialized on the affair whether they knew the truth or not.

Simon came into the kitchen carrying a coffee cup. "Are you up for lunch with Trokev again?" he asked, his eyes earnest.

"Yes." She chuckled. "I thought you were going to pounce on him the last time when he reached inside his coat to get his business card."

Simon's face tightened. "That and a whole lot more if he had produced a weapon."

"I'm so grateful to have you with me." She gave him a smile.

"Thank you." Detecting movement, she looked out the

window as Rhett, their gardener, walked across the patio and knocked on the back door. "It's Rhett," she said.

Simon nodded his approval to Patricia. Simon's rule was rigid. He, and he alone, approved all visitors, even reoccurring ones.

Patricia opened the door and Rhett came in with a big stone in his hand. "There was some vandalism in the garage last night, Mrs. Falcon. A broken window. I found this rock inside."

Vandalism? At a time like this? As if she didn't have enough problems. Annoyance mounted at the piling on of problems.

"I'll take that," Simon said, his voice bristling. He wrapped a paper towel around the rock.

She turned to Simon. "I didn't hear an alarm."

"It's a detached garage," he said. "I'm not sure it's alarmed. I'll check and if it's not, I'll set it up."

"We keep our cars in there. Why wouldn't it be alarmed?"

"Human error," Simon said, his head hung low.

"That's unacceptable, Simon." Patricia turned to Rhett. "Thank you, Rhett. Board up the window and arrange to have a replacement installed as soon as possible."

"Yes, ma'am."

After Rhett left, Simon held up the smooth, cabbage-sized rock. "Where would something like this come from?"

Patricia recognized the distinctive rock. "It's a ballast stone. Old clipper ships used the stones as ballast when sailing here empty, then left them behind when they returned to England laden with the local cotton. The stones are plentiful down by the harbor. River Street is paved with them."

"Any of them around Falcon Square?"

"Not that I know of."

"Interesting choice of weapon." He cleared his throat.

"Whoever did this could have used a brick. There are plenty of those in this neighborhood. But no, someone brought this stone all the way from the harbor. This was no spur of the moment prank." He laid the towel-wrapped rock on the granite counter and headed for the back door. "I'm going to take a closer look around the garage."

"What's going on?"

"I don't think this was vandalism."

The back of her neck tingled. "Me neither."

"I'd say it was a message."

\* \* \*

SIMON STUDIED THE EXTERIOR OF THE DETACHED GARAGE. No damage except for the side window facing the street. He took a smartphone from his back pocket and snapped a couple of photos, then went over to the broken window, carefully watching where he stepped so he wouldn't trample any evidence. The upper window was undamaged. Based on the fragments remaining in the lower frame, the rock had hit the bottom pane more or less dead center. Good aim ... or luck. He'd go with good aim. He took close-up shots, then returned the phone to his pocket.

No one should have been able to do this undetected. Yet, because he'd failed to provide protection for the garage, someone had. They had penetrated his defenses and, in the process, gained access to Patricia's car.

It wouldn't happen again. He'd have security cameras and alarms up on the garage before lunch. And he'd switch out the car and have the cleanup crew go over this one with a fine-toothed comb.

Simon made a call to the Coalition for an immediate vehicle exchange, and then shoved his hands in his pockets and studied the window again. From the glass shards on the window ledge, it didn't appear the perpetrator had entered the garage from that point. The window was still locked in place, and jagged glass remaining in the lower frame precluded entry through the bottom pane.

Unless the person used the jagged hole to open the window, entered the garage through the window, done whatever to the car, exited the window, and relocked it.

Okay. He had to accept that possibility. In which case, switching out the car was an excellent idea. If the car had been altered, the intruder may have left something in or on the car that could be traced. He'd leave that up to the forensic guys.

If something was found on the car, that would provide the *why* for the incident. If not, the question remained to be answered. Was the incident intended to test the home's defenses? If so, the perpetrator learned that the garage was unprotected.

Or was the incident designed to trigger the Falcon security system and then determine how they would react to an intrusion. In that case, the intruder had failed, and another attempt would surely be made ... soon.

All led back to the reason someone would want to test the Falcon security system. Simon's jaw tightened. There was no innocent answer to that. Someone wanted to get inside again. And the use of a specific type of stone might indicate they wanted him to know it.

*Why* again became the focus. To hurt or kidnap Mrs. Falcon? Or was there something inside the house the perpetrators wanted? Hard to say which, but neither alternative was good and it was his job to make absolutely certain neither occurred. No more fumbles.

Who was responsible for this intrusion? The rock and the car might have fingerprints. And why would they haul the rock six blocks. Maybe they were staying on River Street and didn't want to take a chance on not finding something suitable in the Falcon neighborhood.

Simon put on plastic gloves and pulled a hand-sized fragment of glass from the frame. The shard was thicker and heavier than normal. Possibly high tensile, hurricane-resistant type. If so, whoever threw the stone would have a powerful arm. A well-conditioned person. He'd have the neighbors interviewed to see if anyone saw someone hanging around or heard glass shattering.

About ten feet from the window, Simon found a cigarette butt - black wrapper with a Russian imperial eagle emblazoned. *Sobranie.* One of the oldest tobacco brands in the world, but unusual for this country. Sloppy and careless to discard a butt. Not something a professional would do. Except on purpose. He placed the butt in an evidence envelope. With any luck his forensic guys would get DNA off the filter end.

He searched for other trash, footprints, and snagged fabric. Finding nothing, he returned to the house.

Fifteen minutes later, Simon was back in the garage with his thoughts whirling and four pea-sized, wireless security cameras in his hand. High-tech, high-res equipment pulled from the drone program. After installing two inside the garage, he went back outside. He scanned the yard, seeking good locations for the two external cameras. Using an extension ladder, he placed one camera ten feet high in an old oak. No one looked for surveillance cameras in roadside trees. He placed the other camera in full view above the garage window. Should the perpetrator return, this camera would announce that new security measures had been taken. And should it be tampered with he'd be alerted, then the camera would self-destruct, spraying the intruder with permanent dye.

As he headed back to the house, he scanned the area for a good place to hide and observe for the next several nights.

* * *

PATRICIA'S JAW DROPPED AS GRIGORY CAME INTO THE MAIN dining area of The Black Lantern accompanied by a bull of a man. She'd never seen anyone so large and yet so fit. Huge shoulders. Massive arms. Rectangular face with a square chin. His deep-set eyes darted from side to side.

She swallowed and stood.

The giant took a table just inside the entrance, not far from where Simon sat studying a menu.

Grigory offered his hand.

She wasn't comfortable with his hand kissing, but since she needed his cooperation she gave him a smile and placed her hand in his.

He bowed ever so slightly, brought her hand to his mouth and, pale blue eyes on hers, kissed the back of her hand. This was different than the first time. More elaborate. Like the first time had been a rehearsal, and this was the real thing.

Still smiling, he gestured to the table. He held her chair while she sat, then rounded the table and sat opposite her.

"How are you coming with getting your hotel restarted after the bombing?" she asked.

"Slow progress."

She hadn't expected an opportunity to soften him up with an offer to help. "I know people with a lot of experience in construction. Let me know if I can be of any assistance."

"Thank you, Mrs. Falcon. That's very kind of you."

A waiter appeared.

"Do you mind if I order a beverage for us?" he asked. "Perhaps champagne?"

She didn't want alcohol to slow her down but making a

glass of wine last the entire meeting would appear hospitable. "Champagne would be nice."

He ordered Dom.

Was this a date or a business meeting? She hoped she hadn't misled him. If she had, lunch could prove to be awkward.

"I hope your search for your husband is going well."

"Not well at all. That's why I asked to speak with you again."

The champagne arrived. It was sampled, approved and poured.

Grigory raised his coupe. "To your husband's speedy return."

As she raised her glass, her eyes welled at the thought of what Trey might be enduring. She returned the coupe to the table without drinking and dabbed her eyes with her napkin. "Please pardon me. I'm still having trouble with his absence."

"I'm terribly sorry, Mrs. Falcon. I should—"

"No need to be sorry." She picked up her champagne glass and raised it. "To my beloved husband, wherever he is. May his return be swift."

Grigory raised his glass. "Well said."

She again noticed his distinctive signet ring. "That's an attractive ring. Quite unique."

He looked at his own hand as if seeing it for the first time. "It is Armenian. An antique dating to the early Middle Ages."

"Does the cross and arm symbol have any particular significance?"

"It's the symbol of a secret Catholic relic cult that dates to the Middle Ages."

"How interesting." She toyed with her champagne glass as her dinner conversation with Father John's daughter crossed her mind. "Are you a member?"

He smiled. "Oh no. Not at all. The cult disbanded centuries ago."

"How did you come by the ring?"

"I collect Eastern European religious artifacts. I have several with me at the hotel." His eyes sharpened. "If you're interested, I'd be happy to show them to you."

How ironic Father John was researching relics and this guy was a collector. "Perhaps after my husband returns."

He nodded. "How may I assist you with that?"

"It would be most helpful if you could tell me what business you discussed with my husband."

He waved his hand dismissively. "Our business has nothing to do with his disappearance."

What business would Trey have with a crime boss other than Coalition business? "It might."

"I assure you, Madame, it doesn't."

"Did it involve a third party?"

"Most assuredly."

"Who?"

He tilted his head. "Someone who knows how to oil the machine."

"A prominent member of Savannah society?"

"Perhaps."

"Was Trey aware of that person being involved?"

He took his glass and stared at it for a moment. "I don't believe so."

"Did that person know Trey was involved?"

"Yes."

"Would that person have any reason to hurt my husband?"

"I don't know that *hurt* is the right word, but I do know my partner wasn't fond of Mr. Falcon. That's why I handled all the discussions."

Trey had enemies among the movers and shakers. And

now one of them was teamed up with this guy. Not good. "I'd really like to know who this person is."

"Believe me. I'd like to help you, but giving you his name is quite impossible."

"Why?" she said, fighting impatience.

"Why? Because my business is in the process of some very large acquisitions. If my local, shall we say, affiliations were to be revealed, it would jeopardize those negotiations."

"My inquiries would be discreet. I'd just like a name to follow up with." She brought her palm to her chest. "I'd not tell a soul."

He raised his hand defensively. "You know very well there are no secrets. It's best for all involved I don't tell you his name. Besides, my associate is not a violent man. Doing something harmful to your husband would not be in my associate's nature. Not at all. The answers to your husband's disappearance are elsewhere."

Frustration mounted. She didn't like failure, but her social schooling made confrontation unthinkable. Besides, she didn't have a clue how to pull off something as crude as that. Simon, Lucius and Trey would. Probably Isabel and Meredith. But not her. She shook her head. "You won't reconsider?"

Their salads arrived.

"No. I've already said too much about the matter. By the way, do you know that gentleman over there?" He gestured toward Simon.

"No."

"Oh. I thought he might be your bodyguard."

\* \* \*

Traveling a block behind with his headlights off, Father John watched Trokev ease his car to the side of the road. John jerked his Hummer to the curb and stopped well back. He consulted the GPS. They were on the edge of Bonaventure Cemetery, not far from Saint Augustine Creek.

Trokev, dressed in black, emerged from his car and headed down a dark, dirt lane canopied with old oaks. Strange time for a walk. Where are you going, Grigory, and, more importantly, why?

John, also dressed completely in black and now wearing state-of-the-art night vision goggles, stepped from his vehicle and, camera in hand, followed from a distance. Every few seconds, he glanced behind to assure he was alone.

What was Trokev doing out here? The man had to have people who did 'errands' for him. Why was this errand so important? The need for secrecy? From whom? John swallowed hard. Who was Trokev afraid of?

At the end of the lane, Trokev knocked on the front door of a log cabin. When a tall Hispanic man in dreadlocks appeared, John zoomed the lens of his ultra-sensitive camera and clicked off several shots of the two before they disappeared inside.

John moved closer, then circled the cabin. One door and two curtained windows in the front. The other three sides, nothing but logs. No windows. No doors. No outbuildings.

He returned to the front of the house and attached a surveillance microphone to the window. Sound filled his earbuds as he retreated to the shadows. Two voices. He adjusted the receiver until the conversation became intelligible.

One voice was heavily accented.

The other spoke perfect English. Trokev had spoken without an accent at The Amber House.

" ... returned intact," Trokev said.

"Like for like," Dreadlocks said.

"Once I authenticate it."

"Understood." Receding footfalls echoed. "Would you like to see it?"

"If you don't mind," Trokev said.

A thwack, then a thud.

Moments later Trokev emerged from the cabin carrying a two-foot-long wooden box.

John snapped more photos, hoping they'd be the key to learning what just happened in there, then tailed Trokev back to his hotel.

# CHAPTER 15

*M*inutes before his nine a.m. meeting with Trokev, Benjamin Hempfield stood quietly in a debris-laden construction zone that had been the ornate lobby of The Amber House. He'd been through hostage negotiations before, so he knew it helped to appear calm and collected.

Trokev wouldn't like the ultimatum. Produce Trey or have his global string of brothels taken down one by one. Sure, the ultimatum was a form of terrorism. The Coalition had learned long ago to fight dirty when necessary. The big unknown was how Trokev would react. Well, they were about to find out.

Maria, petite but no doubt as deadly as a viper, escorted him into the scanning room. From there they moved to a small office with an intact window, where a scowling Trokev stood beside a desk. A manager's cubicle, not a CEO's office.

Trokev, dressed in a trim black suit, grey shirt, and a black silk tie, leveled piercing blue eyes on Benjamin. If he was going for intimidation, it was a wasted effort. What was the worst thing Trokev could do? Kill him? So what? Death would end the guilt and nightmares. Death would reunite him with his wife and daughter and bring the beginning of eternity with them.

Trokev extended his pale hand. "I hope you bring me good news, Mr. Hempfield."

Benjamin shook Trokev's hand stiffly. It was best to stay formal and keep his distance. "News is rarely good in this business."

Trokev removed his gold-rimmed glasses and narrowed his eyes. "So you are going to be unpleasant? I must warn you, I have not had a good day." Trokev gestured to a pair of high-backed, brown leather chairs in the corner.

Benjamin remained in place. Bad news was best delivered standing. "No. I'll keep things cordial and brief."

"Fine."

"You have detained our negotiator. That is hostile behavior."

Trokev shrugged. "You have plowed that ground. Do you have anything of substance to say?"

"I consulted with my associates. We wish to go back to the beginning. Start fresh. We'll return everything to you and will reimburse your investment in our community at full cost, despite the fact that your property is badly damaged. Furthermore, we will give you a relocation allowance of one million US dollars deposited to the bank of your choice or, if you wish, in gold or cash."

Trokev nodded. "Most generous. What do you expect of me?"

"We merely require two things: the swift return of Mr. Falcon, unharmed, and the relocation of your Savannah businesses elsewhere."

"When Mr. Falcon made me a similar offer, I said no. Why would I now agree?"

Benjamin walked to the window and looked out at the

serene town square across the street. If only people knew what really went on behind the scenes to give them the peace they took for granted. The time. The money. The sacrifices. The ugliness. He turned from the window. "When you turned down our original offer, you might not have been fully aware of the consequences of doing so. Unfortunately, you were naïve and doubted our resolve. You know better now."

Trokev tilted his head. "I do recall Mr. Falcon was vague regarding consequences. Do you intend to be similarly vague?"

"No." Benjamin returned to the desk. "There will be no doubt about consequences this time."

Trokev nodded.

Benjamin removed a folded, letter-sized sheet of paper from his jacket pocket and handed it to the Russian.

Trokev's brow furrowed when he saw the content. "How did you come by this?"

"How is unimportant. The document assures you we are well aware of the intimate details of your global business operations."

"Most impressive. But hardly a negotiating tool." Trokev, his formerly pale face now flushed, went behind his desk, put the document in a drawer and sat. Clearly an attempt to seize some measure of control of the situation.

Benjamin leaned forward, palms resting on Trokev's barren desk. "I agree. The financial summary merely serves to reinforce my statement of the consequences of not accepting our offer."

Trokev settled back in his chair and scratched his stomach. "The consequences being?"

"Should we not come to agreement today, we will completely destroy your business interests. Not just swimming pools. We will assassinate your managers, reduce your facilities to rubble and drain your bank accounts. Division by division. The first being your brothels, your largest and most profitable division. It is not a threat. It is what will surely occur. Would that get your attention?"

Trokev leaned forward, scowling. "Would killing Mr. Falcon get *yours?*"

*Oh hell.* Benjamin, unwilling to show vulnerability, shook his head. "Not in the least."

"What about Mr. Falcon's family? His delightful wife, who visits me daily, and his lovely daughter."

Benjamin shrugged.

"Plus you and your family."

Benjamin clenched his jaw. He needed to get Trokev off this subject. "Grigory, besides having faulty information on my family, you're missing the point. We are patriots in service to the 350,000 residents of metropolitan Savannah. There is no higher honor for us than to die serving our fellow men."

Trokev gave a hearty belly laugh. "Do you really expect me to believe such drivel?"

Benjamin unbuttoned his shirt to expose stigmata scars on his chest. "No, but perhaps you will believe this."

"I see."

"I'm glad you understand we embrace a higher calling. Death is a blessing for us. So. Do you accept our offer?"

Trokev seemed to consider the question. "It's not my decision."

"You run the brothels. No one else."

"Your information is correct."

"Then make it happen."

"This situation is unique." Trokev closed his eyes briefly, then opened then. "I have a partner, a local sponsor. A person with whom I must consult with before making a decision of this magnitude."

"Then take my offer to your partner."

Trokev reached under his desk. "I'll do better than that. I will take you to him and you can present your demands to him in person tonight."

Maria came into the room, gun in hand.

Benjamin smiled. "She's not going to need that. I'll be happy to speak to the man. However, before we speak further, I'd like proof Mr. Falcon is alive."

"I thought you didn't care about his survival."

"He's a soldier. If he dies in service, fine. But he's a good soldier, and I'd like to keep him in service for as long as possible. So, I want proof of life."

"I don't think you understand, Mr. Hempfield. You are my prisoner. You are not in a position to make any demands."

"Grigory, Grigory, Grigory. Do you recall what happened the last time you said that?"

The Russian gestured dismissively. "Swimming pools. So what?"

"I'm afraid it's no longer swimming pools." Benjamin maintained his smile. "Call your Thailand operation and see if they're happy with the fire. Oh, just to let you know ... no local firefighters will be dispatched to that location. You're now out of business in Thailand. Also Portugal and Ireland. If you wish to stay viable at the remaining locations, I suggest you produce proof of life within the hour."

Trokev's face flamed.

"Now. Take me to the man I should have been talking to all along."

* * *

"PATRICIA!" SIMON SHOUTED.

Patricia, seated on the sofa writing checks for bills, jerked her head toward him. What was going on? Simon never shouted. She pulled her purse, and the gun it contained, closer.

He rushed into the room. "It's Trey. He's on Skype."

Patricia jumped to her feet, scattering correspondence. She took the phone from him and turned it so she could see the screen image of her beloved husband.

The air left her lungs. Tears welled, blurring her vision. She brushed them aside. It was him. Trey. Alive. In a heavy coat and hunched over a table. Smiling. "Hello, honey," she croaked. "Are you okay?"

There was a considerable time lag before he nodded and said, "I'm fine. How are you?"

Simon scribbled on a pad and held the note for her to see. It read: *Time short. Ask about sleep.*

She nodded her understanding to Simon, they'd been over this previously. She forced her concern for Trey to the back of her mind. "I'm having trouble sleeping. How about you?"

"Light sleep. Just getting four hours at a time, then I wake up and can't get back to sleep," he said.

She knew that meant he was lightly guarded and had seen only four guards.

Simon held up a second note with 'food' written on it.

"Are they feeding you well, honey?"

"Sure 'nuff it isn't your home cooking. I miss your baklava and roasted turkey. It would be nice to have some goulash. They give me country-style bread. How's Hayley?"

The prearranged code that Simon said all Coalition members used meant Trey thought he might be in Greece or Turkey ... and somewhere out in the countryside. His mention of goulash startled her and she wondered if that was idle talk to hide the code or an intentional message. She'd check with Simon when the call was over.

"Hayley's visiting her first grade teacher." Simon had said that Trey would probably ask about Hayley and that her answer of 'first grade teacher' would let Trey know that Hayley was under the highest level of protection the Cotton Coalition could provide. After the time lag, Trey nodded his approval ... and then the screen went black.

She shoved the phone at Simon and buried her face in her hands, letting out her pent-up emotions. Fear. Joy. Terror. Tears poured, burning her eyes and stuffing her nose.

Simon handed her a tissue, and then left. There was no consoling hug from him. It wasn't in his character.

She soaked tissue after tissue until she had cried herself out. Her head throbbed. She headed to the kitchen for water, passing through Simon's control center on the way.

He sat before a large monitor, advancing the video recording of Trey's call frame by frame.

"Did you get much?" she asked.

He looked up with a rare smile. "It's a goldmine of information. We finally have something to go on."

Her heart leapt. Since Trey's disappearance good news had been scarce. A broad smile stretched her lips. It felt great to have even a sliver of hope. "How's that?"

"Trey mentioned Greece or Turkey. I didn't get a complete trace, but I had the source narrowed to Armenia before they cut him off. They were smart to limit his time on the call, but it was the only smart thing his kidnappers did. They made too many mistakes. They're not pros."

Trey had often said that one man's mistakes were another man's opportunities. Hope swelled, then morphed into anticipation that these mistakes could speed Trey's return. "Mistakes are good. Right?"

"The portion of the call I was able to trace wasn't routed through anonymous servers. That allowed faster tracing." Simon paused the video, zoomed in on something. The close-up picture was too pixilated to tell what it was. His fingers went to the keyboard where he tapped some function keys. The picture sharpened. It was Trey's eye and it reflected a faint image of someone in front of him. Simon captured the image, then resumed reviewing the video frame by frame. "Of course, allowing questions was also a blunder because that permitted Trey to provide the coded answers. Also, allowing Trey to use his hands was a mistake. Throughout the video, he was using sign language. Whoever was handling the video camera was zooming the camera in and out, so I didn't get it all. Overall, a real amateurish job by them."

"That's good."

"Good and bad. It's harder to predict what amateurs might do."

Anticipation faded, but hope remained. Hope for a solid clue. "Was there anything useful in the background?"

"Nothing obvious. But once I finish going through the frames one by one on a macro basis. I'll repeat the process examining each frame on a micro basis. That takes much more time, but that's where hidden clues might appear in the background."

If something was there, Simon would find it. He just needed the time. "There wasn't a ransom demand."

"No. There wasn't. This was what we call a proof of life call. It's designed to make our side more amenable to negotiation."

"But we don't know who we're negotiating with yet."

"Yeah. That might take some time. Meanwhile we know that Trey is in good condition, and that he's somewhere in the Armenian countryside under light guard."

"He mentioned goulash. Any idea why?" she asked.

"I noticed that too. Does he like goulash?"

She nodded. Armenia. Trokev's ring. Goulash. Trey meeting with Trokev. Everything pointed back at Trokev.

She just knew Trokev was behind this, but how could she pin it down. "Trey orders goulash when he eats at The Black Lantern."

"It was probably just something he said to cover his coded answers. But I noted it in my report. We need to look into that."

* * *

As soon as Trey's video call to Patricia was terminated he was handcuffed, then his escort led him through the house, out the front door, and into a black van.

It was the first time since his arrival he'd been outside the walled compound, which was the only habitation in sight. It stood on a sizable plateau at the foot of snow-covered mountains. The van started up and headed from the compound. The road leading across the plateau to the compound was hardly a road. Just two dirt tracks in browned-out grass. The thumping tires pierced the silence within the van.

There were just the three of them in the van. The host sat beside him in the backseat. The driver, a frail old man, sat by himself.

"What kind of van is this?" Trey asked as the vehicle pulled away from the compound.

"ErAZ," said his escort. "We will pass the old plant on the way to the airport."

Airport? Trey stiffened. He'd been able to pass some information about his existing location to the guys back home, but now that information had become irrelevant. He had to hand it to his captors. Moving him around was going to make finding him much harder. Harder, but not impossible. He looked out the back window, hoping against hope to see a drone on their tail, but wasn't surprised to see nothing but empty blue sky.

# CHAPTER 16

*S*eated at her desk in the study, Patricia clicked on the browser's search icon and, recalling what Simon had said, typed *Armenia*.

She assumed Simon had done the same thing, but she knew from past experience he wouldn't share the results of his search. She couldn't settle for that. She *had* to know where Trey was.

The proof of life call showed he was alive and seemed to be well. But he was being held captive half a world away, and she had no idea what, Lord forbid, might have befallen him after the call. *Please, Lord, keep him safe ... and speed his return.*

During her search, she stumbled across a page of Armenian symbols and meanings. Recalling Trokev's signet ring was an Armenian antique, she decided to see if the ring's arm and cross symbol was among those on the image website.

She found the cross-arm symbol in a photo taken at an Armenian monastery of Saint Gregory the Illuminator. She heaved a sigh of relief at finally making a connection.

Further research placed the monastery not far from the

Mount Sebuh sanctuary in Upper Armenia, where Saint Gregory spent his final years. Trokev said the signet ring identified members of a defunct Armenian relic cult. And the symbol on it was carved on the wall in a monastery where Saint Gregory had died.

*Wait a minute.* Father John mentioned looking for relics of Saint Gregory at dinner. She would ask John about the relic cults associated with the saint. But when would she be able to speak with him?

Instead of waiting to talk with John, she Googled the subject and found several references to the saint's relics being of interest to cults over the centuries. The cults gathered the relics, protected them and made them available for veneration.

Further investigation revealed there was a long history of illicit commerce in religious relics. Trokev claimed he was a collector. Was he involved in trafficking stolen relics? He mentioned he was willing to show her part of his collection at his bed and breakfast.

Out of curiosity, she ran a search on Trokev and wasn't surprised by reports of his worldwide criminal enterprises, reports that suspected him of being a senior leader of Russian organized crime. Simon had said as much. But Simon hadn't said that Trokev operated a global string of exclusive brothels.

Oh my. Was *that* what the man was doing in Savannah? Bed and breakfast? Yeah, right. Score one more for Willy. She swiveled away from the desk, stood on unsteady legs, and shuffled back to Simon's control center.

Still dressed in his armored vest, he looked up, brows raised. "Do you want something?"

"Did you know that Trokev operated brothels?"

Hand frozen over the keyboard, he nodded.

Curiosity tempered her frustration at having information withheld. "Why didn't you tell me?"

"No need to know," he said, his voice and manner restrained.

Her cheeks heated. "No need to know? You gotta be kidding. You've allowed me to meet the man twice for lunch. It would have been useful for me to know what his business was. Jeez, Simon. The man invited me to go back to his hotel to look at his religious artifacts."

His eyes narrowed. "Did he?"

She nodded.

"And your common sense kept you from accepting his invitation?" He cocked his head.

"At the time." She chose not to tell Simon about the relic cult connection. She didn't want him taking it and excluding her. It was her clue, and for the time being she alone would pursue it. When necessary, she wouldn't hesitate to bring Simon into play.

"Not that I would have let you, but it was smart to not even consider it."

"How can someone just fly into Savannah and set up a brothel? Right here. In the historic district, in plain sight?"

"It takes connections," Simon said.

"Does Trokev have connections?"

"I suppose."

She raised an eyebrow. "Suppose ... or know?"

He blinked. "No comment."

"Come on, Simon, humor me," she said, fluttering her eyelashes. Mama always said 'charm your way to success.' "Hypothetically, how would someone do it?"

"Hypothetically, they'd bring some fabulous women to town and discreetly introduce them to the movers and shakers. Men who could be deemed as the right connections. Once the right men became deeply involved with the women, the organization would become immune from prosecution. Then the women would go more public."

"As in the bachelorette dating auction and gala?"

"Yes, that might work."

"It's that easy?"

"Yes. Mind you, I'm not suggesting that any of this is actually happening."

*Was this what Trey was discussing with Trokev?* "If it was occurring, would the Coalition intervene?"

A sheepish look came over Simon's face. His lips tightened, as if he worried he'd said too much.

"Come on, Simon. Would the Coalition intervene?"

He nodded so slightly she might have missed it.

"Trey?"

His eyes blazed. "Drop it, Patricia. The Coalition is working on securing your husband's release. That's all you need. Knowing more puts you in jeopardy."

She winced at his rebuke. "I've had lunch twice with the man who is probably behind Trey's kidnapping and you don't want me to know what's going on. My house has been broken into and my garage vandalized and you're concerned about putting me in jeopardy? If anyone has a need to know, it's me."

"Crime bosses like Trokev prefer that people don't know their business. They react violently when their activities are publicized."

She spread her arms, palms up. "There are stories about Trokev all over the internet."

"First off, those stories lack substance. Second, if you look closely at those reports, a lot of the information is recycled, much of which is disinformation made public by Trokev surrogates. Third, the small amount of truthful information is from public records on the rare instances members of his organization have run afoul of the law."

She sat in a chair next to Simon. "I suppose the Coalition has plenty of non-public information on Trokev."

"We know more about his businesses than his accountant."

"You said Trokev reacts harshly to people who know too much. Isn't the Coalition concerned? You let me have lunch with him. Twice. Were you using me?"

"They only punish those who make it public. We keep our information to ourselves."

Eyes fixed on his, she leaned forward. "Did Trokev kidnap Trey? Come on, Simon." She brought her palm to her chest. "I'm his wife. I *need* this information. No, I'm *entitled* to it."

"I'm not at liberty to say. I'm sorry." He grimaced. "Now, if you don't mind, I have to get back to this job. Your husband's life may depend on how fast I can get it done. Surely you understand."

"What I understand is that you damn well better succeed, Simon." Patricia clenched her jaw. Of course she wanted information, but getting Trey back was what really mattered.

* * *

AROUND LUNCHTIME, PATRICIA HEADED TO THE BACK OF THE house, keeping a wary eye out for the unexpected. Taking nothing for granted, she scanned the back study for signs of disturbance before going in and, once in, checked the backyard.

Rhett, her gardener, was seated, back to her, on a bench in the far corner taking a break. He was a hard worker, and the mid-day temperature was well above normal for September.

Patricia returned to the kitchen, retrieved a bottle of chilled water from the refrigerator and went out the back door into the muggy air. Her sundress and sandals suited the weather.

Not wanting to startle Rhett, she called out to him as she approached, but he didn't respond. When she rounded the bench, she stumbled in shock.

"Oh, my God!" Bile surged. The right side of his head was gone. She dropped the water. Her heart thudded. She cringed, then retched. A stump remained where his right hand should have been.

Screaming, she ran for the house, though the dash felt like she was plowing through thick mud. This was a nightmare come true. She fumbled with the doorknob. Finally it caught. She surged in, resetting the security system once inside.

"Simon! Simon!" Patricia shouted in a squeaky voice. *Where was he?* "Simon!"

He rushed into the study. "What? What?"

"Rhett ... Rhett—"

"Rhett what?"

"He's dead." She pointed to the backyard. "Killed."

He pulled her into the hallway, put his body between her and the back window. "Who killed Rhett? Where?"

"He's dead." Her body quaked with shock and sobs trying to get out. "They killed—"

He took her by the shoulders and brought his face to hers. "Where?"

Tears so thick she could barely see him filled her eyes. "Ba ... backyard. Bench. Oh, Simon, what the hell is going on? They butchered him."

"You'll be all right." He removed his phone and punched the assist shortcut, then led her to a chair and helped her sit. "As long as you're inside and away from windows you're not in danger. Understand?"

She shook her head. "No. I don't understand. And no, I'm not safe. First the snake, then the garage. Now this. Rhett.

Why Rhett? He doesn't have—" She sniffled. "He doesn't have anything to do with any of this. Why, Simon? Why?"

"I wish I knew. But right now, sit here and don't move."

She shivered.

He touched her forearm. "Your skin is cool and clammy. You're probably in shock." He grabbed a blanket from the sofa and handed it to her. "Cover up. Lie down with your feet up."

She went to the sofa and did as he asked.

"Where's your purse?"

"Purse?"

"Gun. I want you armed."

"Kitchen. Next to the coffee maker."

Moments later, Simon, now carrying an automatic weapon, returned with her purse and a box of tissues. After he handed her the tissues, he removed her gun and checked it. He handed the Kimber to her. "Safety's off. Keep this with you at all times."

She nodded.

"You stay here," Simon said. "I'm going to check on Rhett."

After Simon left, a new wave of fear swept over her. Was Rhett's killer still out there? Was he in the house? Shivering uncontrollably, she scanned the room. Did the dark doorways conceal killers? How many were there? She listened for footfalls. She glanced down at her trembling hands. She was useless. She couldn't hit anything with her hands shaking like that. Forget it. Forget it all.

She wanted to run upstairs and hide in the safe room. Rhett's killers couldn't get her there. But Simon had told her to stay there. So she'd stay there and wait for the bad guys to come kill her. She shouldn't think like that, but she couldn't help herself.

Though she massaged her damp eyelids, her eyes continued to sting. What had the Falcon family been thinking to get wrapped up in trying to defend Savannah? What business did ordinary folk like Trey have going against cold-blooded killers? She'd seen the hole where half of Rhett's face once was and the stump of his arm. The Coalition had bitten off too much this time, and they were going to get themselves killed. All of them. Including Trey. Their families. "Hayley! Oh my God, Hayley!" Tears came again. Her sobbing intensified.

Simon returned.

She put her gun on the sofa and sat up. "Rhett?"

"I've called—"

"The police?" she asked.

"No. A clean-up crew."

"Why not the police?"

"This isn't a police matter." Simon propped his rifle on the coffee table and sat on the sofa as well.

"What do you mean? Rhett's dead."

"Precisely. Rhett's dead. End of matter."

"How can you be so cold?"

"Not cold. Professional. I'm sure Rhett's death is somehow involved with Trey's abduction. When we apprehend Trey's kidnappers, we'll also have the person responsible for Rhett's death."

"I want Rhett to have a proper burial."

"His family—"

"He doesn't have family. I want him buried at Bonaventure."

"I'll see what I can do."

"Simon. It's important to me."

He nodded.

"Am I supposed to just sit here?"

"No. You don't have to stay here. Just stay away from windows and don't go outside. And don't worry about the backyard. The crew will be discreet about the clean-up."

"I 'preciate that."

"So. Are you okay?" he asked.

She bristled. Rhett had done so much for her family. He was a lost soul when he arrived in Savannah, and had found himself in the city. "No. I'm not okay. I'll never be okay with this business, but I'll manage. For Trey's sake, I'll manage."

# CHAPTER 17

$S$hortly after dusk, Augusta met Doctor Snake in the back of Bonaventure Cemetery to discuss the arm. Snake stood on the bank of the Saint Augustine Creek. A full moon hung on the horizon, casting a silver shine on the still, black water.

Snake, shrouded in a dark robe, put his flat palm just below his chin and opened his mouth. A big, fury spider scurried out.

Augusta gasped.

He placed the spider on the ground, then gestured to the elaborately carved tombstones that stood to his left and right, marble sentinels as far as the eye could see. "I be happiest surrounded by ghosts. Can ya heard dem?"

She listened. "I only hear cicadas."

"Dem ain't no cicadas, child. Cicadas they don't come for long time, don't cha know? Maybe next year. Not now. What choo be hearing is ghost talk. Sho 'nuff."

She shivered in the warm air. Fact checking on the life cycle of cicadas in Savannah was definitely in order as soon as she returned to the office.

Snake sat on a white marble bench facing the creek. Augusta settled on the other end of the bench and stretched her back. He was a strange person. He heard ghost voices in night sounds the same way people imagined animal shapes in rock and cloud formations. It probably suited his life's mission. There were certainly enough shadowy shapes in the cemetery to fill anyone's imagination.

"Dem ghosts say dey like ya."

"I'm glad to hear that," Augusta said, hoping to conceal her disbelief.

A squirrel, nose twitching, crept from the dark shrubbery, then scurried to her feet.

On hearing rustling to her side, she turned to see Snake shaking a small paper bag. *What was with the bag?*

"I call dis squirrel Licorice cause he likes de roots." A smile filled Snake's wizened face. "Don't that beat everything? A squirrel what eats roots. Here. Give him one." Snake shook the bag.

Augusta pulled a thin three-inch root from the bag and tossed the treat in front of the squirrel.

Licorice looked at the root, then at Augusta, but didn't touch the offering. "Isn't he hungry tonight?"

"Dat's no way to feed good ole Licorice. Ya got to hold it out, and when he be good and ready he come get it from ya." Snake held out a root.

The squirrel's eyes darted to Snake's offering. Nose twitching, Licorice quick-looked right and left, then dashed forward, stood on his hind legs and clamped the root in his jaws. Once he'd retreated to a safe distance, he gnawed on the bark.

A large shadow plunged from the oak canopy above them, an owl hurtling toward their squirrel friend. It would be over in seconds. Morbid curiosity kept Augusta's eyes open, even as her head pounded with horror.

At the last moment, Licorice jerked to the right, barely escaping the owl's talons. He scampered back into the undergrowth, still clutching the root in his mouth, as the owl rose once more and merged with the shadows.

"The creek be still right now," Snake said.

She looked up. Marsh grass stood in dark silhouette against the glassy, obsidian water. Stately oaks draped in moss framed the view.

"Shame we couldn't have dat party Saturday night. But don't cha know, we cain't have no spirit party without Buzzard's arm."

At the mention of Buzzard's arm, she looked at him and waited with anticipation for him to deepen the conversation.

He removed his sunglasses. His one yellow eye seemed to glow in the moonlight. As before, his piercing gaze penetrated her soul, worming into it so thoroughly she felt exposed. But, unlike the last time, tonight his expression was friendly. This time she welcomed the connection. He could comb through her soul as much as he wished. She had nothing to hide from him.

She couldn't take her eyes from his. He controlled her attention. She was comfortable with his inspection of her soul, but control? Her heart sped. She didn't like the sound of that. Suddenly uneasy, Augusta realized she'd stopped breathing.

Snake squinted, reached over and touched her hand. The connection was surprisingly calming. "Yous okay, child?"

"Yes." Her face heated. "About Saturday night. Why was your gathering cancelled?"

"Dat's why I axed you to come see me. I want you to write a story so that de people can help me get my mantel back."

She tried not to get too excited about the important news story in the making. Everyone in the Lowcountry knew of Doctor Buzzard. Surely a story about what had ultimately become of his body parts would be published. The regional news wire might even pick it up. "Get it back? Did something happen to Doctor Buzzard's arm?"

His face drew tight. He nodded as he put his sunglasses back on. "A man done come to my door last night and said he was a bone collector. There ain't—"

"Wait." She knew she wouldn't remember all the details. With just moonlight, writing legibly might be a problem, but she had to try. "Do you mind if I take notes?"

"Not 'all, child. I want dis story be told far and wide. You take all dem notes you like, ya hear?"

She nodded while removing her notebook and ballpoint pen from her pants pocket. "Okay."

"So, da man what come to my door tells me he be a bone collector. I axe him if he be a root doctor or something, and he done say no. Now I'm a wondering what a bone collector doing at my door. I don't sell no bones."

"He arrived unannounced, right?" Augusta asked.

"Yes indeed. That be correct."

"Had you seen him before?"

Snake shook his head, bouncing his dreadlocks. "Never seen 'em and don't rightly care to ever see 'em again, except to get my stuff back. Anyways, he tells me he gonna pay a gawd-awful large amount of money for any of Doctor Buzzard's bones I might have."

"The arm?" Augusta asked.

"He don't mention no arm, but I got it in my head that it might be a good idea to hear the man out. I mean, this fella was talking big money. Upwards a million for an arm or leg. Now my mantle just be the forearm, so I figures half a million. Man, that's walking money."

"Walking money?"

"Like retirement. I could live large on dat, piece a cake." He stared at the moon. "I've been thinking 'bout retirin', but I ain't got but beans to my name. So anyways, this guy be axin' what I have. Well, don't cha know that when I mention I have Doctor Buzzard's arm, the fella gets all excited."

"I bet."

"So we have sum tea, though he didn't drink much beyond a sip. And he starts preachin' 'bout only payin' if he can au-then-ti-cate the arm. Now I'm a right honest fella, but I knows a man has to be careful, so I shows him the arm. Bam. I'm out cold. When I wake up, Buzzard's arm and dat man be gone."

A shudder hit her. She fought to keep him from seeing it. "And?"

"I don't know what to do to get my bones back so I calls you. Can you tell da people? Spread da word? Can you get dem city folk to look every which a ways for my arm?"

"It's an interesting story. I'll write it up and see if my editor will run it."

He nodded. "I'd be most grateful."

"By the way, did you report the theft to the police?"

"No."

"Why?"

"Dey don't take kindly to doctorin' without a license."

"Can you describe the man?"

Snake smiled. "He be da one what be carrying a long box wit my arm in it."

She chuckled. "Hair? Eyes? Build?"

"I don't know. Nothin' special. A white guy. All dem white folk look the same to me. Specially when I got these on." He gestured to his sunglasses.

"Long hair? Short hair?"

He pushed his dreadlocks behind his shoulders. "Short."

"You're pretty tall. Where did he come up to you?"

Snake gestured to his shoulders.

"Jewelry?" she asked. "A watch? A wedding ring?"

161

Snake paused for a moment as if trying to recall. "No watch. Just a ring wit some bones carved on de top. Come to think 'bout it, don't dat beat everythang. Dat bone collector done got himself a ring wit bones."

She scribbled a brief description of the thief's ring. "Anything else about him?"

"He done smell funny."

"In what way?"

"He just didn't smell like regular white folk."

"Tobacco smell?"

"Not dat. Sort of spicy."

"Which spice?"

He shook his head. "Nothing from here 'bouts."

"What kind of car did he drive?"

"Don't rightly know. Come to think about it, I never saw a car."

"Language. Southern boy or Yankee?"

"Definitely not a Southern boy." Snake looked out over the glassy river as if gathering his thoughts. "Not really a Yankee either. Sounded like a foreigner. Yeah. A foreigner. But dat boy spoke well, like he had him a proper ed-u-ca-shun."

"Anything else?"

"Not dat I can conjure up dis minute."

"Okay. If you can think of anything else, have Eustis contact me. I'll get to work on this as soon as I get back to the office."

"Bless you, child."

\* \* \*

THE ROOM FOR BENJAMIN'S MEETING WITH TROKEV'S BOSS was a Spartan place in the back of Bubba's Ribs, a working-class barbeque joint on the West side. The back room was as cold as a morgue. Too cold for an extended meeting.

Seated at a fold-up picnic table that had seen better days was a creepy-looking cowboy with bad theatrical makeup, a lopsided handlebar moustache, and an ill-fitting black felt hat pulled down low over his forehead. There was just him and the cowboy clown.

Benjamin blinked and looked again. A weird situation. Not at all what he'd expected. Obviously this clown had chosen this outfit to throw him off ... and it had.

Benjamin gave the man a frown. "Halloween?"

The cowboy grinned through partially blackened teeth and shook his head. "Impromptu disguise. I thought Trokev was going to handle everything. That's what he assured me. But it looks like you and I will have to work this out before the mad Russian takes Savannah apart. I mean, you really pissed the man off."

"Do you have a name?"

"No."

"Okay, Mr. No. Here's the deal. Trokev may have you running scared, but he doesn't have us diving for cover. We'd like you to take your brothel elsewhere. I'm sure Trokev has filled you in on the details."

"He has. And I understand he has likewise told you the brothel is here to stay."

"Thus the meeting." Benjamin sat across from the man.

Mr. No leaned forward, elbows on the table. "You're aware Mrs. Falcon's gardener is no longer with us?"

"Yes. His death was unnecessary."

"Quite the contrary. Mr. Trokev suffered severe business losses because of you. Tit-for-tat."

Benjamin cocked his head. "The man had nothing to do with our business."

"The man was inside what you considered to be a

completely secure perimeter. As is Mrs. Falcon. That's not very good security if we can so easily eliminate the man. You escalate. We escalate even more. Understand?"

Benjamin nodded. They were stalemated and not going anywhere. No point getting more innocent people killed. Frustrated at the lack of progress, Benjamin looked at his watch. "Look, I think we both have better things to do than faceoff like this. And, despite the chilly air conditioning, I imagine your get-up is mighty uncomfortable. My associates will find another way of accomplishing our objectives."

"What's that supposed to mean?" the cowboy said in an acidic voice.

"It means this conversation is getting us nowhere."

"I agree. So where is the compromise?"

"Open Savannah to your brothel and Lord knows what else? No way. I'm afraid there'll be no compromise on that point. As for destroying additional brothels, we won't do that. I expect Mr. Falcon will continue to be kept safe and there'll be no more killings of innocent folks."

"What about my ... Trokev's frozen assets?"

"I'll deliver your assets as soon as you give me Mr. Falcon and pull out of Savannah. Can we agree to that, and a date? Like today?"

"Mr. Hempfield, what exactly is your objection to our brothel? You've never taken any action against existing pros-titutes in Savannah. Why now?"

Hempfield paused for a moment to give the impression he was about to provide a well-considered response. "Our objection is not to prostitution. It's organized crime we object to. Since you're such a student of our activity, I assume you know we have always been swift to act against organized crime. And we have been, to a large degree, successful."

"That you have. Until recently. Tell me, Mr. Hempfield, have you not permitted Vladimir Olneki to operate openly in your fine city? Surely you must know he heads a vast criminal enterprise?"

Vladimir was certainly scum. But there were only so many fires the Coalition could fight, so they focused on those in Savannah and cooperated with others leading the fight elsewhere. So far, no one had requested help with Vladimir. "His enterprise is not engaged in any criminal activities in our city. He simply uses our port for transportation."

"Transportation of criminal goods into Savannah. You tolerate that, but not us?"

"Let me put it in a different way," Benjamin said. "We would have no objections to you using our international airport to bring your employees into the Southeast, provided you immediately transported those women to other counties. In our opinion, that is the type of thing Vladimir is doing. He's also agreed to work with us around the world to further our interests. In short, he cooperates."

"Our brothel in Savannah is entirely unacceptable to you?"

"Precisely." Benjamin was anxious to terminate the circular conversation.

Trokev came in to the room with an expectant look. "Well?"

"No progress," Benjamin said. "We're going to let things settle down for a while."

The cowboy shrugged.

"You want me to kill him?" Trokev asked in a sinister voice.

The cowboy roared with a familiar laughter Benjamin couldn't place, though the voice-recognition program they would use on the meeting audio might.

"That was a good joke," Mr. No said. "But just so you're

clear, I want Mr. Hempfield alive. We have business to conclude, eventually, and I like him."

"Thank you, Mr. No," Benjamin said. "I 'preciate the vote of confidence."

The cowboy winked and a slight smile appeared. "It's well-earned. I'll noodle on this problem we have and get back to you shortly with fresh ideas. Meanwhile, just so we understand each other, you'll be leaving Trokev's brothels alone, and you'll not make any attempt to impede the reconstruction of the ones you destroyed?"

"What about delivering Mr. Falcon today?"

"That's not going to happen." The cowboy leaned forward. "Do we agree to a truce regarding the brothel?"

"You understand correctly, provided Mr. Falcon remains untouched, and provided you document his condition with daily, real-time proof of life video to Mrs. Falcon."

Nodding, the cowboy pushed an envelope across the table. "Tickets to our gala. It's a VIP table of ten. Bring your friends as my guest. You'll see I operate legitimately. And it would be a fun night for y'all."

Benjamin took the tickets, though he had no intension of using them. "Thank you. We might just do that."

# CHAPTER 18

*W*hen Trokev's green Jaguar XJ left Bubba's Ribs' parking lot, Beau Simpson eased his rental SUV in well behind. Traffic was light and the glow of Savannah lit the night horizon. Beau smiled. As rewarding as his cardiology practice was, he much preferred Coalition clandestine work.

"Does Trokev have partners involved in his other brothels?" Beau asked Father John, who was seated next to him.

"No other partners that I know of. I have to say, Trokev taking on that damn cowboy disturbs me."

"Why would he do such a thing?" Beau passed a delivery truck blocking his view of the Jaguar.

"Trokev's extremely independent. He must be desperate for more capital."

"His balance sheet looks good." Beau clenched the steering wheel. "Could this be a harbinger of things to come?"

"That's what I'm wondering. If he's planning to go global with this partnering, it could provide massive new funding for his operations. Hopefully, it's just unique to Savannah."

Trokev's Jag stopped at a red light.

Beau eased his SUV into a lot fronting a convenience store, then pulled out again when the light turned green. "Either way, we have to get on top of this development. With Isabel tailing Trokev's boss, maybe we'll get a break there."

"Yeah," Father John said. "Though I would've preferred to have a tracking device on the cowboy's truck. Too bad he didn't call ahead and let us know which one was his."

Beau, shaking with laugher, followed the Jag up the entrance ramp to I-16. "Looks like Trokev's heading back to town. Maybe The Amber House. I think he's still living there, despite the construction."

"That's where he ended up last night."

"Have you been following him?"

Father John adjusted the air vent. "Lucius asked me to keep an eye on him in my spare time."

"I've been thinking, now that we're talking directly to Mr. No, we don't have to play nice with his boy Trokev. Since Trokev's the one who detained Trey, he's our greatest hope of finding our man. What do you think of abducting Trokev? I'm sure drugs could overcome his reluctance to speak freely with us, and he wouldn't remember anything. Taking him would be a small change of plan that could make a big difference."

"Mr. No wouldn't like that," Father John said, his tone clipped.

"Mr. No wouldn't have to find out."

"How would you prevent that?"

"Mr. No seems to have given Trokev plenty of room to operate on his own," Beau said. "I suspect the two just communicate on an as-needed basis."

"I don't know. They've already shown they can penetrate our best defenses and are willing to kill. If we escalate by taking Trokev, they would escalate. Who would they kill next? Mrs. Falcon? Benjamin? His family? They're all sitting ducks, Beau."

Though he should have kept focused on the road and Trokev's car, Beau turned to Father John. Glow from the control screen illuminated the priest's rugged face. "So you suggest we stick with the plan?"

Father John flashed him a smile. "I don't think it's wise at this point to provoke anyone in that organization. Simon's narrowing the possibilities of where they're holding Trey. Let's give him time. And we have tails on these two guys."

Beau nodded as he guided his car off I-16 and headed, still behind the Jag, toward what he supposed would be The Amber House.

Trokev's Jaguar made an abrupt u-turn at the first light, catching Beau hanging back in the right lane and unable to respond.

Beau smacked his palm on the wheel as the Jag raced by, window down and a broad smile on Trokev's face.

\* \* \*

IN ISABEL'S MIND, IT HAD BEEN BIZARRE WATCHING MR. NO AS he left the back door of the barbeque joint. She knew the clown in the cowboy outfit was Mr. No because of several comments Benjamin made about the guy's costume during his meeting. But his comments hadn't prepared her for ... well, she didn't know what to call it. A freak show, perhaps?

Ten minutes later, she was still chuckling to herself as she followed the cowboy's beat-up Ford F-350 pickup into town on I-16. It was night, and she hadn't seen a gun rack in the truck, but she'd bet a dozen Krispy Kreme doughnuts he had one.

She slipped in behind him, got his license number and called it in to Simon. He came back moments later with a name and address in Richmond Hill. If Mr. No was heading to Richmond Hill, he was taking the scenic route.

No one had guessed Trokev had an accomplice in his brothel business, much less a local partner. That changed everything, and the Coalition was now temporarily operating in a reactive mode, something her father, Lucius, trained her to avoid at all costs.

She followed the pickup off I-16 and pulled to the curb to avoid stopping behind Mr. No at the light. She hoped he hadn't noticed. Normally, on a tail like this they'd use multiple vehicles, but there hadn't been time.

The light turned green and the pickup went through the intersection. Once Mr. No was a block away, she eased out and followed. The risk of losing Mr. No was heightened by staying so far back, an experienced driver could easily drop a tail that remote, particularly one as inexperienced as herself. But Mr. No apparently lacked experience. She snickered. Yeah. No was no pro. Not with *that* disguise.

Who was this clown? Hold it. She'd have to stop thinking of him as a clown. Her father insisted she respect her opponents. So, who was this opponent? And why did he want to sponsor a brothel in Savannah? Daddy often counseled her to follow the money trail. They didn't have a money trail ... yet. So they were following the man.

She winced as her side window shattered inward, and heard the distant second shot that collapsed the rear window, as Mr. No turned into a city parking garage and slid to a stop at the gate. "Shots fired," she shouted into her clip-on microphone.

"You okay?" Simon asked through her ear-channel receiver.

She pulled up to the gate, grabbed a parking ticket and drove in. "I'm okay. Subject just entered the parking garage on Liberty. Do you have anyone in the area who can cover the exits? Even covering one exit will help."

The truck disappeared at the top of the ramp, complicating matters immensely. The place had several exits and multiple ramps. Tight quarters, too. Easy to be spotted-or trapped, with no easy exit in an emergency. She slid her purse closer and removed her gun.

"Beau's in the area. I'll get him over there. Might take a minute or two."

"Thanks, Simon. Subject went up, so the exits are momentarily out of play. Let me know when Beau gets here."

"Your signal's breaking up, Isabel. Did you say subject is on a higher floor?"

"Yes."

"Got it. Beau's on his way."

She guided her car around the top of the ramp. Her eyes snapped right and left. Oh shit! No truck. Her mind spun, considering options. There weren't many. She accelerated to the next level. No pickup there either. Bewildered, she pounded the steering wheel. Heat washed over her face. "Simon. I've lost the truck."

"You're breaking up, Isabel. Say again."

She jerked the car into an empty spot close to an open wall. "I've lost the tail. Tell Beau to keep an eye out. I'm heading down. Then I'll work my way up, checking parking spaces to see if Mr. No abandoned the pickup."

"Got it."

"I'm sorry." She set her jaw.

"Nothing to be sorry about," he said in a soft, even tone. "Sometimes we get the rabbit. Sometimes not."

"I 'preciate that."

* * *

Trey tensed as the van stopped at a rusted iron gate beside the airport runway. The sun hung high in a cloudless sky. An armed sentry came out of a shabby, unmarked guardhouse and conversed quietly with the driver in a language Trey didn't know. The grim sentry nodded a lot and, at times, seemed terrified.

Soon the sentry unlocked the gate and pushed one of the iron barriers to the side.

The van inched through and drove to a remote hanger where an unmarked private jet awaited. Though Trey was familiar with private jets, he didn't recognize the make of this one. Not that it mattered. The van stopped at the foot of the fold-out stairs.

A crew-cut, thickset man in a black leather jacket and black trousers clomped down the stairs and opened the van door. He wore square-framed sunglasses that looked expensive and sported dark, day-old stubble. There were no markings on the glasses or jacket to indicate their country of origin. The man had no distinctive scars or tattoos.

Trey's escort narrowed his eyes and indicated for Trey to get out of the van. Once out, the guy in black patted him down, uncuffed him, and then gestured for Trey to board the jet.

When Trey went up the steps, Blackie didn't follow. Whatever. The guy didn't look like he would be good company anyway. Trey stepped into the aircraft. The stairs folded up, turning the plane into a flying prison. Or was it a death chamber?

# CHAPTER 19

*P*atricia awoke from a restless night with a stabbing migraine. Trey missing ... and a damn migraine. Nausea threatened as she got out of bed and shuffled through the dimness into the bathroom. After turning on the bath, she went to the sink and gulped down two Excedrin tablets to fight the pounding in her head and a Prilosec to keep her stomach settled.

During the warm bath, the Excedrin kicked in, erasing her migraine. If only she could erase her melancholy so easily. Allison and Rhett's deaths gnawed on her, and there was no escaping her fear for Trey's well-being.

She stepped from the tub and dressed casually in khakis and a blue cotton blouse. No makeup. She wasn't going out, no visitors were scheduled and, well, Simon didn't count. She went downstairs and headed into the dining room where Simon, still wearing yesterday's clothes, labored over his computer.

"Mornin'," he said without looking up.

"Do you need a refill on your coffee?"

He nodded and handed her his cup.

When she returned, the dining room was flooding with chipmunk-like voices.

"What's up?" She handed him the cup of coffee.

"I'm running Mr. No's voice through the NSA voice recognition program."

"Mr. No?"

"He's an unidentified person who may have something to do with Trey's abduction. He met with one of our people last night. Of course, we recorded the meeting."

Her mind sharpened at the possibility of progress. "Any success on matching the voice?"

"Not yet, but they have 800 million voices catalogued and combing through all that data takes time." Simon sounded tired and his bloodshot eyes looked like he'd been up all night. "Admittedly, the chance of getting a match with a muffled voice like Mr. No's is remote, but we have to check all possibilities."

Her shoulders slumped. "Did you get any sleep at all last night?"

"Just a quick cat nap here and there. I had too much on my mind to sleep. Like I said yesterday, we have some good information on Trey's whereabouts. He's definitely in Armenia. I've requested a satellite be moved over the country to help on the next call intercept. Once we get a specific location, we'll dispatch a drone over him as well."

"Thank you for all you're doing." She put one hand on her hip. "What's this about a next call?"

"We've asked for at least one proof of life call a day."

Her heart surged. "He's going to call today?"

"I certainly hope so." Simon's phone blared.

"Is that him?"

Simon glanced at the display and stood. "Sorry, no. Excuse me. I have to take this." He walked to the front of the house.

From her chair, Patricia leaned forward and watched one of Simon's monitors as the security system paged through the video feed of the grounds. Everything looked so tranquil, but she knew better. The estate was a fortress, not a city park. And poor Rhett's murder had exposed its vulnerabilities. She shuddered.

Patricia saddened when the security feed of the bench where Rhett had died filled the monitor. She hadn't seen that part of the yard since discovering his mutilated body. Staring at the screen through tears, she so hoped the person who killed Rhett roasted in hell. The monitor display changed to the next camera. Patricia wiped the back of her hand over her eyes.

Though the video feed moved on, her anger boiled. Why did God permit a good, innocent man like Rhett to die? Why did God let his killer go unapprehended? Did 'love one another' mean she had to love Rhett's killer? She couldn't do that. She couldn't even forgive the man ... yet. Maybe never.

Simon came back with a DVD and put the disc into his computer.

"What's that?"

"We had a tail on Mr. No last night. Apparently he became aware Isabel was following him and escaped into a parking garage. This is a copy of the security videos from the parking garage. A courier just delivered it."

"You think of everything."

He shrugged. "I try."

"How will you know it's him?"

"He'll be wearing a cowboy hat and a fake handlebar moustache."

She put her elbows on the table as the monitor filled with a driver's face. "So, you can get a close-up photo of this cowboy?"

"That's the idea. As you can see, when a driver stops to

take his parking ticket, the video starts. Everyone faces the machine to get their ticket. The ticketing area is intentionally well lit. Thus we have a sharp, full-face video of each driver entering the garage. Also the same thing when he leaves. We'll pull photos from the video and send them to—"

"That's him," she said, leaning forward to get a better view.

Simon stopped the play, backtracked to slightly before Mr. No appeared, and punched a red button labeled 'record.' The video advanced in slow motion. "Too bad he's still wearing that hideous makeup. Fortunately, facial recognition depends on measurements, so if he's in the database we'll get a match with or without makeup."

Patricia watched as Mr. No reached out in slow motion to take a parking ticket. Shocked, she straightened. He wore a signet ring identical to Trokev's. The ring was a clue, possibly a critical clue. Trey's return hung in the balance. She glanced at Simon. He didn't seem to have noticed the ring.

"Simon, I have to tell you something."

He paused the video, looked away and massaged his eyes. "Go ahead."

"Mr. No and Trokev wear identical signet rings."

The corners of his mouth rose a tad. "Fraternity brothers?"

"Hardly. The rings are associated with a Middle Ages relic cult."

He folded his arms across his chest. His biceps bulged beneath his black tee shirt. "How do you know that?"

"Trokev told me."

He hesitated for a moment. "Let me get this straight. You're saying Mr. No and Trokev are members of some ancient cult?"

"No. I'm not. In fact, Trokev said the cult disbanded

centuries ago. I'm simply pointing out that they both wear a ring associated with the cult."

"Duly noted," he said. "Anything else?"

"No." Though she wanted to shake some sense into him, she knew it would be futile. Instead, she'd keep her mouth shut. She'd given him the information. Now this was her clue and she could work it. After all, it wasn't like she was impeding him.

As soon as Mr. No's face left the screen, Simon put the security video on fast-forward to the exit videos. One by one, drivers exited the parking garage. They got to the end of the exit video without seeing Mr. No.

Simon cued the DVD back to the beginning of the exit sequence. "Something happened in there. Either Mr. No didn't exit, or he exited without his makeup. I'll go back to the entrance shot and see if I can get a fix on the make and model he drove, then see if the vehicle exited. If I don't get an exit shot, it's not a problem, mind you. The entrance video is very sharp. We don't have to have the exit shot. But if he exited without makeup, I'd love to have that shot as well."

"How long until you get results back from facial recognition?"

"Twenty-four hours, max."

Finally. Progress. "What if Mr. No doesn't show up on the exit video?"

"Then he parked the truck and walked out."

"Didn't Isabel check the unattended vehicles last night?"

"Yes. A quick pass. She might have missed the truck. We'll send someone over today to walk through checking each vehicle. I want to recover that truck. It could have Mr. No's fingerprints or DNA." He took a sip of coffee.

"What if he took off his disguise and drove out?"

"With Isabel on his heels, he wouldn't have much time for that," Simon said. "But I suppose it's possible."

"Can you compare the facial measurements of Mr. No's entrance photo to the physical measurement of all those leaving?"

"Sure."

"You know, Simon, he had to buy that costume somewhere. I doubt he had an outfit that gross hanging in his closet. Have you checked Acme Costumes?"

He gave her a rare smile. "Good idea. You're thinking like an investigator, Mrs. Falcon."

"That's what Trey tells me from time to time." Her eyes stung a moment and she blinked. She touched his ring. He had to be alive. She couldn't wait for his next call. *Dear Lord, keep Trey safe*. The call. What would she do if his captors didn't let him call? A shiver went through her. "Simon?"

"Yes."

"How does Trokev communicate with Mr. No?"

"We're checking out Trokev's phone information as we speak."

* * *

SEATED IN HIS OFFICE, TROKEV STARED AT WHAT HE HOPED were Doctor Buzzard's arm bones, feeling the energy pulsing from the bones, feeling the strength build within him. This mystic power was what he loved above all else.

As far as he knew, no one had previously measured and catalogued the doctor's relics, so there was no reliable way to authenticate his prize. But this arm's journey to Doctor Snake was well known to numerous insiders he'd interviewed.

Having photographed the assembled arm from several angles, Trokev set about meticulously measuring and recording each bone. While placing a caliper on the first bone in the little finger, he recalled doing so with other bones as a child after his family's "skeleton hunts" throughout Eastern Europe. Those were marvelous weekend trips with his father and grandfather to hallowed shrines and black markets and old gravesites, a family tradition that yielded a relic collection that rivaled all but the Vatican's. As the collection grew, so did the Trokev family fortune and power. His grandfather had assured them the relics conferred good fortune on their possessors. And so it seemed.

Grigory inherited the ancestral collection years ago and added to it, selling off lesser relics to finance his pursuit of more important pieces. He purchased, at enormous expense, all the major relics available on the black market. When that supply dried up, he took to searching for lost relics, focusing on prized ones like Doctor Buzzard's right arm.

The brothel business was good cover for his relic searching. Sex was universal. Brothels were easy to establish if you had a reliable supply of good women. He'd been well mentored in the supply end of the brothel business by a fellow relic collector, whom he rewarded with bones purged from his ancestral collection.

Once established, the brothel profits fed his real obsession, the prized relics. The bones and their power excited him in a way no woman ever had. An obsession.

He had come to Savannah in search of two different arm relics. He now possessed one of them. The location of the other, Saint Gregory the Illuminator's arm, remained unknown. A mystery he intended to unravel before returning to Armenia.

Holding up his own hand, he examined the signet ring. The cult was everywhere and had been searching for Saint Gregory's arm ever since church authorities had quietly decided that the Cilician one wasn't authentic. A fact known to the cult, but not to the public.

He'd joined the cult a few years ago in Armenia, the very country Saint Gregory converted to Christianity. The country Saint Gregory had died in, high in the mountains not far from Trokev's Russian birthplace.

After intensive research, he'd traced the saint's lost arm to Savannah, and through the cult leadership he'd located and befriended a Savannah member of the organization. The person was also searching for the arm, but was totally inexperienced in such things-a sincere believer, but not a collector-a believer to partner with. An ambitious man looking for cash flow to fuel his dream of high political office. A local partner who provided Trokev access to the very people who might know the Savannah whereabouts of the saint's arm.

All had been set in place for his greatest find, the lost Saint Gregory arm relic, until Trey Falcon and that damn civic organization got in the way. Trokev put down the caliper lest he damage a bone with the anger coursing through him. How could they be so obstinate? He had to keep the brothel open. Photos of clients in compromising positions gave him leverage over key players in Savannah. Leverage that, applied properly, would eventually produce leads to the saint's arm. Without the brothel he had no leverage and, consequently, no relic. No. He had to get the brothel reopened and keep that damn Coalition at bay. The current standoff suited him very well.

Besides, winter was coming to Armenia, turning the high plateaus into frozen tundra. Savannah seemed a much nicer alternative ... and Mrs. Falcon was certainly delightful. Naive, but delightful.

* * *

FATHER JOHN'S HUMMER ROLLED INTO THE GRAVEL DRIVEWAY of the address he had for the registered owner of Mr. No's

Ford pickup. The beige, vinyl-sided ranch had an attached garage that had been converted into living space. Covered parking had been added on the side. There was no vehicle in sight. A tool shed sat behind and to the right of the house.

John clicked the safety off on his concealed pistol, walked, business-like, to the front door, and rang the bell. No answer. He pounded on the door without response. He twisted the doorknob. It was locked. Draped side windows kept him from looking in. He went to the back of the house and peered in the kitchen window. The lights were out. No one appeared home.

He checked the mailbox out front. It was full of mail. Same name as the one Simon had given him. Chances were the pickup had been stolen while the owners were gone. Was Mr. No familiar with the owners? Or was the theft random?

\* \* \*

THE JET TOUCHED DOWN ON A WASHBOARD LANDING STRIP running along the banks of a wide river. To Trey, seated inside the jet, the area seemed sparsely populated. Deer grazed in the fields. There were terraced hills on the horizon. No snow-covered mountains.

The plane stopped close to a black Mercedes limousine, the jet engines silenced, and the stairs deployed. A big, scowling guy with dark hair and an ugly scar that disappeared beneath the collar of his black overcoat stepped out of the passenger side of the limo and looked expectantly up the stairs.

Showtime.

Trey put on the pea coat and headed to the hatch. He paused at the top of the stairs where cold air sliced through him and took his breath away. All of it. After buttoning the coat with stiff fingers and turning up the collar, he barreled down the stairs and into the limo, hoping they had the heat turned up high.

They did. As stiflingly as Savannah in July. He shed the coat. The big guy ducked into the passenger side and the limo rumbled off.

Trey looked skyward and figured, from the low sun, it was late in the afternoon. The flight had been long enough for them to be anywhere in Europe.

"Cold outside," he said.

"Ya," the big guy said with a German accent.

"Snow?"

"Soon."

As the limo left the crude runway and turned onto a paved two-lane road, Trey spotted a road sign that proclaimed the road to be *Berghoff Strasse.* Maybe Germany.

"Sprechen sie Deutsch?" he asked, using his best collegiate German.

"Ya," said the big guy.

Mercedes. German road sign. German-speaking host. Germany? Switzerland? Austria? Probably Germany. But where in Germany?

About an hour later, a medieval castle on a hilltop came into view. The limo turned at a sign that said *Schloss Wilheim.* Trey wondered why his abductors were so careless in allowing him to see the street signs. A siren wailed. He looked back and saw a police car approaching. The Mercedes slowed and pulled to the shoulder, just as the police car flashed by. *Wilheimdorf Polizei.*

The Mercedes eased from the curb and headed up a narrow, serpentine road that led to the hilltop. At the castle, the big guy led him inside to a well-furnished period bedroom and left. Trey tried the wooden hall door, not surprised to find it locked. So was the leaded window over-looking a courtyard forty feet down. Too high to jump.

Trey crossed the stone floor and collapsed on the bed. The warm air and the long flight made him drowsy, but he forced his mind to stay active. He wasn't about to give up. He had to escape. But how?

He stood and, aware his abductors were probably watching him, prowled the room, looking for vulnerabilities, fixing the interior layout in his mind so he could maneuver without lights when it got dark.

In the distance, he heard bells chime six times. He went back to the window and looked for a clock tower. He saw none. There was just a wall and turrets below him, and a farmhouse in the distance. He turned back to the room and spotted a recessed, ceiling-mounted video camera in the corner.

The lock clunked and the hall door swung open. The big man from the car filled the doorframe. He wore a black t-shirt, black jeans and motorcycle boots.

"You come," he said.

Trey followed him down a wide hall and into a cavernous room where two men stood beside a video camera on a tripod. The camera was aimed at a huge medieval dining table with a single chair behind it.

"Sit," the big man said. "Your wife wants to speak with you. Remember, if you say the wrong thing you lose a finger."

# CHAPTER 20

"Patricia, it's Trey on Skype," Simon shouted from the library doorway. Simon rushed through the room and, his face tense, shoved the smartphone into her hand.

Her heart flip-flopped when Trey's smiling face popped up on the phone display. Thank God, he was still okay. "Hi, honey." She studied his rugged face. "I ... I miss you."

"I miss you too, sweetheart." He brought one hand to his cheek and started barely perceptible signing.

Her heart snagged. She wished she could read the message he was sending.

Simon was glued to his monitor watching the inbound call and furiously making notes on a tablet. Apparently he could read Trey's hand signals.

Patricia forced a smile. There was so much she wanted to say to him, but she knew the code questions had to come first. "Are they feeding you well?"

"A steady diet of bratwurst and sauerkraut."

Simon raised an eyebrow and started clicking away on his keyboard, frowning as he typed.

"Is something distracting you?" Trey asked.

Cringing, she returned her gaze to the smartphone camera, gathered herself, and said, "No. Sorry. Are you getting plenty of rest?"

"It's hard to say. Some nights are good, some are bad. Last night I slept well. A good, heavy sleep. If I didn't have to get up for breakfast, I could have slept for at least ten hours. Maybe more. How's Hayley?"

"She says she ran into her first grade principal. He's doing great."

"That's good to hear. I've always liked Gregory."

Since Hayley's first grade principal had been a woman, Patricia tried to think of who or what he might be referencing. Certainly Grigory Trokev qualified, but so did Saint Gregory's relic and Saint Gregory's cathedral.

"How's the cotton crop?" Trey asked. It was a coded question referring to the progress the Coalition was making on his rescue.

"With all the cold weather, they were talking about getting the Armenia crop in, but I think they've changed their plans. The weather here in Savannah is—"

The screen went blank.

Patricia's hand tightened on the phone as if by doing so she could squeeze one more moment of Trey from the device. Anger at being cut off almost overwhelmed her. "So he's in Germany now. What did he sign?"

"He messaged *Castle Wilheim* and a crossroad named *Berghoff Strasse*. Because of the crossroad, I was able to locate the castle. A huge stroke of luck for us. The castle is not far from our Ramstein Airbase. I'm currently working on getting a drone and a fast response force over there." He pumped his fist. A victory pump. A rare display for Simon.

Might Trey finally be rescued? "How long?"

Simon glanced at his monitor, now filled with roadway

schematics, building icons, and moving rectangles on the roadways. "Estimated time of arrival, ten minutes, maybe fifteen, depending on the traffic."

"Those are military assets. How'd you manage to get them deployed for our use?"

Simon smiled. "It's how we do things. We both have the same objectives. We help them. They help us."

"What about Trey's safety during the rescue?"

"They're pros. His safety is their highest priority. Don't worry, Patricia."

She gestured toward his screen. "Impressive graphics."

"This is a Department of Defense enhanced satellite view."

"How do you get this kind of video access?"

"It's routine. Most of the work we do for the government is classified."

She sat in a chair next to his.

He pointed to the center of the screen. "The castle. Once the drone gets into position, we'll have an actual image." He indicated four icons moving toward the castle. "The fast response team. Twelve men. Three per van. Ten combat. One negotiator. And a local policeman. After they enter the castle we'll have the video feed from their helmet cameras as well."

Combat? Live? Her stomach churned. "We're going to watch this happen?"

"You can leave if you wish," Simon said.

Terror and anticipation gripped her. "I ... I have to watch."

One of the vans left the other three and circled to approach from behind the castle.

"That team is blocking any escape out the back."

The three remaining vehicles turned off the main highway and onto a secondary road ending at the castle. The monitor flickered and real imagery replaced the icons. As the vans drew closer to the castle, the picture slowly zoomed in.

By the time the three vehicles came to a stop outside the castle, a stone fortress filled most of the screen. Six people left two of the vans and approached the entrance to the complex on foot. The third unit drove through the entrance and into the courtyard. One person dressed in a grey business suit got out of the van and walked to the door.

"The guy at the door is the negotiator," Simon said in a monotone.

"He doesn't look military."

"That's the idea."

"Is he armed?"

"Of course."

The monitor flickered and a high-def, color picture she guessed was being transmitted from the man's chest or eyeglass camera came into view. The door opened to reveal a young woman.

"Do you speak English?" a man's voice asked.

"Yes," the woman said. "How may I help you?"

"I'm here to pick up Mr. Falcon."

Patricia's heart caught.

"I'm sorry," the woman said. "You must have the wrong place. We do not have anyone staying with us with that name."

"Is this *Schloss Wilheim?*"

"Yes."

"May I speak to a manager?"

"Certainly."

The door closed. After a period of time, an older woman in black appeared at the door. "May I help you?"

"I am here for Mr. Falcon."

"As my receptionist told you, we do not have a Mr. Falcon staying with us." The door began to close.

"Miss, I have a search warrant." The negotiator held out a letter-sized document.

The door opened a tad. The woman took the warrant and read it.

Patricia gritted her teeth. *Come on. Please find him. Please. Please. Please.*

"This permits the entry of eight people to search for Mr. Falcon."

"Yes, ma'am."

She frowned. "I'll call my lawyer."

"You can call your lawyer if you wish, but I must insist you comply immediately. If not, I have a member of the police in my car who will arrest you for not honoring a lawful court order."

She dipped her head and swung the door open to reveal a couple of massive, broad-shouldered men. Men similar in stature and appearance to the person who accompanied Trokev to The Olde Pink House restaurant the second time. Body guards, no doubt. "Please come in and search."

"I'll need keys to every room," the negotiator said.

She went behind the desk, returned, and handed a key ring to the negotiator. "Master keys."

"There are only six keys."

"Those are all I have. We're a small hotel."

Patricia heard the negotiator say, "Okay. Let's do it."

Bodies in black uniforms passed by the negotiator, and as they did more individual pictures came up on the monitor until there were eight. The men proceeded to systematically enter and clear rooms, placing a green glow stick at the door of each room cleared. The manager was on hand to explain to the four guests, all older men, whose rooms were searched. The remaining guest rooms were vacant.

Patricia waited eagerly for the first view of her husband's liberation. But with each room cleared without a trace of Trey, she began to worry.

No. She had to remain optimistic. As long as even one room remained unsearched, she had to hope.

Once the guest rooms were cleared, every remaining nook and cranny was searched.

An hour later, the camera views began to click off the monitor one by one, as the searchers left the facility. Each departure deepened the pit of dread in her stomach.

She gave a strangled sob. What was going on? He was there. She'd seen him. He had to be there. Why were they leaving? Tears welled in her eyes when the final team member thanked the manager and the door swung closed on the opportunity.

Tears came in a torrent.

Simon laid a hand on her shoulder. "It happens this way sometimes. We won't give up, Patricia. It's not the end of the game."

She dabbed her eyes. "What do you think is going on?"

Simon paused. "Apparently they're moving him between call-ins. Across continents."

"Private aircraft?" she asked.

"Most likely. We have an Interpol alert out for Trey should his name show up on any passenger manifests."

"Have you checked private arrivals and subsequent departures from the closest civilian airport to *Schloss Wilheim?*"

Simon keyed in a command. Moments later, a map showing airfields in the vicinity of the castle appeared. Simon tapped the icon closest to *Schloss Wilheim*. A list of ten arrivals and departures appeared. Only one aircraft had both arrived and departed in the appropriate timeframe - and it had arrived from Armenia. "Got it," Simon said, keying another command.

"How could they be so dumb?" she asked.

A screen of data appeared.

"What's that?" she asked.

"The departing aircraft's flight plan. It's on its way to Cairo." The printer came to life. "FlightAware will provide me updates on the jet's progress in case they change their destination." Another screen appeared. "I've entered the aircraft's beacon identification number into our satellite tracking system—"

"Our?"

"Department of Defense," he said. "If it's in the air, we're tracking it." The screen changed again. "German Immigration indicates one person, a male named Conrad Frasier, entered Germany from that inbound flight, and a totally different person left on the departure."

"Trey didn't leave on the flight?"

"They're probably moving him around using different passports," Simon said. "They'd guess we'd contact Interpol as soon as we realized Trey was overseas. Without a name match on immigration records, Interpol would report no records of Trey anywhere."

"They're using a lot of resources to keep Trey beyond our reach."

"I suppose they feel what they want from us is worth it."

"How long until Trey arrives in Cairo?"

Simon keyed his computer. "Four hours. Time enough to get Egyptian authorities to the airport to intercept Trey when he steps off the plane."

"It's that simple?"

"Sometimes." He shrugged. "Sometimes not."

"What's that supposed to mean, Simon?"

"It means I don't want you to get your hopes up. These guys are clever and using everything in the book to evade us. Anything could happen in the next four hours. Meanwhile, we keep pursuing other leads."

She made a fist. "This uncertainty is maddening."

"Do you need something to ease your anxiety?"

"No. I'm not taking any drugs. I just want Trey safe. I want this over and done with."

"So do we, Patricia. We're doing everything we can to get him back. You just have to be patient."

Tears returned.

He gave her a stiff hug.

She closed her eyes and bowed her head. *What have we done to deserve this? Please Lord, find Trey and bring him back to safety.*

Shame rose. Shame at being impatient. Shame at being ungrateful for the work and sacrifice of so many. Shame for questioning God's way. She needed to pray for forgiveness. She needed to back off and let God take charge. She needed to go to church, humble herself, and get right with the Lord.

"Simon, I want to go to Saint Gregory's."

"The cathedral?"

"Yes."

He shook his head. "It's too dangerous. And, even if I could arrange it, the visit would take me away from finding Trey. We're close to getting this done. I'm needed right here, right now. So you're not going to church. If you need Bishop Reilly to come over, I'd be happy to call him and see if he's available."

"I'd appreciate it."

"I'll get to it in a moment," Simon said.

An hour later, the bishop arrived. After exchanging greetings, escorting him to the library and pouring tea, Patricia made the sign of the cross and said, "In the name of the Father, and the Son, and the Holy Spirit. My last confession was one week ago. I've been prideful, impatient, and critical of the Lord, Your Excellency."

He touched her forehead. "God, The Father of mercies, through the death and resurrection of His Son, has reconciled the world to Himself and sent the Holy Spirit among us for the forgiveness of sins; through the ministry of the Church. May God give you pardon and peace, and I absolve you from your sins in the name of the Father, and of the Son, and of the Holy Spirit."

"Thank you." She let out a sigh. "It's hard to live in the Spirit during stressful times like this."

"God understands. He's with Trey, giving him the strength to continue, just like He will for you. God provides all we need, Patricia. There is no need for you to fret over anything other than the exercise of your own gifts."

Patricia shook her head. "What gifts do I have?"

"You have many. For example, you're a wife and a mother. A caregiver."

"I haven't given Trey much care lately."

"You might be surprised, Patricia."

"And I haven't even spoken to Hayley since all this started."

"Why is that?"

"She's in Atlanta and I didn't want to worry her."

"I suspect Hayley needs you, and that you need her."

Patricia's eyes welled. After the bishop's visit, she'd ask Simon if she could go see Hayley.

The bishop folded his hands in his lap. "The Lord works in mysterious ways. Sometimes all we can do is trust that everything is going according to his plan."

"It's hard."

"Hard, but not impossible. You can do it, Patricia. Have faith."

"But, Trey—"

"The Lord will watch over him. Of that you can be certain. Now, is there anything else I can do for you?"

"Are you familiar with Saint Gregory the Illuminator?"

Bishop Reilly's eyes widened. "Yes. Why?"

"Father John mentioned a lost relic."

Bishop Reilly nodded. "It's likely one of the saint's relics is in Savannah. We're working with Father John to find it."

"Have there been relic cults associated with his relics?"

"I suppose so, though I'm not personally aware of any."

"How would I find out if there were any current cults centered on his relics?"

He narrowed his eyes. "Why would you be interested in that?"

"Ever since Father John mentioned the missing relic, I've been interested in the relationship between the cults and the relics they venerate."

"You'll find scant public information on relic cults. They tend to be secretive. It's one of the ways they protect the relics. But, the Vatican keeps records of the relic cults. I could check for you."

"Thank you, Your Excellency."

After Bishop Reilly departed, Patricia went to Simon. "I'm concerned about how well Hayley is doing."

"I've received daily reports that she's doing well."

Patricia shook her head. "I want to spend some time with my daughter."

"I'm sorry, Patricia. Now's not the time. It puts more people at risk."

"Look, Simon. When we had to leave Savannah last year, Trey arranged military transportation for us. I've seen you in action. I know you could arrange military transportation to Atlanta for me, so it's not dangerous, nor time consuming. I'm Hayley's mother. She needs time with me ... and I need time with her."

"If you're not here when the next proof of life call comes in, we'd blow an opportunity to find Trey."

"They've already called today. They won't call again until tomorrow. I can be up and back before dinner." She knew the visit would be brief, but it was something she had to do.

"Why not Skype her?"

"It's not the same thing. Just arrange it, Simon."

Simon keyed his computer. "Okay."

\* \* \*

As instructed by Bishop Reilly, Father John went down the stone stairs to the cathedral's basement and traversed a dimly lit, wide hall to the end. The noticeably cooler basement air had a musty odor. After knocking, Father John opened the door on a room labeled *Archives Office* and went in.

A thin, pale, older man in clerical clothing came from behind a cluttered desk, hand extended and a smile on his face. "The bishop said you'd be right down. How may I help you, Father?"

"I'd like to see records for 1939 and 1940."

The archivist gave him a hard stare from deep-set eyes framed above with bushy eyebrows and bracketed below by dark circles. "There are several categories of records for each year, Father. Might I ask what specifically you are looking for?"

"Certainly. I'm looking for records of a shipment received during that period of time from a parish in Armenia."

The archivist held his gaze momentarily, then left the office through a dark doorway behind the desk. "Thirty-nine and forty?" the archivist said from the doorway.

"Yes."

"This might take a while."

"How long?" Father John asked.

"Well. There are a lot of boxes to move. I—"

"I'd be happy to help you move the boxes."

The archivist gestured dismissively. "I can manage fine. Actually, I'd prefer to do it myself. It's the only real exercise I get down here. Oh, that and going up and down the stairs. So I'd say it might take half an hour. Would you like to come back later, Father?"

"I'll wait."

"Suit yourself. There's a pot of coffee in the kitchen." The archivist gestured to a side doorway with light spilling through, then shuffled into the darkness beyond his office.

While wondering what the priest had done to be relegated to this vocation, Father John checked his smartphone and wasn't surprised to see that it wasn't receiving a signal within the thick walls. He went into the kitchen. A small metal table with folding chairs sat to one side. A brown-stained coffeemaker with a partial pot of coffee sat on a Formica countertop that had seen better days. Father took a ceramic mug from the overhead cabinet, poured coffee and sat at the table.

Recalling his time in a similar kitchen while attending seminary, he took a sip and found the strong coffee satisfying. He'd rather be helping to find Trey Falcon, but he was under Papal orders to find the relic. He thumbed through the old magazines stacked on a corner of the table, only finding real interest in the parish magazine. The parish historian had submitted articles for each issue documenting the early years of the Savannah church. Father John made a note of the author's name and phone number. The historian might have some idea on what became of the relic or who to talk with that might know.

The archivist returned with two bound ledgers. He went straight to the coffeemaker and poured himself a cup, then offered a fill up, which Father John gratefully accepted. The cold damp basement was getting to him.

The archivist sat across from him and blew on the top of

his coffee. He probably didn't get many visitors. He pushed the two ledgers across the table. "If we acquired or disposed of anything in those years, it would be recorded in these property ledgers."

"Do you mind if I take them with me?" John asked.

"I'm afraid you'll have to use them here. Rules, you know. Not mine."

FIVE HOURS OF INTENSE READING LATER, FATHER JOHN RUBBED his eyes. The 1939 property ledger lay open before him. Still two more hours before the archival office would close.

John stood on legs numbed from sitting so long, wobbled to the coffeemaker, and poured another cup. The warm mug felt good on his arthritic fingers. He returned to the table and sat, eager to make a breakthrough before shutting down for the day.

The archivist, dressed in black with a white collar, came into the kitchen, carrying a cup. He flashed a smile. "Any success?"

"Every page forward is progress, but the sloppy writing makes careful reading mandatory."

The archivist's eyes glimmered. "So you read Latin?"

"There aren't many Latin notations in this ledger but, yes, I'm comfortable with Latin text."

"It's a shame so few are learning Latin these days."

The archivist seemed to want to converse. But John had work to do and no time for idle conversation about the modern curriculum. John turned the ledger page and looked down, hoping the man would get the message.

"And so few seek religious vocations. Sometimes I wonder if—"

John looked up. "I'm afraid I must get back to my research."

The man's eyes widened. "But of course." The archivist poured coffee and left.

John returned his attention to the next page, yellow and old. He'd grown familiar with the author's handwriting, such that what had been somewhat illegible had become reasonably readable, though John had to occasionally guess at a word or two ... and the man's spelling was atrocious. Nevertheless, John was able to pore over page after page, sensing the end as the November entries morphed into December.

Suddenly a shiver went up his spine. In Latin, the entry read, *A relic from Saint Gregory the Illuminator Church, Yerevan, Armenia. 49. 74. 65.* In the margin to the left of the entry was a drawing of an arm superimposed on a cross. John hadn't seen that symbol anywhere in the previous ledger pages.

Was the wording of the entry intentionally vague to mask the importance of the relic, or had more than one relic been sent to Savannah for safekeeping? The only way to tell was to continue searching.

# CHAPTER 21

*L*ucius Alton, seated at the table in the Coalition's subterranean conference bunker, scanned the somber faces of Benjamin Hempfield, Roland Potter, Beau Simpson, and their aides, standing behind each. "Before we start, let's take a moment of silent prayer for Trey Falcon and his family."

Lucius bowed his head, closed his eyes and privately prayed. On completion, he waited for the others to finish. Once he had their attention, he cleared his throat. "Trokev is stronger than we thought. He's beating us at every turn. We're failing Trey. Benjamin, where do we stand with Trokev?"

"He'll return Trey if we let him operate the brothel. If we continue to interfere, he'll take more violent action against Trey's family and us. He has demanded we concede by the end of the week."

Lucius glanced at the calendar on his monitor. "Why the deadline?"

"He has an elaborate gala to introduce his escorts to high rollers and wants his brothel fully operational by then."

Lucius shook his head. "I assume Trokev understands the brothel is unacceptable."

"Yes. That's where we're at. A standoff. Meanwhile, he's repairing the hotel damage and plans to reopen in a day or two."

"Where's Trokev getting the money?" Roland's eyes widened. "We've frozen all his Savannah assets. He's too new to get credit from his contractors. Yet he's moving forward on reconstruction. And Trokev is spending a bundle moving Trey around. We need to find out where his funding is coming from and shut it down."

"I can check on that," Beau said. "This new funding is either coming directly from offshore or from a third party like Trokev's boss. I'll contact the contractors doing the hotel repairs and find out how they're being paid."

Lucius' head seemed to be floating. Was it side effects from the cancer drugs? Perhaps. Fighting the lightheadedness, he took a breath. "We can't use force on Trokev until we get Trey out of play. Once we have Trey, we can get tough with Trokev."

"Hold on, Lucius," Roland said. "We have families. Trokev hit Patricia's home, killed her gardener. Our families might not be safe. We need to find out if Trokev has any loved ones before we get rough with him."

"Will you follow up on that, Roland?" Lucius asked.

"Sure." Roland made a note. "What do we know about Trokev's boss?"

"Trokev mentioned that he's local," Benjamin said. "I met with him once. He didn't seem to be a heavyweight. I'm guessing he's the money, and Trokev is the muscle." Benjamin passed each man an eight-by-ten photo. "This is an artist's representation of what Trokev's boss looks like without a disguise."

Lucius picked up the drawing. "You've seen him without a costume?"

"No," Benjamin said. "But we have a clear photo of him in disguise. The artist used that as the starting point."

Lucius examined the photo without recognizing the subject. "Have you subjected the photo to facial recognition?"

"No hits so far," Benjamin said, "but the system is still processing."

"Anyone recognize him?" Lucius cocked his head.

No one responded. Just a sea of blank faces.

Lucius coughed and blew his nose, noticing some blood on his handkerchief before putting it away. *Lord, please keep me going until we get Trey back.* "Okay. Let's see. Money. I suppose the local guy is in this for the money."

"Lucius, we just met this guy," Benjamin said. "We haven't established his motive yet."

"What other motive could there be?" Roland asked.

"The motive might be blackmail to achieve non-economic purposes. Or to get power over a specific person. Or to get political influence. Or to set up a new old-boy network in Savannah. Or to achieve vengeance. We just don't know."

"Prostitution and drug sales are usually low-level businesses for organized crime." Lucius coughed again. The exertion made him dizzy. His vision blurred, then restored. "As the mob becomes more powerful, their streams of income diversify. If this local guy is investing in brothels, he's got to have his eyes on a bigger objective. Find out what that is, and we'll make sure we become his suppliers. Once he has what he's after, Trokev and his brothel become obsolete."

Benjamin nodded. "I'll explore that with him."

"We need to keep in mind that their higher goal might be more onerous than organized crime." Lucius took another look at the artist's rendering. There was something vaguely familiar about the face. Nothing he could nail down.

"What could be worse than organized crime?" Benjamin asked.

"Terrorism," Lucius said. "Economic chaos. A meltdown of law and order."

"I don't understand why they refuse to relocate," Beau said. "They can make money from prostitution anywhere. What's their attachment to Savannah? Maybe as difficult as we're trying to make it for Trokev here, it's even harder other places. How do other communities keep this sort of thing out? Or could there be something else they want in this specific city?"

Benjamin shook his head. "Neither Trokev nor Mr. No have mentioned any material objective other than the brothel."

"Mr. No?" Beau asked.

Benjamin smiled. "It's the name we're using for Trokev's unidentified boss."

"Roland and Beau are on to something." Lucius stroked his chin. "We're stalemated because we're not discussing their main interest."

"I agree," Benjamin said. "I'll push hard and see what I can come up with in my next meeting."

"Okay." Lucius consulted his laptop. "Let's move on. Beau, where are we with rescuing Trey?"

"Simon's doing a masterful job. We only missed grabbing Trey by minutes this morning. We're getting our daily proof of life calls, but Trokev's no fool. After the last two calls, he immediately moved Trey. That takes coordination and a ready supply of secure locations to accommodate Trey. The last location Trey was at is one of Trokev's brothels. We suspect he's shuffling Trey between his brothels. If so, that's a break for us."

"Since those brothels are international, you'll need help," Lucius said. "I doubt the United States has personnel in all those locations. Most of the brothels are adjacent to resorts. Not your typical place for a CIA outpost. Are you thinking of requesting assistance from the Vatican?"

Beau's aide handed him a note. "Simon's tracking a private jet that could be transporting Trey to Cairo. He's arranged for Egyptian authorities to intercept Trey on arrival."

"What a break." Lucius smiled. "When will the jet get there?"

Beau consulted his watch. "Less than three hours."

"What's your backup plan?" Lucius asked.

"Father John arranged with Vatican security to stake out all ten of Trokev's European brothels. If Trokev is brazen enough to walk Trey into a place in plain sight, we'll get a heads up. But I don't think it's going to be that easy. The plan is to spot them leaving with Trey immediately after the next proof of life call and follow them to the next location. Once there, they should remain in place for twenty hours or so."

Roland leaned forward. "Why not detain them on the ground en route?"

Beau turned to Roland. "Our friends don't have the necessary capture assets to cover every brothel location."

"What about using local authorities for the capture?"

"Unreliable in some locations."

"So once we know where he is being held, how do we plan to extract him?"

"A European Joint Ops fast response team can get to anywhere in Europe in an hour or so." Beau drummed his fingertips on the table. "Trokev's only moving Trey once a day."

"How's security for Patricia and Hayley?" Lucius said.

"Patricia's security was beefed up after the breaches. No

further incidents there. She's mourning her gardener."

Lucius' shoulders slumped. "What a marvelous man Rhett was. So generous with his time. Besides working for the Falcons, he tended the parish garden that supplied the soup kitchen. A good soul. Make sure his family is taken care of."

"No family. Mrs. Falcon arranged a proper burial," Beau said. "As I mentioned, we've corrected the security breach. Seems the house next to the Falcon's is unoccupied. A sniper secured a second floor position with a full, unobstructed view of the Falcon backyard and killed the gardener. Simon has since installed full security in the unoccupied house, including a novel arrangement that allows Patricia to lock all her second floor doors from the safe room in the event of an intrusion."

"What about Hayley's security?" Lucius raised an eyebrow.

"She's in a level-one safe house not far from her college," Beau said.

"How's she handling this?" A smile came over Lucius' face as he recalled the tantrums Hayley used to pitch years ago when things went wrong.

"She's a college student." Beau shook his head. "Full of energy. Questioning everything. Being locked up in a safe house doesn't suit her, but she's accepting. Smart woman. She's keeping up with all her studies through an anonymous server, but she's anxious about her father's safety and her mother's emotional state."

"How is Patricia's emotional state?" Lucius asked.

"Simon says she's holding up as well as might be expected." Beau crossed his hands. "Good days. Bad days. She appears rested, and she's taking a lot of interest in Simon's work, which keeps her mind occupied. She's performing beyond expectations on the proof of life calls."

"Patricia's safety is paramount," Lucius said, saddened

that Patricia had to go through this again. "Should we go after these guys, she's likely to be their primary retaliation target."

"Understood," Beau said. "Do you want her in a safe house?"

Lucius paused for a moment. He knew she wouldn't go for that. "Not yet. Okay, if there isn't—"

"Lucius," Beau said. "Your nose is bleeding."

Lucius, his head hung, swiped his nose with his handkerchief. A bright red smear. He sagged. He knew what the blood meant, and it had taken the heart from him. He looked up and made eye contact with the others one by one. They knew too. He shook his head. "I wish I could have had more time with you," he said slowly.

Benjamin brushed a tear from his eye. "You have done so much, Lucius."

Lucius shook his head. "Not nearly enough." He shook his head. "Not nearly enough."

"You've given far more than anyone in your condition should have to give," Beau said.

The pain in Lucius' chest started up again. He closed his eyes. The pain killers would take the pain away, and his mind with it. No drug.

"Lucius?" Roland said.

Lucius opened his eyes and met Roland's gentle gaze.

"You must think of yourself." Roland's eyes welled. "We can manage."

The pain. The blood. The cancer had won. "My good friends, I'm afraid it's time for my daughter, Isabel, to take my seat."

He looked at them once more, one by one, recalling how each had changed over the decades they had worked together, remembering how their predecessors had retired and died, knowing his Coalition work would cease, but not his close friendship with each. They were brothers in the war against crime, bonded by unthinkable common experiences and unimaginable secrets.

He rose and offered his chair to Isabel.

Flush-faced, she hesitated.

"It's time, Isabel," Lucius said. "Please sit."

She gave him a wordless hug and took a seat.

Lucius handed her the security token to his Coalition laptop, and then left the table to attend to his nosebleed.

\* \* \*

Simon made a tight fist as he watched the Egyptian authorities leave after searching the private jet, then slammed the fist down, rattling his coffee cup. Not a trace of Trey. He opened and closed his hand to relieve the pain.

Trokev's mistakes weren't mistakes-they were freaking diversions. Diversions Simon had fallen for over and over.

Unable to sit still, he stood and paced the room. The Coalition and their partners had superb resources and were deploying them as well as they could. They had Trokev's brothels staked out, and Lucius said the Coalition was exploring other ways to force the return of Trey. But nothing they'd done so far had worked. Nothing at all.

He'd earned his Coalition position by outthinking brilliant criminals. But this time the criminal was outsmarting him ... and the entire Cotton Coalition. If he didn't turn the tide on Trokev, they could lose Trey, and Savannah could fall prey to organized crime. Once rooted in Savannah, Trokev's organization could take their corruption throughout the southeast. Neither the Coalition nor their government backers would tolerate that.

They had to beat Trokev in Savannah, but how? What were they missing? Simon paused, looked out the back window, and clenched his fists. An innocent man had paid the supreme price out there for Simon's stupidity.

From now on, skepticism was in order. He'd seek the truth beyond the obvious, or behind it, but definitely not in it. He wouldn't just react to circumstances, he'd try to think like Trokev and move ahead of circumstances.

If he was Trokev, what would he be doing right now with Trey? Hmmm. He'd be taking him somewhere as far from Cairo as possible. Would he use a private jet? Maybe not. There were plenty of commercial international flights available, but a commercial flight would give Trey much more opportunity to escape. If he were Trokev, he wouldn't take that risk. He'd stick to private jets, just not the obvious ones.

Simon sat at his computer and searched for private aircraft departures within one hundred miles of *Schloss Wilheim*, narrowing the search to long-range jets that had filed international flight plans to countries where Trokev had brothels. There were several that had departed that morning within three hours after the proof of life call.

Simon contacted Father John to let him know of the failure at Cairo and the most logical destinations for the next proof of life call.

After talking with Father John, Simon stared at his monitor. If he were Trokev would he continue the proof of life calls? Yes. They were very effective in keeping the Coalition off base. So it was important the Coalition continue to appear to be falling for Trokev's diversions. And once they sighted Trey, they needed to grab him before Trokev could resort to a contingency plan. If he were Trokev, he'd certainly have a contingency plan or two.

What was Trokev's contingency plan if the Coalition got close enough to rescue Trey? Kill the rescuers? Failing that, kill Trey? Simon massaged his throbbing head. This could end very badly.

# CHAPTER 22

*P*atricia made the day trip to Atlanta with nothing more than a lipstick and a hundred dollars in cash. Everything she wore, right down to her underwear, had been purchased for the trip and meticulously scanned for electronic implants.

Simon drove her to Hunter Army Airfield and parked next to a small military transport jet.

"Are you sure you want to do this?" he asked.

She nodded. "I don't want to be here two days from now regretting I hadn't gone."

"I agree they're looking for Hayley, but she's safe up there."

"She's only safe if she stays there. She's a rebel and independent. I'll not believe she's safe, and that she'll stay put, until I see her and talk with her face-to-face. This is a ticking time bomb. Every day they don't return Trey, Hayley could bolt. I need to go eye-to-eye with my daughter. Now."

She stepped from the car and boarded the military transport. Her mind whirling, she sat in the front of the empty passenger compartment. Her and a dozen empty seats. Alone.

She knew she had to go to Atlanta, to see Hayley, to explain, to reassure, to somehow get Hayley to bridle her rebellious nature and stay in place. It was necessary. Critical. But only when she left Simon on the tarmac did it occur to her she would make the trip alone. She looked around. Utterly alone ... and without her gun.

If something happened—she gripped the armrest—she would be defenseless. Like Rhett. The horrible image of his shattered face reared up like some Dante demon and consumed her. She shook her head. Was she next? Instinctively, her hand went to her purse. Her new purse. The purse with nothing but lipstick and money. No gun, no safety, no—

Someone came into the passenger compartment.

She could only see the silhouette against the open hatch, but the person was big and broad-shouldered and they were coming for her. She squinted, trying desperately to see if they had a gun or a knife.

"Good morning, Mrs. Falcon," the silhouette said. "I'm Captain McDonald. My co-pilot and I will be taking you to Dobbins. We'll be departing momentarily. Please keep your seat belt fastened until I tell you it's okay to remove it. Your life vest is under your seat. The nearest exit is the hatch you came in. Any questions?"

She shook her head.

He turned, closed the hatch, and went forward into the cockpit.

Patricia's jaw clenched. What was she going to say to Hayley? How should she say it? Should she tell her daughter everything? Doubt crept in. Maybe Hayley would be better off kept in the dark?

No, Patricia thought, Hayley was now grown up. It was time to ease her into reality. Her father had been abducted and the family gardener was murdered. How the hell did she ease her into that? Despite her doubts, she couldn't keep Hayley in the dark. Ignorance could be life threatening.

A squared-jawed, middle-aged man in casual civilian clothes, who introduced himself as Robert, met the jet at McGuire and drove her into the city.

"This is it," Robert said, pulling up in front of a brownstone apartment in Atlanta. Although no students were present, the overgrown landscaping strewn with empty beer bottles screamed 'off-campus housing' for the nearby Emerald University.

Robert came around and, his shoulder-holstered gun readily apparent, held the door for her as she stepped out. Murky gray clouds coated the sky. Pedestrian and vehicle traffic was lighter than she had expected. Discreetly scanning right and left, Robert led her through the ivy-covered gateposts and up the crumbling stairs. He paused at the steel door and made a call.

A portly older woman opened the door. Robert excused himself and left. The woman led Patricia down a narrow dark hall, scratching her head and chatting incessantly about city politics, then pointed at a door near the end. "Your daughter's room."

"Thank you."

The woman nodded and left.

She knocked on Hayley's door. The door opened to reveal Hayley, dressed in a black shirt and snug black jeans. No makeup. Hair pulled back. Hayley blinked. "Mom?"

They embraced. A warm, lingering hug full of love and concern. Patricia held Hayley tightly, inhaling her familiar vanilla scent. An awkward silence ensued.

"Daddy?" Hayley asked in a weak voice.

"He's okay. So far."

Hayley squirmed and stepped back. "Then why are you here?"

The serious look on Hayley's flushed face and her rigid pose told Patricia that her very clever daughter knew it wasn't a social visit. Patricia gestured toward the upholstered, overstuffed sofa, an inviting piece in a nicely furnished room. They sat side-by-side. She gazed in Hayley's narrowed eyes.

"Why didn't you call?"

"Security." Patricia touched Hayley's shoulder. "The kidnappers still have Daddy, but they seem to be taking good care of him."

"What are you doing to get him back?"

"Lots of people are doing everything possible to bring him home to us."

"When?"

"Don't know. Soon, I hope." Patricia took Hayley's hands. "There's been a lot going on. I thought it best to come up and fill you in personally." Patricia paused to collect herself. "They killed Rhett."

Hayley pulled her hands away and folded her arms into herself.

Patricia wrapped her arm around Hayley's shoulder and held her tight. "I'm so sorry."

Hayley's chest heaved. She sniffled, then wiped her eyes. "His family—"

"No family but us. I've taken care of everything."

Hayley quivered. Her shoulders heaved up and down as she silently cried. "I'm scared."

"I understand. The threat is real." Patricia wiped the moist trail from Hayley's cheek. "That's why you're under so much protection."

"It's stifling."

Patricia stroked Hayley's hair. "It's necessary."

"I know." Hayley wiped at her eyes again. "It's just that it's hard doing this by myself."

Patricia nodded. "It's safer for you if we're apart. If trouble came, I would be their main target, not you. And they need me down there."

"I want to come home." Hayley grabbed her purse. "I could be packed in minutes."

"You're safer here."

"What if they find me?" Hayley said in a squeaky voice.

Patricia gave her another hug. "I don't know how they could. Simon was very careful in moving you."

"But you came here. They could have followed you."

Patricia pulled Hayley closer. "I came by military transport. The people involved in this are Russians. They don't have access to our military operations."

Hayley pulled away. "How do you know that?"

"I guess I don't. I just assumed—"

"That's what I mean, Mama." Her gaze skittered around the room. "We don't know anything. They could have followed you. They could be outside right now."

Patricia shook her head. "You're letting your imagination get the best of you. Has anything bad happened to you since you came to the safe house?"

"No. Not yet."

"Then a bit of trust should be in order."

Hayley scowled. "They took Daddy and killed Rhett, and you're asking me to trust you? You have to be kidding."

"Hayley, sweetheart. What happened to your father has nothing at all to do with your safety. Daddy went to a meeting with the people who abducted him."

"Just like that?"

"Honey, you need to understand. They didn't infiltrate anything. He was available, and they took him. As for Rhett, Simon made a serious mistake in failing to secure the house next door." Patricia dabbed her eyes. "Unfortunately, mistakes happen. But that's no reason for you, sweetheart, to assume the people who operate this safe house have made a mistake that could cost you your life. I believe you should trust that the folks here will keep you safe."

"I don't know," Hayley said, shriveling into herself.

"Do you remember how I was after the accident?" Patricia asked.

"Yes. You were completely paranoid."

"Was my behavior appropriate?"

"No."

"Is your paranoia appropriate regarding this place?"

Hayley crossed her arms over her chest. "Yeah."

Patricia gestured toward the front down. "Look at the steel-reinforced door. And you have bulletproof windows with imbedded intrusion alarms. Check the cameras, if you can find them all. Do you honestly think anyone unauthorized could get through those formidable defensive layers?"

Hayley shrugged. "Probably not."

"So?" Patricia asked.

"Why did they take Daddy?"

"He was discussing business with them and the discussion wasn't going well." She stroked her daughter's hair.

"Isn't that bizarre? Civilized people don't act like that."

"I agree," Patricia said softly. "But not everyone plays by the same rules we do."

"Mom! Rules or not, you can't do business like that."

Patricia shrugged. "Apparently they did."

"What kind of clients is Daddy dealing with?"

"All kinds."

"Can't he just limit his practice to safe clients?"

"There's no such thing." Patricia recalled those who betrayed her a year ago. "Even people you think you know well can turn on you."

"Like the people who took Daddy?"

"Yes indeed."

"Do you think they'll actually hurt him?"

"It doesn't appear so," she said, though she didn't really know.

"I'm relieved to hear that." Hayley paused for a moment. "How do we get Daddy back?"

"Give them what they want."

"That sounds straight forward. Why not do it?"

"It's not that simple."

"Why?"

"What they want is illegal."

Hayley sniffled. "So they're not going to release him?"

"We're working on a compromise." She wanted to tell Hayley about the rescue plan, but because of the risks and uncertainties involved didn't want to worry her unnecessarily. "Daddy will be okay." She swallowed back a lump in her throat and forced a smile. "By the way, how's your course work going?"

"It's going well. I'm doing a lot more studying and the material is making much more sense. I suppose the lack of distractions helps."

"Have they provided your burn cream?" She ran her fingers over Hayley's scared forearm.

"Oh yes. Exactly as prescribed."

"How's the food?" Patricia asked.

"Much better than—"

There was a sharp knock at the door.

*Had the hour already passed?* Patricia stood. "I think that's my ride."

Hayley stood and embraced her. Patricia stroked Hayley's back, savoring their last moments of the too brief visit. Tears welled. She didn't want this to end. Not yet.

Another knock sounded.

Stepping back, she brushed the tears away. "I'm going to miss you, sweetheart."

"Me too."

They went to the door.

Robert nodded. "I'm Robert. I'm here for Mrs. Falcon."

Patricia and Hayley stepped out into the hall.

Robert turned to Hayley. "It would be best if you said your goodbyes here. I don't want you anywhere near the front door when we go out."

"Give us a moment, please." Patricia hugged Hayley.

"Thank you for coming, Mama." Hayley tightened the hug. "I don't like what's going on at all, but you've given me strength to carry on."

"I want you to promise me that you'll stay here no matter what happens in Savannah."

Hayley cringed.

"I'm still carrying a gun. Your grandmother carried a gun. This is what I do. I can find him. And your part to help me is to stay safely hidden away so I can focus on getting Daddy back. Will you do that?"

"Yes. I promise to stay safely hidden if it helps you and Daddy."

So coming to Atlanta was a good thing. Thank God. "I'm glad to hear that. I'm hoping we'll get this all taken care of soon and we can get your life back to normal."

"I don't think my life will ever be normal."

Patricia throat tightened. "I'm sorry."

They embraced one final, tearful time, and then Patricia walked with Robert down the long hall to the front door. Patricia turned and, though her eyesight was blurred with tears, looked back at Hayley. "This will pass, sweetheart. Trust me." She waved to her daughter, and then, not knowing when she'd see her precious daughter again or under what circumstances, stepped out on to the porch.

As soon as the door clunked shut, Patricia burst into sobs.

* * *

AUGUSTA STRAIGHTENED AS WILLY FINISHED READING HER piece on the theft of Doctor Buzzard's right arm. His face didn't give a clue at what he actually thought of her story. She recalled he'd been skeptical of the whole relic storyline when she first proposed it, and now she'd combined the relic storyline with a theft.

He placed the story on his desk and smiled. She knew the stilted social smile meant nothing. The man changed faces as often as well-dressed Southern ladies changed hats.

"Good job," he said.

She puffed up. "Thank you."

"But it needs some work before I'll consider passing it on for publication." He ran fingertips through his comb-over.

Her shoulders slumped. She pulled out her notebook and pen. "What kind of work?"

Willy rubbed his chin, reminding her of that 'Thinker' statue, but she doubted he was thinking. A man like him always had the answers before the questions came up. So why was he rubbing his chin? Drama? Perhaps. "If it's true, this is an important story. Therefore, you'll need at least two independent sources on each key fact. For example, you said you saw this arm skeleton in Doctor Snake's possession. Correct?"

"Yes, sir."

"I'd like you to document at least one other person who also saw the skeleton—"

"Relic," she injected.

He leveled a scathing look on her. "It's just a bunch of bones until you prove it's a relic, and until you have that proof, you don't have a story."

Her face heated with embarrassment. He was right, of course. She'd have to prove the arm was Doctor Buzzard's if she wanted to label it as such in her story. That meant a lot more research. More interviews. A lot of work, but she could do it. She crossed her fingers, hoping he was done with his critique.

Willy raised an eyebrow. "I want to know exactly how Doctor Snake acquired the skeleton, and I want a second source on that aspect of the story. Preferably the person who gave him the skeleton. If that person's unavailable, I'll need a person who witnessed the transfer."

Her hand shaking with frustration, she scribbled the requirement in her notebook, wondering if she'd ever be able to satisfy him.

"I also want a full biography on Snake." Willy's eyes sharpened. "His real name. Birth date. Birthplace. I don't want to put a story out featuring a known con man or serial killer looking for headlines, so make sure you do a thorough background check on him."

She flipped the page on her notebook and continued writing.

"A picture would punch up this story, preferably one of the skeleton. Make sure it's at least 600 DPI. If you can't find one of the skeleton, get one of him—"

She held up a hand to stop him. "I don't think he's going to agree to a photo of himself."

"Does he want his skeleton back or not? Push him. We need a picture, and a signed release." Willy took out a cigarillo and stabbed it into his mouth, his well-understood signal that the conversation was over. "You think you're up to all that?"

Augusta nodded.

"Get it done by tomorrow morning." He scowled at her.

A sinking feeling invaded her. She knew better than to ask for extra time. "Yes, sir."

"By the way, do you have a ball gown?"

"No." She shifted in her seat. "Why?"

He pushed an envelope across the desk. "You and I are covering the bachelorette auction gala in a couple of days."

# CHAPTER 23

Father John sat across from Connie in The Sentient Bean coffee shop, savoring a cup of steaming coffee while waiting for a breakfast burrito. His daughter, her long blonde hair pulled back in an elastic band, had ordered the vegan quesadilla. She'd grown into a fine woman, and he was proud to be her father.

Whenever possible, John liked to spend the first couple of hours of each day with Connie. They used the time to relax and gathered their wits. Business paid the bills, but he'd learned over the years family time was more important.

Their order came, and Connie's eyes widened as she took in the size of the quesadilla. She smiled when she caught him observing her amazement.

He loved to see her happy. Fresh-faced. Bright-eyed. What father wouldn't be? It hadn't always been like that between them. Thank God they had long ago settled their differences over his frequent absences.

"How was your run?" he asked.

"Delightful." She took a sip of her strawberry smoothie. "I'm so glad we relocated to Savannah. This part of the city is made for early morning runs. Wide sidewalks marked with running lanes. Cool air. Sunlight trickling through the oaks."

While they ate, they chatted about the advantages of now being based in Savannah. And he kept an eye out for the usual suspects. Or, more accurately, for anything unusual.

As soon as John finished his burrito, he leaned back in his chair and enjoyed watching Connie attack what remained of her quesadilla.

She soon finished the last carrot crisp and, over his objections, cleared their dishes.

When she returned to the table, he said, "I wish you'd let me take care of myself."

She gave him a bright smile. "Where's the fun in that? You want more coffee?"

"Yeah." He stood. "And I'm getting it myself."

When he returned from the coffee station, he asked, "What happened to my napkin?"

"A busboy came by. He cleaned the table and left you a fresh one." Her smile deepened. "He was sort of cute."

"How's the research on Saint Gregory the Illuminator going?"

"You've heard of the Bavarian Illuminati?"

He nodded. If he never heard another word about the Illuminati, it would be too soon. Contemporary novelists had taken a positive eighteenth-century movement and rebuilt it to suit their fictional purposes. Unfortunately, their readers sometimes confused fact with fiction. "Sure. I've heard of them."

"Most historians feel the Order of the Illuminati was founded in 1776 in Upper Bavaria by Adam Weishaupt. There's no question of what followed, it's well documented by multiple sources. What I've learned is the Bavarian Illuminati could have deeper roots, perhaps back to the fourth century and Saint Gregory the Illuminator."

"Illuminator. Illuminati. I see the naming similarity." He scanned the room to assure no one was listening. "Is this connection a theory, or have you proven the linkage?"

"I've found some solid links and some broken links. So, no, I don't have irrefutable proof. But here's the deal. There are those who claim the Bavarian Illuminati have continued into modern times masterminding events and seeking to influence world affairs."

"I'm fully aware of the conspiracy theories. The Vatican keeps close track of such things and, when appropriate, documents them. To my knowledge there has been no evidence to support the present existence of such an organization."

Connie rolled her eyes. "Dad. Lack of evidence doesn't necessarily signify lack of existence. It could signify lack of detection. As you know, historically the Illuminati have recruited some of the brightest people in their era, people who could easily develop means to avoid detection."

He nodded. "All right. Apparently you've bought into the conspiracy theories. What does this have to do with the arm relic of Saint Gregory the Illuminator?"

"I think maybe the Order of the Illuminati is a relic cult that venerates the relics of Saint Gregory the Illuminator, believing that possessing those relics is the source of their ongoing power. If this is true and they have the missing right arm of Saint Gregory the Illuminator, we're going to have a hard time finding it, much less recovering it."

"An interesting theory and a plausible explanation, Connie. I'm impressed."

Her eyes lit up. "Thank you, Dad."

"You did so well, I have some new work for you to start on today."

A smile broke out, revealing those gleaming white teeth he'd spent a fortune to straighten. She took a pen and small notebook from her purse. Pen poised over paper, she said, "Okay."

He reached out and took the pen. "Let me borrow this."

After again scanning the room to confirm no one was observing, John took a napkin from the nearby dispenser and drew the 'arm over cross' symbol he'd seen in the ledger. He pushed the napkin across the table. "I want you to research this symbol."

The drawing triggered vague recognition. She couldn't place when or where she'd encountered it before.

"You've seen this symbol?" John asked

She shook her head. "I don't think so. But maybe in my research. Where did *you* see it?

"Doesn't matter."

"It matters. Where would help me pinpoint it faster. General research takes longer."

"You're going to have to start broadly then."

She held up the napkin.

He pushed her hand down.

She tapped her finger on the napkin. "Does this symbol have anything to do with our search for Saint Gregory's relic?"

"Yes, and one more thing," he said, keeping his voice low. "I want you to check Savannah newspaper archives for December 1939 and see if there was a story on the arrival in Savannah of a religious relic."

She nodded. "Anything else, Dad?"

"No, that will do it for now."

He opened his napkin to clean up spilled coffee and found a message: *If you value your daughter's life, get out of the relic business.* He schooled his features to show no reaction, refolded the napkin, and put it in his pocket. Had they been overheard? Was there a listening device under the table?

"Okay," he whispered. "Let's test your observation skills."

"Dad. Come on."

"If you're truly interested in this work, I need to give you a lot more hands on training. I've committed to the Pope to give him a fully trained agent. So, what did the busboy look like?"

"Which one?"

"The one who cleaned the table while I was getting coffee."

"Hmm. He was cute. College age. Asian. Lean waist." Connie starred at the ceiling for a moment. "Long, black hair. Glasses. Average height. Black shirt. Black pants. Muscular forearms like he worked out."

John looked around nonchalantly at the others in the room. No Asians. Delivering the message must have been the only objective. John excused himself, citing a need for more coffee, then stepped to the counter and asked for the manager,

"I'm the manager," the counter clerk said.

"Do you have an Asian busboy working today?"

"No."

John scanned the ceiling for cameras. Saw none. "Security video?"

"None of your business."

John flexed his hand. "Bless you, my son." He filled his cup, then returned to the table.

Connie pushed her hair behind her ear. "What are you up to today?"

"Back to the catacombs."

"All day?"

"Probably."

"You might want to consider taking carryout from here for lunch."

"Good idea."

"And make it healthy, Dad. I don't want to have to go into

those creepy catacombs to haul you out."

"I want you to go straight back to the condo," he whispered. "If anyone follows you, dump them before you get to the condo. Once you get there, lock it down, and stay there until I come home."

"What's up?"

"I'll explain later. Just do as I say."

She nodded.

* * *

FATHER JOHN ARRIVED AT THE ARCHIVAL OFFICE SHORTLY AFTER it opened. The archivist had the 1940 property ledger and a fresh pot of coffee ready. After putting his lunch in the refrigerator, John poured coffee and sat at the table. He opened the ledger to the first page and read one acquisition record after another. Mundane purchases interspersed with donated items. The down-to-earth business of a large parish. It was going to be a long day.

John didn't mind the long hours or the isolation. He was a warrior for the church and a loner. The problem was that reading every entry was boring. Intently staring at the text, a purchase of institutional cookware for the soup kitchen, he tried to make the record interesting, but failed.

When noon came around, John pushed the ledger to the back of the table and brought out his lunch, a pesto and mozzarella panini.

The thin archivist walked in to the kitchen and, after returning the ledger to its protective pouch, sat at the table next to John. John offered him half of the sandwich, but the man declined. No wonder he was so frail.

The archivist sat there, hands flat on the table, and watched John eat his entire sandwich as if John was some sort of circus act, and the archivist didn't want to miss one second of the show. After John finished eating, he dumped the wrapping and paper bag in the trash.

The archivist frowned. "Is this going to be your last day?"

"Depends."

His bushy eyebrows rose. "Depends on what?"

"It depends on if the bishop in 1939 kept a personal diary. And if you have the bishop's diary here."

"I can tell you, if he kept a personal diary we would have it in our archives. If you'll excuse me, I'll go see if there's one back there."

Ten minutes later, the archivist returned clutching a beautiful black leather-bound book with gilded edges. The tooled cover depicted Jesus on the cross. The archivist held the book out and, face beaming, said, "Bishop Justine's diary."

John's heart sped as he thumbed through the book. The elegant handwriting was perfect and the entries reflected the vocabulary of a well-educated man. The content suggested a detailed, focused person.

As much as John wanted to read through the December 1939 entries, he realized there might be key information on the relic well before or well after that date. The shipment to Savannah of something so important would have been preceded by correspondence with the local church. And there was no telling when the relic was found missing. Perhaps years after being received.

It would take days to read the entire diary, and he would take the time after he finished reviewing the 1940 property ledger. His best chance of locating the relic was finding every possible record regarding its movement in Savannah. He had no doubt records would be there; he just had to find them.

He handed the diary back to the archivist. "Thank you, Father. I'll start reading it tomorrow. Also, would you mind pulling the church correspondence from June to December 1939?"

\* \* \*

THOUGH PATRICIA LOOKED UP WHEN THE FRONT DOORBELL chimed, she remained seated in the study and waited while Simon searched Isabel. Knowing Isabel and her resources, Patricia was sure that if Isabel really wanted to test their defenses she could bring in anything she wished. If Isabel could, who else might penetrate Simon's security?

She recentered a crystal vase of white Fuji mums on the glass-topped coffee table just as Isabel, dressed in a stylish beige pants suit, strode into the study. Her vermillion lips and nails contrasted nicely with her suit. Isabel usually dressed more austere, causing Patricia to wonder what was up. Delighted to have company, she came around the table.

They embraced and did the requisite cheek kisses. Isabel, a tall woman, seemed taller. New heels? Isabel normally wore flats to compensate for her height. Something was definitely going on.

Patricia stepped back and, after exchanging greetings, gestured to the sofa where they took their seats.

Patricia turned her eyes to Isabel's, which were slightly bloodshot. "Would you care for tea?"

Isabel nodded.

Patricia took the heirloom sterling teapot, poured tea into two bone china cups, and handed one to Isabel.

After a polite sip, Patricia said, "How have you been, Isabel?"

"I'm fine, but Daddy's health has taken a turn for the worst and ..." She sniffled. "He's stepped down the Cotton Coalition."

Patricia's blood chilled. "Last I saw your father he seemed to be tolerating his treatments very well. I'm sorry."

Isabel's eyes welled.

An awkward silence simmered. She took Isabel's hand. "I'm so very sorry."

Isabel shook her head. Her chin quivered "They say this might be it."

Patricia stroked Isabel's hand.

"He's strong, but he's not Superman. He won't take pain killers. Says he wants to keep his mind clear. Oh, Patricia, I hate to see him suffer." Tears spilled.

"Is there anything else the doctors can do?"

"No." Isabel sniffled. "The cancer's gone too far."

"Oh dear. What I can do for you?"

"You're such a dear friend, Patricia. So kind and generous. Here in the midst of your terrible situation you're comforting others. You are truly a blessing."

She shrugged. "I can't imagine watching a loved one slowly die. What torture that must be."

"It's not as bad as you might imagine. I just get emotional when I talk about his condition. We made arrangements well ahead, and assured every minute together was fully lived. That makes it easier to ride out the sorrow."

"If there is anything you need, just let me know." Patricia handed her a tissue from a sterling silver box she kept on the side table.

"Thank you."

She patted Isabel's hand and changed subjects for the poor woman's sake. "You said Lucius has stepped down from the Coalition?"

Isabel, pain etched on her face, straightened. "Yes. He has. In accordance with the by-laws, I've been given his seat, which is why I asked to speak with you."

Patricia sat back. She didn't like the sound of that. "Is everything okay?"

"Not as long as Trey is being held hostage. I just want to assure you, we're doing everything in our power to get him back." Isabel paused to take a sip of tea. "I realize Daddy didn't keep you informed about the details of what we were doing to find Trey. He felt it best to wait until he could deliver good news. I never agreed with that approach. So I'm going to brief you daily on our activities, starting today."

Patricia squeezed Isabel's hand. "I appreciate that."

"The short version of the news is that we're stuck."

Patricia gasped. She brought her hand to her mouth. Her cheeks heated. She'd never once heard Trey use that word regarding Coalition business. They had all those resources. "Why?"

"First of all, as long as we keep getting the proof of life calls we're able to say Trey is okay. And I want to assure you we will not do anything to jeopardize his safety. Now, while the people who took Trey have not shown violence toward him, they did murder your gardener in retaliation for our destruction of three of their brothels. We regret our action resulted in Rhett's death and have ceased using any force against these fellows, lest they kill again."

"You did that?"

Isabel nodded.

Patricia drummed her nails on the armrest, grateful to know the circumstances behind Rhett's death. She wondered how much Isabel knew about the rings. Isabel was sharing, but was she sharing everything?

"We just learned we've been negotiating for Trey's release with a secondary player, the man you know as Trokev."

Patricia didn't think Trokev was secondary.

Isabel looked out the back window for a moment, then returned her attention to Patricia. "We've now opened negotiations with Trokev's boss. Unfortunately those negotiations have stalled."

Patricia grabbed the end of the armrest and dug her nails into the fabric. "Why?"

"Neither of us will budge." Isabel closed her eyes and massaged her forehead. She opened her eyes. "As it stands, we get Trey back only when we permit Trokev's brothel to operate in Savannah. Our concern is, considering the owner of the brothel, doing so would open the door to organized crime here. The Cotton Coalition isn't going to do that."

Patricia, shaking with rage, made eye contact with Isabel. "So you're doing nothing to get Trey back. Nothing at all."

"For the time being. Now, it's possible the other side doesn't see the stalemate as a problem. After all, they get to operate their brothel. At least temporarily. But I suspect they're thinking long-term and realize we are working hard to come up with a viable means to stop them."

"Force?"

"Not as long as Trey is their captive."

Her stomach clenched. "So?"

"We are pursuing a two-pronged approach. One is to use the proof of life calls to find and free Trey. The other is to give the brothel owners whatever they hope to gain from having a brothel here."

"You said they wanted a foothold in Savannah."

"I'm not convinced getting organized crime started here is their primary objective. We're a relatively small community as major American cities go. There are much more attractive places for organized crime to take root. No, I believe the brothel owners are in Savannah for something else."

Should she share the ring connection? No. Best to hear Isabel out. "What are they here for?"

"We don't know, but now that we're talking to the top man we've asked our negotiator to try to find out. And that's where we are today."

"I appreciate you being up front with me."

Isabel slid forward on the sofa and turned more toward Patricia. "One more thing."

She didn't like the sound of that. "Yes?"

Isabel took Patricia's hand and held it for a moment. "The other side forced a stalemate by taking Trey. We're concerned they might try to force a permanent concession from us by abducting more Coalition members and their families."

"Oh hell."

"No need to overreact, Patricia. I'm just trying to help you understand the—"

"Understand?" Patricia bolted up and paced. "What I understand is there have been at least two breaches of security here. And now you tell me, in effect, the Russians are coming. Overreact? Damn right I'm going to overreact."

Isabel stood, coming face-to-face with Patricia. "Maybe Daddy was smart to suppress bad news."

Patricia held her hand up apologetically. "I'm sorry, Isabel. You're doing the right thing here. It's just ... there's so much to absorb."

"I know." Isabel nodded. "I know."

"Do you need me to do anything different?"

"No." Isabel headed for the foyer. "Just follow Simon's instructions to the letter."

At the door, Isabel said, "I notice you don't carry your purse when you move from room to room. You're in constant danger. You might want to consider a holster for your revolver, so you'll have it with you at all times-and I'll ask Simon to order an armored vest for you. Do you mind?"

Patricia's cheeks flamed. "Considering what you've just told me? Not at all."

After Isabel left, Simon entered the study. "Come into the dining room. I want to show you body armor on my computer."

In the dining room, he gestured to a chair next to his. She sat and looked at the monitor, which displayed some attractive vests. "Armored?" she asked.

He nodded. "Take your pick."

"I had no idea they made designer armored vests for women."

"Wait until you see the pink shoulder holster."

She paged through the dozen or so vests, finally selecting a beige one with a snakeskin print. "I like that vest."

He keyed the information in. "It'll ship today with overnight delivery. Are you ready to look at those pink holsters?"

# CHAPTER 24

*L*ucius, noticing Isabel had returned to the living room, placed his book of Elizabethan poetry on the mahogany side table. Isabel had left to answer an urgent phone call from Simon. Now that Lucius had stepped down from Coalition leadership, Simon reported to her.

Lucius knew he'd done the right thing in passing the reins to his daughter. Isabel had been well schooled in Coalition activities. She had more than sufficient knowledge and experience to handle her new responsibilities. And, standing over six feet and sporting a broad-shouldered, athletic build, she was as physically impressive as anyone in his inner circle.

"How's Simon?" he asked.

"He just had a breakthrough." She started for the kitchen.

"Are you going to tell me what the breakthrough is, or do I have to drag it out of you?"

She turned to face him. Her eyes sparkled. "Daddy, I'm still not sure how much involvement you want in Coalition business."

"I backed out of leadership, but not out of involvement. I put most of my adult life into the organization. I'd like to stay abreast of key events." He huffed. "Especially those involving my friend's life, so I can pitch in when my experience or expertise can help."

She gave him a warm smile. "In that case, I'm sure you'd like to know that Simon got a match on facial recognition. It's ninety-eight percent reliable Mr. No is Preston Somerset."

A shiver ran through his back. It always shocked him when one of the good old boys went bad. Bad apples happened often enough, he thought he'd be used to it. "Any idea why Preston has taken up with a Russian mobster?"

"No." Her jaw worked back and forth. "But as soon as I got off the phone with Simon, I called Benjamin. He's going to set up a meeting with Preston."

Lucius grabbed his cane and stood on stiff legs. "I know the boy. His father and I were once close friends. I think it would be better if I spoke with Preston."

Her face distorted into a disdainful look as she shook her head. "Benjamin's our negotiator."

"And I have a relationship with the boy."

"He's not a boy," she said with a stern voice that echoed a tone he'd often taken in reprimanding her. "He's a man. A dangerous man from the look of things."

There were times, like today, when he regretted teaching her to speak her mind. But, despite her iron will, she was no match for him. "All the more reason I should go. How does Preston pose a danger to me? What's the worst he can do? Kill me? The cancer's already doing that."

She gasped.

He took a small, unsure step toward her. "Let me talk with Preston and see what he's up to. One meeting. What do you say?"

She paused. "If you insist. Should I ask Simon to go with you? Do you need a ride?"

"Heavens no. Simon's busy, and I've been traveling these streets since before you were born. I suppose I can manage a few blocks to Preston's office."

"At least let me set up the appointment for you." She reached for the phone.

"You do that. I'm going to change into something more appropriate for a meeting with one of Savannah's up-and-coming lawyers."

\* \* \*

AN HOUR LATER, LUCIUS, DRESSED IN A LIGHT GREY FLANNEL suit, hobbled into the lobby of Preston's law office. After announcing himself to the attractive receptionist, he settled into a high-backed leather chair in the corner and kept an eye out for Preston's approach.

It had been quite a while since he'd been in the Somerset Law office. Maybe ten years or so. That was when Preston's father and he had clashed over whether or not the Somersets could reclaim the Coalition seat relinquished by Preston's grandfather. Lucius shook his head. What a monumental battle that was. An unfortunate incident that cost both men their friendship. Good friends were hard to come by and the loss of even one troubled him.

Preston, tired-eyed and dressed in a pale blue seersucker suit, stepped into the lobby, greeted Lucius with a too-firm handshake, and escorted him into a small conference room. "Would you care for something to drink?" Preston asked from the bar.

"No, thank you." Lucius flexed his fingers, still smarting from the young man's aggressive handshake.

Preston indicated a chair at the circular oak table and, when Lucius was seated, took a seat next to him. "What brings you here today?" He raised a trimmed eyebrow. "My secretary told me you said it was urgent."

Lucius didn't like how today's youngsters rushed into business, disregarding the well-established, genteel way of doing things. He understood the days of leisurely conducting business in smoke-filled rooms were long gone. It was the abandonment of civility that troubled him. Well, if the boy wanted to get down to business, he'd oblige. "I understand you're now in the brothel business."

Preston's jaw dropped. "How did—"

"I'd like to think that a bright man such as you would know better than to traffic with a Russian mobster." He shot the flustered young man an icy glare. "That's opening the door to organized crime right here in Savannah. Do you have any idea what that would do to our city?"

Preston's face reddened. "It's not like—"

"Your father, bless his soul, must be turning over in his mausoleum watching you destroy everything he and his forefathers worked so hard to build. Why, in the name of heaven, would you do such a thing?"

Preston appeared ready to explode.

"Answer me, boy."

The young man's eyes narrowed. "I can see why Daddy avoided discussions with you. When you get rolling, you don't stop for anything."

Lucius leaned back, reining in his desire to continue lecturing the boy, and flashed him a gratuitous smile. "It doesn't make sense to me why you, of all people, invited that Russian criminal to Savannah."

"I didn't invite him." Preston folded his arms. "He found me and made an attractive financial offer."

"He says you're the boss."

"He misled you."

"Then why did you meet with Benjamin?"

"Because Grigory asked me." Preston's manicured fingernails tapped the arm of his chair. "He said he needed time to work some things out."

"What things?"

Preston shrugged. "Don't rightly know."

"You have no idea what he's doing?"

"Just prostitution. High-end. Discrete. Discerning. Satisfying a need for those who can afford it."

"What do you get out of this?"

"Money. Lots of it."

"You've got plenty of money."

"I do okay, but I don't have enough to run for a judicial position."

Lucius lifted his head. "You're bartering Trey Falcon's life so you can be a judge?"

"Trey? What's Trey got to do with this?"

"Trokev has ... *detained* Trey."

Preston's jaw muscle twitched. "I don't know anything of Trokev's activities beyond the brothel."

Lucius clenched his fists. "You'd bring organized crime into Savannah so you could sit on the bench and preside over the destruction of everything decent in this city?"

Preston held his hands up, palms out. "Hold it, Lucius. You're making a big leap from a brothel to citywide crime. That's not going to happen."

"For sure it's not going to happen." Lucius coughed, then wiped his mouth, noting the bright red blood on the handkerchief before putting it away. He hoped he'd live long enough to see the boy's grand plan shut down. "Look, Preston, I know people. If you'd drop this brothel business, we could get you appointed to a vacant bench or arrange to have you run unopposed for the court of your choice. How's that sound to you?"

"It sounds good." Preston nodded. "Very good, but it may be too late to stop the train."

"Why?"

Preston turned his flushed face toward the window and stared into space. "I don't think Grigory will shut down the brothel."

"Why?"

"When he originally approached me, he spoke of the two of us joining forces to find a major religious relic he's seeking in Savannah. I'm not aware of any major religious relics in Savannah, and I told Grigory so. That's when he offered me an equity position in his business in exchange for introducing him to my friends." Preston stared at him expectantly, as if seeking approval.

"So what does this have to do with getting Grigory to leave Savannah?"

"I don't think he's going anywhere until he finds what he's looking for."

"And that is?"

"The right arm of Saint Gregory."

So that was Trokev's objective. "The dead pope's arm?"

"No. Saint Gregory the Illuminator's arm."

Lucius shook his head. "Never heard of him."

"He brought Christianity to Armenia in the Fourth Century. Armenia was the first country to convert."

"And this arm is in Savannah?" Lucius' pulse sped. Was the church aware?

"Grigory thinks so. I wouldn't know."

He bit back the urge to scold the boy for being so naive. "Thank you, Preston. If I put you on a bench, will you disengage from Trokev?"

"In a heartbeat."

\* \* \*

ONCE AGAIN, AUGUSTA MET DOCTOR SNAKE AT THE BACK OF Bonaventure Cemetery at night. As before, they sat on the marble bench down by the creek. His full cheeks, broad nose and thick lips shone in the moonlight. Waves slapped on the shoreline. The sweet jasmine-like aroma of tea olive blossoms filled the air.

"Ya come troubled," Doctor Snake said softly.

"I can't submit the article about your lost arm without some proof," Augusta said.

He twisted his mouth. "What kind of proof be dat?"

"I can't identify the arm as being Doctor Buzzard's unless I can prove it's his."

"Call it what you will, Miss Augusta. Don't matter much. It be Doctor Buzzard's arm sure as shootin'. I ain't 'bout to lie 'bout sumthang like dat. There be no reason fo' you to doubt me. None at all."

"I'm not questioning the arm's authenticity. I just have to prove it, and I need your help to do so."

"Like how?"

"Who gave you the arm?"

"That would be Buzzy hisself."

Augusta took out her notebook and wrote down the name. "Who is Buzzy?"

"He be one of Doctor Buzzard's sons."

"How did you and Buzzy come to meet?"

"Years ago, he done come down to one of my Hoodoo parties out here." Snake paused, then nodded, looking out at the creek. After a moment, he turned to her, smiling. "He walks up to me with his father's purple sunglasses on and tell me who he is. Now I done heard stories of Doctor Buzzard, but I ain't heard of no Buzzy. So I axe folks, and dey say he be the real thang. So we talks 'bout cures, and I can tell he know de magic."

"When was this?"

"I come to Savannah in ninety-two, so it be in ninety-three. Maybe."

"When did Buzzy give you the arm?"

Snake stroked his chin. "It be a couple of years afta. In between, Buzzy done gave me some powerful cures. Man dat boy sure nuf know his stuff. So anyway round 'bout fall of ninety-five he gave me de arm, his bestest magic."

"Why did he give the arm to you?"

"Dat boy, he say I be de most worthy one of da bunch. Ain't dat something?"

"Yes indeed." She made a note, then looked up at Snake. "Where'd he give it to you?"

"At the Hang Fire Bar, or maybe the Life Everlasting Bar. No, I think it be the Hang Fire."

"Saint Helena's?" The breeze blew a lock of hair in her face

"Yes indeed."

"How can I contact Buzzy to verify this?"

"Cain't. Ole Buzzy done passed in ninety-seven."

She clenched her teeth. One less witness. "Was anyone else there when he gave you the arm?"

Snake gazed at the creek for a long while. "There be lots of folk there, but I only 'member one. Minerva. She be there. Maybe Della, too."

She hoped both were still alive. "Minerva saw Buzzy give you the arm?"

"Oh yes. She thought she was gonna get Buzzard's arm. She was one unhappy lady dat night."

"How can I contact Minerva?"

"We ain't friends after dat. Don't rightly know where she be right now, but I know who do. I'll let cha know. Okay?"

"Yes." She didn't like the delay in getting verification, but she had no option. "As soon as possible."

Snake gave her a toothy grin.

She tapped her pen on her notebook. "Um ... where is this Hang Fire bar?"

"It done burnt down long time ago."

"But where was it located on Saint Helena's?"

He shrugged. "Don't rightly recall, only been there once, but folks over there can tell ya."

Augusta glanced at her notes from her meeting with Willy. "I need some personal information."

He nodded.

"Your real name?"

He tensed. "Why? There ain't nobody here abouts what knows me by dat name."

"To verify your story."

He nodded. "My birth name be Stanley Gabriel Hernandez."

"Where were you born?"

"Trinidad, in the province of Sancti Spiritus."

She scribbled, then looked up. "Cuba?"

He answered with another nod.

"When were you born?"

"December 23, Founders' Day, 1962."

"When did you come to the United States?"

"1992."

"Legally?"

"Yes."

"Which entry point?"

"Miami."

"I have one final question." She paused, staring at his face.

"Yous be troubled to ask dis question of yours?"

"Very."

"Why is that, my child? I ain't nevah hurt no one."

"I know. You've been very forthcoming, as well as kind and considerate."

"Den why you be troubled so?"

239

"I need a photo of you for the article."

An awkward silence followed. "You know better dan to ax me dat," he said in an uncharacteristically firm voice.

"No photo, no article. No article, goodbye mantle."

"Oh my, you got a mouth on you, child."

"Well?"

"No photo." He kicked at the ground. "Cain't do dat. But you bring one of them drawing people out here tomorrow night and dey can draw me. How 'bout dat?"

"Sure."

"And den you put my story in yous paper?"

"No guarantees."

"You got the magic." He gave a tooth-filled grin. "I know dis will happen, 'cause you got the magic. Dis I believe."

# CHAPTER 25

*A*fter the lockdown, Patricia created a quiet place in a spare bedroom where she could isolate herself and think deeply about Trey.

No phone.

No TV.

No snakes.

The curtains were drawn and the lighting dim-a soothing place to defuse her pain on those days when she felt utterly lost, as she did today.

Seated in a comfortable chair, she surveyed the well-appointed room. Heirloom furniture acquired and passed down over the generations. A hand-knotted Oriental rug. Antique crystal lamps. All inherited. Each with a story. A connection with the past and beautiful, but also cold and dormant. Nostalgia was over rated. A euphoria for the person she used to be, before she was tempered by fire. Now scared with the frailty of life, wanting only the basics in life, she'd no longer sought material things. Real contentment for her came from simple daily pleasures and her relationship with Trey.

She looked with longing at the photo in her hands, a large close-up of Trey. Taken just a year ago, it had been on her nightstand throughout her recovery. An ever-present reminder of the wonderful man she loved more than life itself.

She closed her eyes and eased Trey's photo to her chest. Her shoulders heaved as the highlights of twenty incredible years of marriage paraded in her mind: the early years, the birth of Hayley, weekends at their Tybee beach house, family vacations, walks in Forsyth Park.

After several minutes, she wiped her eyes and shifted her gaze to the candles she had lit in vigilance for him. The flames danced in the breeze from the ceiling fan, mesmerizing her. A rosary and a Saint Anthony medallion lay to one side. Saint Anthony, the finder of the lost, had recently become her favorite saint. Patricia prayed, "Saint Anthony, please intercede and keep Trey safe."

Standing, she adjusted the bulky armored vest, blew out the candles, and crossed to the door, where she hesitated. She didn't want to leave the room. The space had a settled feeling and a closeness to Trey she needed. But she needed to get Trey back, and knew God and Saint Anthony would help those who helped themselves. She shook herself and went downstairs to Simon's control center.

Simon, looking disheveled, glanced up and brushed his dark hair from his face.

She rearranged the vest a bit to ease the pressure on her shoulders. "The daily call from Trey is overdue."

"There's no fixed schedule." He stood. "I wouldn't worry about it. You look uncomfortable in that vest."

She cringed and glanced down at the stiff armor. "I am."

"With any luck, we'll have Trey back before you get used to the vest."

She shuddered to think of the possibilities. "I hope so."

"Isabel asked me to tell you they've identified Preston Somerset as Mr. No, Trokev's associate. Her father has spoken to Preston Somerset and has come to an agreement with him. Preston is no longer a problem for us."

Isabel. Lucius. Preston. Each a civic leader. Each wealthy, powerful and well connected. Tainted too. Not always on the same personal agenda over the years. Sometimes in conflict. But, when Trey's life was on the line, seemingly able to work together for the greater good. "That's wonderful news."

"Yes. All future Coalition negotiations will be with Trokev. He apparently has more going on in Savannah than the brothel business."

"Meaning?"

"He collects relics."

"I know."

He flinched. "How?"

"Trokev told me at lunch. At the time, it wasn't pertinent."

"According to Preston, Trokev's in Savannah specifically to acquire relics."

She put her hand on her hip. "That's the only reason he's here?"

"Apparently."

"What about the brothel?"

"He's taking pictures to compromise men who might know where the relics are."

"That's clever." Patricia brought her hand to her mouth. This could only mean ... "So, once Trokev gets the relics he wants, he'll return Trey?"

"And close down the brothel. That's the result we'd like to see, but we don't know for sure. Benjamin is trying to set up a meeting with Trokev to discuss the situation."

"Is Trokev after any specific relic?"

"Preston says Trokev is obsessed with one, but may be interested in others."

"All in Savannah?"

"That's what Lucius believes."

"What's this relic Trokev is obsessed with called?"

"The right arm of Saint Gregory the Illuminator."

"That's the same relic Father John is seeking."

Simon's eyes widened. "Really?"

Surprised he didn't know, she nodded.

"I have to pass that on to Isabel right away." He picked up his phone and tapped the display.

To give Simon privacy, Patricia went out to the foyer. While passing the portraits of Trey's ancestors, she paused at the picture of Trey's father. He looked so like Trey her heart fluttered. She studied the painting of Trey's grandfather and saw less resemblance. Then she looked closer at the portrait.

She went rigid. Trey's grandfather wore a signet ring identical to Trokev's and Preston's. How had she not seen that before?

There was no doubt Trokev was evil, and Preston had conspired with him. Was there some sort of secret criminal brotherhood that wore the ring? Was Trey's grandfather a criminal? Damn. She *had* to find the significance of the signet ring. Simon seemed disinterested. Trokev had passed his ring off as nothing. Maybe Preston would be more forthcoming. She'd have Simon set up a meeting for her with Preston.

When Patricia returned to the dining room, Simon was off the phone.

"Isabel thanks you for the tip about Father John's investigation."

"I'm glad to be of assistance." She sat at the table across from him, wondering if she should tell him about Trey's grandfather's ring. Maybe she would after she talked with

Preston. She'd have a better picture then. "I like the openness you and Isabel are showing."

"I wish we had better answers for you."

"The information on Preston was positive. Since he's cooperating, I'd like to talk with him. Would you invite him over today?"

Simon's face tightened. "What do you want to talk to him about?"

"Nothing specific. I won't tip him off. I just feel better when I have a solid understanding of reality. What do you say? This afternoon?"

"Sure. Bishop Reilly is due soon ... and Meredith. How about after your meeting with Meredith?"

"If you can, get Preston in before Meredith."

"Okay."

"I'll be in the study." She walked to the back of the house, pausing on the way to digest a thought about Trey's grandfather's ring. *It may have been passed down. Trey might have it stored in his collection of family jewelry.* Careful to avoid attracting Simon's attention, she hurried upstairs. Inside Trey's closet, she slid the shoe shelves to the side and punched in the code to the walk-in safe.

She couldn't recall the last time she'd been in Trey's side of the safe. Like the man himself, his side was well organized, with each drawer labeled, the jewelry drawers identified by original owner of the valuables.

She searched the names and slid out the felt-lined, heavy metal drawer dedicated to Trey's grandfather, gulping at the array of massive, carved gold rings. They were impressive, though she couldn't imagine Trey ever wearing one. Not seeing the ring she sought, she pulled the drawer further out.

In the back of the drawer sat a maroon felt ring box with an ornate Byzantine cross in gold thread sewn into the top.

She swallowed hard. The cross commanded reverence, and she willingly gave it.

Her hands shook as she removed the box. The sewn gold cross shimmered under the overhead light. She tried to open the lid, but it wouldn't budge. Holding the case to eye level, she turned it left and right. There was no lock in sight. It was jewelry. Why prevent access to it? Patricia shook her head. She was missing something. With frustration mounting, she pushed the felt-covered sides and seams to no avail.

Returning to the drawer, she searched thoroughly and found nothing to suggest how to open the beautiful box. She closed the drawer and, treasure in hand, sat down in the chair to think. The elaborate embroidered cross was worthy of the altar of any Armenian church. Perhaps Saint Gregory the Illuminator would intercede. She closed her eyes and traced her fingertip over the cross. The lid sprung open to reveal the special ring. She gasped.

Her trophy in her palm, she marveled at the power of faith, and the ingenuity of whoever created the box. Bishop Reilly would appreciate the story of how she found the ring, though she doubted she'd tell him. Still, a good story was a good story. "Thank you, God."

She pocketed the ring, returned the empty case to the drawer, and secured the safe.

The simplicity of the solution to the ring box puzzle was astonishing. She'd never been one for puzzles, but Hayley and Trey delighted in them. She fondly remembered Hayley puzzling her way through the Falcon family dollhouse. Four-feet-high with ten rooms of ingenious brainteasers. Not even Trey knew if they ever found them all. There was no master list or clue book, just years and years of adolescent intrigue for each generation of Falcons.

She remembered how Trey had hidden tiny gifts in the secret compartments he knew about as soon as Hayley became interested in attempting the challenges. Patricia smiled, recalling Hayley's shouts of glee at solving a puzzle and claiming its treasure.

Someday Hayley's children would have the dollhouse to explore. Hayley's children. Her grandchildren ... *their* grandchildren. Oh, Trey honey, where are you?

She made her way back downstairs to await Bishop Reilly's visit.

# CHAPTER 26

*P*atricia put *Eversea*, her reality-escaping book, aside when she heard the doorbell. In twenty minutes, she hadn't turned a page.

"Right this way, Your Excellency," Simon said as he escorted Bishop Reilly into Patricia's study.

The bishop's welcoming eyes, gentle smile, and overall personal warmth settled her more deeply than she had experienced since Trey's disappearance. She gestured for him to sit. "Would you care for tea, Your Excellency?"

His smile crinkled the corners of his eyes. He nodded.

She poured and handed him a cup.

He put the teacup on the end table, canted his head, and studied her for a long moment. "You asked about contemporary relic cults associated with Saint Gregory the Illuminator."

"Yes."

"Relics are an integral part of the church. Veneration of the bodies of saints and martyrs dates from the earliest days of Christianity and continues to this day." Bishop Reilly's mellow voice soothed her. "The Council of Trent decreed that God grants benefits to the living through the bodies of the saints and martyrs. Those relics are, therefore, prized and must be protected."

Patricia moved a plate of shortbread cookies between them.

He took a cookie and placed it on the saucer next to his untouched cup of tea. "During the Armenian Genocide of 1915, a secret organization dating to the Middle Ages was revived to hide and protect certain relics of Saint Gregory the Illuminator. That organization is known to the Holy See as The Order of Grigory Illuminati. It is still active in Armenia, and perhaps in the United States, where many of Saint Gregory's relics were sent for safekeeping."

"These people who protect the saint's relics, are they priests?"

"Not necessarily. But they're ordained for their sacred work."

She cocked her head. "So membership in the cult is a religious vocation?"

"Yes."

"Is the secrecy to protect the relic?"

"Yes. Obviously, the presence of a Grigory Illuminati implies the presence of a relic."

"Is Father John a Grigory Illuminati?"

"Not as far as I know." His face hardened, then he glanced toward the back window for a moment. "But he could be."

She didn't think the bishop would lie, but something about her question or his answer had made him uncomfortable. "Father John is looking for a Grigory right arm relic here. Does that mean there could be a Grigory Illuminati in Savannah?"

The bishop's pale cheeks flushed a bit, presumably due to how much she knew about his business. "I suppose so."

More discomfort. She locked eyes with him before asking

her next question. "Do you know any Grigory Illuminati here in Savannah?"

Though he shifted in his seat, his brown eyes betrayed nothing. "As much as I would like to answer your question, I can't. If Illuminati are in Savannah, they're here to protect a relic of Saint Gregory. If they're not in Savannah, and a relic of Saint Gregory is here, the relic is unprotected."

"Was the relic ever here?"

"According to church records, it arrived in December, 1939."

"Do you know where it is now?"

"No, and neither does Father John, though he's working very hard to track it down."

"Are you aware that Grigory Trokev, a Russian collector of religious relics, is in Savannah looking for the relic?"

He nodded. "That recently came to my attention."

"Trokev has Trey."

He nodded again.

He'd been so forthcoming, and now all she was getting was nods. What wasn't he telling her? "The relic could be the key to Trey's release."

"The relic is a part of the Church," he said firmly. "It has no place in a private collection."

"If I had the artifact ..." Her voice was as cold and determined as she could make it. "I'd gladly trade it for Trey."

"And perhaps that's why the order remains secret and the relic was hidden." He frowned. "Patricia, I understand your love for your husband, but as a woman of faith, I trust you'd seek guidance on a matter of such solemnity."

Her throat tightened. His rebuke stung. She had always been so pious, so faithful, and now it could cost her Trey. She touched an index finger to the moist corner of each eye. "We've been friends for a long time. Let's stop the cat and mouse game. They have Trey. What can we do, Your Excellency?"

He took her hand.

His touch was warm.

"We do what we do every day, Patricia, we trust in the Lord."

"And if God should call a person to action?"

"I suppose one would answer that call."

"What would you consider a call to action?"

"The call should be obvious."

Patricia pulled her hand from his and looked into his gentle eyes. He was a good friend, as well as her confessor. He wasn't Trey, but he was wise, and he wouldn't mislead her. "I believe I've been called to action."

His brows arched. "Just like that? Now?"

"No. I prayed earlier to Saint Gregory the Illuminator for help finding and freeing Trey, and he provided this." She handed him the signet ring.

As soon as he saw the symbol, he crossed himself. Then his lips moved as he said a silent prayer.

She shuddered. "Wa ... wa ... what's going on?"

"Do you have any idea what this is?"

"It's a ring that was in Trey's safe. Beyond that, I don't know. But I found it after praying for help. So I believe it will help me find Trey."

He examined the ring in the light from the chandelier. "This is a ring worn by members of The Order of Grigory Illuminati. Why was it in Trey's safe?"

Though she sought assistance from him, she was getting interrogation. Regretting showing him the ring, she put out her hand. "Could I have the ring back?"

He frowned, then placed it in her hand.

She held up the ring. "Would you view this as a call to action?"

"I would say so."

Trey's life depended on Reilly helping her. God had called her. She now had to take the leap of faith for Trey's sake. "We are friends, aren't we?"

He nodded.

She met him eye-to-eye. "Will you help me?"

"Yes, I'll help, but first I want you to tell me all you know about the ring."

She spent the next ten minutes explaining how she found the ring and who the presumed owner was.

The bishop took a sip of tea. "Trokev wants the relic in his collection because he thinks it's available to be found. There are tens of thousands of relics, and he's picked this one to go after. Why?"

"It's an important relic. A prize."

"There are many more important relics. For example, the Shroud of Turin. Certainly the Shroud would be a bigger prize for his collection. Why isn't he going after it?"

She paused while considering the possibilities. Her scrambled thoughts finally focused. "He isn't going after the Shroud because it's too well protected."

"Precisely. He's going after the less protected artifacts. If we get the arm of Saint Gregory the Illuminator locked up in the Vatican, Trokev will move on. And when he does, Trey will no longer be a bargaining chip."

"Wouldn't they punish Trey for that? Maybe kill him, rather than return him?"

"Trokev is a collector and a businessman. Killing Trey out of anger won't get him anything but a relentless manhunt. I assure you, men like Trokev don't want that."

"What about the brothel?"

"Once Trokev's relic hunt collapses, I'm sure he'll be more willing to consider shutting his brothel. I'm told the Coalition can be quite persuasive."

"Okay," she said. "Let's get Father John over here to discuss what we do next."

"Good."

Now that they were working together, maybe he'd be willing to give up more information on the Illuminati. "When we were talking earlier, you were unwilling to discuss the Grigory Illuminati in Savannah. I had the impression you knew more."

"I do."

"And?" she asked, trying to keep her voice from breaking.

"When the relic arrived in Savannah, three men were inducted into the Grigory Illuminati and were charged with the protection of the relic. There were three signet rings. Each was engraved inside the band with a partial code that together reportedly revealed where the relic was hidden. One of the rings has been passed down through the sitting bishop. Until today, I had no idea where the other two rings were."

She noticed he wasn't wearing the ring. Her pulse surged. Three? She knew of four. But Trokev said he acquired his ring in Armenia ... or did he? "So there are only three rings?"

"I don't know how many Illuminati rings exist. The cult has been around since the Middle Ages. But there are only three rings engraved with the location code."

Patricia, her heart hammering, held the signet ring up to the light and looked inside. The letters *SQ* and the numerals *25* were deeply engraved inside the band. She showed the engraving to the bishop.

He examined the band, then handed the ring back.

Patricia clutched the ring, squeezed her eyes shut, and focused every fiber of her being on deciphering the code. Trey's safety rested on her understanding. After a few minutes, she smiled. The answer was so simple. "Since the engraving references a location, could *SQ* stand for *square*, as in the city squares?"

"Quite possibly." He nodded. "The twenty-fifth square to be laid out here was Falcon Square."

"How convenient. What's engraved in the ring you possess?"

He stroked his chin. "The band is engraved with the letters *FO*."

"No numbers?"

He shook his head.

"I don't see how *FO* points to a location."

"I once thought *FO* might refer to *fountain*, but as far as I know there's never been a fountain on Falcon Square."

"Did you tell Father John about the engraving?"

He nodded. "He couldn't figure it out either. But we didn't have the part of the code you now possess."

Unable to reach Father John, Bishop Reilly left with a promise to set up a strategy meeting with the three of them at the earliest opportunity.

Once the bishop was gone, she cleaned the study to prepare for Preston Somerset's visit, then went upstairs and returned the signet ring to the safe.

The ring seemed to be a good talisman, highly likely to be the key to bringing Trey home safely. It was hard to let something that important out of her sight.

But she was about to grill Preston on why he had a Grigory Illuminati ring and what he knew about it. And to be effective, she had to put all thoughts of finding Trey out of her mind and switch into sleuth mode. Trey had encouraged her sleuthing. She hoped he'd be proud of her today.

Patricia returned to the study, turned on the hidden video camera and microphones, and activated the computerized interrogation system Trey had installed last year. The system used the video camera to monitor pulse-related facial twitches, and then calculated heart rate. It was a non-invasive lie detector that would illuminate a small light on the wall behind the person when his heart rate sped.

She paced. Quite possibly Preston had the third Savannah Illuminati ring, but she wouldn't know for sure until she looked inside the band.

# CHAPTER 27

*W*hile Patricia waited in the library for Preston, she went over the information she'd gathered. Something wasn't right. Bishop Reilly's assurance that finding the ring was a call to action had reinforced her feeling to take the initiative to find the relic and, hopefully, Trey. Not that she had a clear idea how to do that. She and Bishop Reilly would make those decisions in consultation with Father John.

But both men were exceptionally resourceful and already focused on the relic's recovery. Why would they need her involvement to find the bones? What could she possibly contribute? The Falcon Illuminati ring? She shook her head. By itself, the ring didn't solve anything. Successive bishops had possessed a ring from the beginning. A lot of good it had done them.

Did Bishop Reilly view Trey's ring as important? It was the second clue of three, but without the third clue it was meaningless. Maybe the bishop was just humoring her, or keeping her out of the way chasing phantoms? After all, as clerics the bishop and John had a much different focus than keeping Trey alive. She'd need to be careful. One thing for sure, the way she found the ring *did* seem to be a heavenly call. Bishop Reilly had said as much.

Footfalls in the hallway interrupted Patricia's thoughts. Simon, who wore trainers, usually came and went without a sound.

"Incoming," Simon said from the doorway. He was dressed in an armored vest over a black T-shirt and black cargo pants. Preston Somerset accompanied him.

Simon excused himself, leaving them alone to talk.

Though Preston was in his forties, he looked younger. His tanned face was smooth, his dark hair fashionably unruly. If he hadn't been a successful lawyer, he could easily have been a model. Preston wore a mint sport coat that matched his paisley bow tie, black dress pants, and black slip-ons. The outline of a clip-on holster was visible through his linen jacket. Simon would have relieved Preston of his weapon at the door.

"Why all the security?" Preston's voice was husky. According to Trey, Preston, a man of questionable honesty, practiced most of his law in back rooms working out shady deals over scotch and cigars. Though they had conversed at functions, she didn't see Preston often enough to know him well. There was some sort of bad blood between the Somersets and Falcons going back a couple of generations. Trey had been secretive about the specifics.

She waved her hand dismissively. "Simon is just conducting a security test. We do it every year."

He frowned.

"Would you care for something to drink?"

His attention went to the sterling tea service. "I'll have tea, thank you."

He sat on the sofa while she poured.

She handed him a cup, then offered him the tray of shortbread cookies. When he reached for a cookie, she noticed his ring, the one she'd seen him wearing in the parking garage photo-identical to the Illuminati ring in Trey's safe.

Heart thudding, she sat across from him with the glass coffee table between them and a good view of the pinhole light that would illuminate if Preston's heart rate shot up. "It's been a while," she said. "How have you been?"

"I've been fine." His eyes met hers. "Thank you for asking."

"Trey says you've done well for your clients."

He took a bite of cookie. "I've been fortunate. How are you and Trey doing?"

Her throat tightened. Surely he knew about Trey. Perhaps not. She'd play along, just in case. She gave him a smile. "Never a dull moment."

"Your daughter's off at college, isn't she?"

If he knew about Trey, if he knew what Trokev was doing, how much would he know about Hayley? Was he playing dumb? Fishing? And if so, for what purpose? "Yes. Hayley's attending Emerald University in Atlanta."

"Does she like it?"

"She's still getting used to being away from home." In an effort to change the subject away from Hayley, she glanced again at his hand. "I couldn't help but notice your ring. It looks old."

His frown suggested he felt the discussion of his ring an annoyance. But the pulse indicator light on the wall didn't illuminate. She hoped he'd have the manners to respond to her interest.

"It was my grandfather's." He shifted in his chair.

"It's so unique. Could I see it closer?" She extended her hand.

He removed the ring and placed it in her palm. She turned the ring to the side as if admiring the profile. In doing so, she looked at the inside of the band, seeing the letters *HO* and the number *9*. The all-important third clue. Filled with joy, she said a silent prayer as she turned the band. Though she was fully familiar with the image on the top of the ring, she made a show of closely examining the symbol. "Is there some significance to the ring?"

"As a matter of fact, there is." He took a sip of tea, then sat back in his chair. "The ring signifies membership. Around the beginning of the Second World War, there was a special Catholic organization in Savannah and my grandfather was a member."

"Like the Masons?" she asked.

"More like the Knights Templar."

"In Savannah?"

"Yes."

"How interesting. What was their function?"

"They were charged with the protection of one of the parish's greatest treasures."

She handed the ring back to him. "Really?"

He slid the ring on to his finger. "Yes."

"It must have been important to have an entire organization protecting it."

"So they say."

"What on earth could be *that* valuable to the church?"

Preston straightened.

Had she been too direct with her questions? Too obvious? *Come on, Preston, just answer the question.*

He opened his mouth as if to speak, then clamped his mouth closed.

Damn. What should she do? Her palms moistened. She folded her hands to keep him from noticing.

He moved forward on the chair. "The bones of a saint," he murmured.

"Do you mean the relic they place on our altar on All Saints Day? How interesting."

"No. Not that one. At one time our parish had another, much more important, relic."

"I thought the parish relic was quite revered."

"It is, but nowhere near as much as this other relic."

"What makes it so special?"

"It's the right arm relic of Saint Gregory the Illuminator. Perhaps you've heard of him? He's the patron saint of Armenia. The organization my grandfather was in was created to protect the relic while it was in the parish."

"How'd they do that? I wonder ..."

Preston's amber eyes jittered. "I'm not certain."

"I've never heard about this arm relic. Does the parish still have it?"

His face clouded. "It seems it disappeared shortly after its arrival. But this organization—"

"Your grandfather's organization?"

"I guess they failed," he said.

"You're wearing the ring. Does that mean you're a member?"

"Oh no. I'm told the organization disbanded after the relic went missing."

"Who else had the honor to serve in this organization?"

"I don't know." Preston frowned. "I checked once and found the parish doesn't have any records of the membership. I do know there were just a few members, and I suspect they were prominent parishioners, like my grandfather. Curiously, I recently met a foreigner with the same type of ring. He said his ring was an antique from Armenia, which happens to be the saint's home country. Perhaps the Savannah organization was a part of a much larger organization based in Armenia."

"This foreigner is a member of that organization too? How curious."

"No. He's a collector of religious artifacts. In fact, he came to town and contacted me to see if I had any information on the missing relic."

Patricia feigned polite interest. "Goodness. How did he know to contact you?"

Preston's eyes widened. "I didn't think to ask. Perhaps there were records in Armenia."

She stiffened and wiped the sweaty palms on her slacks. "If he saw records showing your grandfather was a member, would he have seen the names of all the Savannah members?"

"Perhaps." His eyes narrowed. "Why?"

"Just curious. It's an interesting part of our parish history that I've never heard before." She offered to refill his tea.

He politely declined. His expression morphed into grimness. "Patricia, the Falcons and the Somersets haven't gotten along for years. And I doubt you invited me over today for a social visit. I appreciate your hospitality and courtesy, but could we get to the point of your invitation?"

"The new burn center has run into some regulatory delays," she said. "You've worked with the state, haven't you?"

"Yes."

"Have you done any work with the medical regulators?"

"No."

"Oh. That's too bad. Someone told me you had. They must have been confused. I'm terribly sorry to have wasted your time, Preston." She stood.

He stood as well. "It was no waste at all. In fact, I rather enjoyed our little talk about parish history."

They walked together to the front door.

Once Preston had left she cleaned up the study, then went to her desk and sat. She wrote *SQ 25* on a sheet of paper. Below that she printed *FO* and beneath that *HO 9*.

*SQ 25* had to mean Falcon Square. *HO 9* probably meant house number nine. She didn't think any of the houses on the square were numbered nine, but how were they numbered in 1939? The library might know.

Patricia called the Live Oak Library and posed her question to a researcher. Ten minutes later, the researcher called back to tell her the 1939 Savannah City Directory had no listings for a home numbered nine on Falcon Square.

Well. She hadn't expected the location code to be easy. What other numbering method might the Illuminati have used to identify the homes on Falcon Square? Or did *HO 9* stand for something other than *house number nine*?

Patricia searched the Web and found *HO 229* was a delta-wing, stealth fighter used by Germany near the end of the Second World War. According to the records, the prototype flew in 1944, but could it have been in development in 1939? Was there more to the relic than bones?

Bishop Reilly or Father John might find this new twist interesting. Just as she reached for her phone, it chimed Meredith's distinctive ring. She was due momentarily. "Meredith, am I still expecting you?"

"Yes. I'm on my way. How are you progressing on getting Trey back?"

"For the first time in days, I have some promising leads. Nothing certain, mind you."

"That's hopeful. I pray Trey will be quickly returned without a scratch."

"From your mouth to God's ears," Patricia said.

"On my way over I heard an ad by the Savannah Technical College regarding their certificate program for Crime Scene Investigation," Meredith said.

"Are you considering enrolling?"

"I thought we both might. The instruction would certainly help us become better sleuths and solve more crimes. As good as we are, we can become better. What do you say?"

It *did* sound like an excellent idea. "When do the classes start?"

"They've already started for this semester, but we could begin in January with their second semester."

Surely Trey would be home by then. "Good idea. When everything settles down, let's do it."

"Between the CSI certificate program and the Senior Sleuths organization I'm ... we're working on, we're on course to have a major impact on Savannah crime for a long time," Meredith said. "Hang on, Patricia. I'm just pulling up to your drive now. See you in a minute."

Patricia ended the call, and willed her mind to calm. Between the two of them they might solve the Illuminati ring code today and move one step closer to bringing Trey home.

Moments later, Meredith strode into the study. At six-two and built like a linebacker, Meredith's entrances were always dramatic. Her long black hair and black business suit not only added to the impression, they added depth to it. The woman radiated professionalism and power.

Patricia stood and opened her arms. Meredith did the cheek kiss thing she was so fond of, then she stepped back and met Patricia's eyes. "How are you holding up? Any news on Trey?"

"No news, but maybe between us we can figure out how to get him back."

"I certainly hope so, honey. So, what do you have for me?"

"I need your help in breaking a code to locate a religious relic that's the key to Trey's release."

Meredith raised an eyebrow.

"You've always been good with codes." Patricia handed her the paper with the three Illuminate ring inscriptions.

Meredith studied the note. "These reference a location in Savannah?"

Her stomach clenched. "I had assumed so, but to tell you the truth I don't really know."

"Why did you think the location was in Savannah?"

"In 1939, the relic was sent to Saint Gregory's Cathedral for safe-keeping. It disappeared some time after arriving. I assumed it stayed in the city. Besides, the code *SQ 25* could mean the twenty-fifth square to be established in Savannah ... Falcon Square."

"That's a reasonable explanation for *SQ 25*, and a good reason to believe the relic is in Savannah." She narrowed her eyes. "Do you have any thoughts on the other two inscriptions?"

"*HO 9* could be *house number nine*. Unfortunately, there was no house number nine on Falcon Square in 1939. It also could refer to a German stealth fighter used in the Second World War, but that's not a location."

"Okay." Meredith settled back on the sofa. "Let's think like the code maker. Hmmm. The code maker used the order of creation as the basis for identifying the square. He could have used the same basis for identifying the house. We need to find out what homes were on Falcon Square in 1939, and the order in which they were built."

"The 1939 City Directory lists the homes. They have a copy at the Live Oak Library."

Meredith grabbed her purse. "We can scoot over there right now and—"

"Can't do. Too dangerous for me to go out."

Meredith regarded her, then nodded. "I'll get the addresses, then stop by the County Recorder's office to find construction dates. It shouldn't take long."

"What about *FO*, the third code?"

Meredith looked at the note again. "Do you have any idea what it means?"

"No. You?"

"Not a clue. Let's hold off on that inscription until we solve the house clue. Having the first two codes deciphered might help us figure out the third."

Patricia smiled. It was good to have Meredith with her on this. Not just Meredith's incredible brain, but her company and empathy as well.

# CHAPTER 28

*P*atricia clenched her fists as she watched Meredith's black Escalade pull away. Hopefully her friend would quickly solve the second clue and determine which home on Falcon Square hosted the relic. Were it not for the lockdown, she'd be there with Meredith every step of the way, just like the old days. Patricia shook her head and stepped back into the house as the foyer clock struck one.

The unsolved third clue *FO* taunted her. The other two had been relatively straightforward, but the third one didn't make sense. Had Bishop Reilly somehow misread the engraving? Perhaps she could examine the bishop's ring to confirm what was actually engraved inside the band.

Still standing in the foyer, she called the bishop. His secretary answered on the first ring.

"This is Patricia. Is Bishop Reilly in?"

"I'm sorry, Mrs. Falcon. The bishop is out for the afternoon. May I have him call you back?"

Patricia left her number, trying not to sound impatient.

She needed to see his ring. For Trey's sake, she needed to solve the clues, all of them, soon.

Her stomach growled. Hunger pangs came. As Patricia walked to the kitchen to make a salad, she paused at the oil painting of Trey's grandfather, a young adult at the time of the painting. The age of Trey's grandfather suggested the portrait might date from when he'd been inducted into the Illuminati, not ten or twenty years later. Had the painting been created specifically as a relic clue?

His image filled the canvas. His suit was black. His shirt, white. The only jewelry visible was the Illuminati ring. On closer examination, she noticed a faint image in the background over his right shoulder. The Falcon dollhouse. No other furniture was visible. Why the dollhouse and nothing else?

Then a thought struck her like a ray of sunshine through dense clouds. Trey said the dollhouse, a facsimile of 'Tara' from *Gone With The Wind*, was constructed in 1939, the same year the movie came out-and the same year the relic was sent to Savannah. Trey's father was just a baby then and, as far as she knew, he had no siblings. A dollhouse for a family with only a son? And at four feet tall, the structure could easily hold the arm bones.

But Hayley and Trey had spent hours finding secret compartments and hidden nooks. Surely they would've found an area large enough to hide bones.

Trey had said, however, the dollhouse was full of secret compartments with clever locking devices, many more than he or Hayley had ever discovered.

Patricia raced up the stairs to the playroom, yanked the dust cover from the dollhouse, and, heart pounding, rolled the structure into the middle of the room.

Everything about the dollhouse was extravagant. There

was a ballroom with polished cherry floors and onyx-topped side tables. Light reflected from the miniature crystal chandeliers. In the dining room sat a mahogany table with six chairs and a matching china cabinet. Bookcases with tiny leather-bound books filled two walls of the library. A miniature sterling tea service sat regally on a polished mahogany table. In the foyer stood a working grandfather clock. Patricia used to wind the clock for Hayley and listen to it chime, it was tradition each and every time they played with the house. But, with Trey's life in the balance, tradition would have to wait.

Starting with the attic, she looked for the sacred bones in each room, including the built-in closets and large pieces of furniture, finding nothing but empty space. She sat on the floor and stared at the dollhouse, feeling suddenly stupid for thinking she'd find something in the old toy that Hayley had loved so much.

Wait. There *had* to be something there. Patricia twisted Trey's ring on her thumb as she tried desperately to recall where any of those hidden compartments were or actions that needed to be taken to open them. Perhaps putting the picture and the house side by side would help.

Trying not to alert Simon to what was turning out to be a silly project born of desperation to get Trey back, Patricia snuck back down and gingerly eased the large painting off the wall. She took it back to the playroom. With a full wall of floor-to-ceiling windows, the light was better there. She sat in a chair and methodically examined every square inch of the canvas. Then she reexamined the painting with a magnifying glass, finding nothing. Still, she was convinced the dollhouse was being shown on purpose.

Maybe a clue for finding the relic resided within the house itself. Again Patricia scoured the structure from top to bottom. This time she noted a number of places and objects that could be locked secret compartments, each a puzzle in its own right. She examined every miniature painting and the little rugs to see if they contained directions, but still found nothing guiding her clue search to a specific location within the dollhouse. She blew hair out of her face.

If the dollhouse held a clue, it had to be hidden in one of those compartments. So opening every puzzling secret chamber was critical. Trey's life depended on it. Meredith could probably figure out how to get into them, but first Patricia had to make sure she knew the location of every hidden compartment. She wished she had x-ray vision.

She smiled. Of course. She'd do the next best thing. She'd have the dollhouse x-rayed, then have Meredith solve the puzzles as quickly as possible.

Simon came into the playroom. "What's the painting doing up here?"

"I'm looking for the relic."

"Up here?"

"In the dollhouse." She pointed to the painting.

He examined the canvas. "Clever. Did you find anything?"

"No. But I think x-raying the dollhouse might be worthwhile."

Patricia called Beau Simpson, a close friend and the Chief Cardiologist at Falcon Memorial. He explained that a conventional x-ray would only be marginally useful, but by adjusting frequencies he could probably identify the hidden chambers and possibly verify their contents. He sounded fascinated by the challenge and said he'd oversee the procedure.

Simon had a security courier pack up the dollhouse and deliver it to the hospital.

Once the courier left, Patricia returned to the study and tried to relax, but her mind raced. She went to the bookshelf and arranged a row of books. What could she do to find Trey that she'd overlooked? She clenched and unclenched her hands. How was Trey? She had no idea when or if she'd hear from him again.

Patricia fought the mounting urge to ask Simon why Trey hadn't called yet. She paced the study. Simon probably didn't know why today's call hadn't come. And if he did, he'd have a good reason for not telling her. Feeling light-headed, Patricia sat and took a deep breath. A wave of nausea hit.

With everything going on, she hadn't been sleeping or eating properly. She went to the kitchen and made a crab omelet with egg whites, sliced up a fresh peach, and poured a glass of water. Just as she was finishing the omelet, Simon strode into the kitchen and handed her the phone. "Trey's on the line."

Heart hammering, she took the phone. She turned the screen toward her for what would certainly be a bittersweet moment.

Looking intently, she saw his smiling, gentle face. A tremor ran through her. Tears welled. She touched the screen, then sniffled and forced herself to breathe slowly. Seeing him didn't fill the cavity inside her. It made the hole deeper. Darker. He was so far away, held by criminals who made the rules and set the agenda of her life. People who would kill whomever they wanted. Trey's life for a brothel? They didn't care.

Simon waved his hand before her face.

She looked up.

His eyes bored into hers. He screwed up his face and pointed at the phone.

She grabbed a tissue, blew her nose, and then said, "I'm sorry, Trey. It's just that I miss you so very much."

"Stop wasting time." Trey's voice was harsh. He looked distracted. The camera zoomed in on his face. "Tell Benjamin to give Trokev what he wants. If Trokev doesn't get what he wants, he'll kill me." Trey's face soured. "Life means nothing to Trokev. Move quickly. Please. If you want to see me back alive, do this. Soon."

Something wasn't sitting right. The words weren't his, the delivery stilted. The pressure in the library seemed to have increased. The air felt heavier. "Trey, honey, how—"

The screen went blank.

"What the hell was that?" She held the phone out to Simon like it was a poisonous snake. "Simon, we have to get Trey out of there."

The doorbell sounded. Simon nodded toward the front of the house and departed.

What had they done to Trey? What else could they do? She shivered. *Please, Lord, help me.*

Five minutes later, Simon returned and handed her a large envelope.

"X-rays?" she asked, surprised Beau had accomplished the task so fast. Being the founding contributor of the Falcon Hospital had its benefits.

"Yes. I had the courier return the dollhouse to the play room." Simon left.

She opened the envelope, removed one of the several films, and held it to the light, astonished at the number of secret compartments evident. "My goodness," she said. There were hidden compartments everywhere. She removed a second film, a different view, and saw more hidden chambers. Small. Large. Most in unlikely places. Finally a roadmap to—

Her cell rang Meredith's distinctive tone.

Patricia answered the call.

"It's your house," Meredith said.

A chill ran up Patricia's spine.

"Your house was the ninth built on Falcon Square."

"Great work, Meredith." Patricia eyed the envelope of x-rays. "I found another clue. Can you come back and help me solve it?"

"I'm just pulling up."

Patricia went into the dining room. "Meredith's coming back."

The doorbell rang.

Simon stood. "I know it's only Meredith, but I still have to get it."

Moments later, Meredith entered. "So, what's this new clue?"

## CHAPTER 29

Simon leaned back from his computer, disappointed by the lack of architectural data available to him. Between public, private, and secure governmental databases, he could usually get detailed information on almost anything. Not so this morning.

He finished off his first cup of coffee of the day, tapped Father John's call icon on his phone display, and pressed the cell to his ear. As a papal covert operator, John had access to data and people unavailable to Simon ... unless asked for.

"Hi, Simon. What can I do for you?"

"I have a theory on how Trokev is moving Trey in and out of those Skype broadcast locations undetected by us." Simon headed to the kitchen to refill his cup.

"I've been wondering about that too. What did you come up with?"

"Underground passages," Simon said. "I've exhausted my resources trying to document that he has them at his brothels and have come up empty. Could you have your people check to see if Trokev's brothels are in buildings with escape tunnels? I'll bet the next call comes from one of them."

"Good thinking. Besides fooling us, those tunnels would be an effective way to assure his well-heeled clients didn't have to endure the publicity of using the front door. It's no problem for us to check, but it may take a while. Some of those foreign municipalities don't keep good architectural records, but we'll be thorough. If there's a need for a physical inspection, we'll do it. I'd like nothing better than to spring Trey and trap those rats escaping in a tunnel."

"Me, too." Simon refilled his cup then headed back to his command center in the dining room. "The other thing is, I've identified your daughter's harasser. It's our friend Grigory Trokev." Finding Connie's harasser had taken more time than Simon planned since locating Trey was his top priority.

"Damn."

"Yeah. The Russian seems to be at the center of a lot of our troubles." Simon brought up his search screen. "What's Connie looking for?"

"A missing relic."

Simon stopped typing. "The arm relic of Saint Gregory the Illuminator?"

"Yes. How'd you know?"

Simon settled in his chair. He relished when pieces of a mystery began to converge. "We recently obtained reliable information Trokev is obsessed with adding the saint's bones to his private collection. The relic is likely the major reason he's in Savannah. He's already killed Patricia's gardener over it. Connie's been warned and is clearly in danger. You should pull her off that research."

"I agree," John said. "Who's your source on Trokev's intent?"

"Preston Somerset, an attorney who was helping establish Trokev in Savannah. We've neutralized that relationship."

"Nice work," John said.

That meant a lot coming from a man like John. "Why was Connie researching the arm?"

"She was working for me."

"What's your interest in the relic?"

"The church wants it found and put into secure storage."

"Any leads?" Simon asked.

"No."

"If I hear anything more about Trokev's search for the relic I'll let you know," Simon said. "Meanwhile, don't be too hard on Grigory for harassing your daughter."

Laughter erupted from the phone. "What are you, Simon, a mind reader?"

"No. I just know you well enough to know Grigory will pay in some way."

* * *

FATHER JOHN STARED DOWN AT THE NEWSPAPER LYING OPEN TO the article on the theft of Doctor Buzzard's arm. Having witnessed Trokev enter Snake's cabin and leave with a box, John, who had no love for Trokev, had decided to recover the stolen relic and return it to Doctor Snake. With the revelation that Trokev was Connie's harasser, John now had a second reason to punish the Russian. Until this discovery, he had planned to spend the day on research in the archives. He gulped his coffee and headed for the garage, archives, then Trokev's later-much later, after two a.m.

After a fifteen-minute drive, John descended the worn stairs beneath the church. With anticipation mounting, he traversed the musty, dimly-lit hallway to the archives. He'd start reading the bishop's journal today. Intuition told him the answer to finding the missing relic was written on those pages ... somewhere.

As he raised his hand to rap on the office door, he

wondered if Trokev had even thought of looking in the church archives. Or, perhaps, the Russian had already searched the archives without success.

John knocked.

"Come in," the archivist said.

John swung the door open, and gasped. The entire office was in shambles. "What the hell happened?"

"I opened up this morning and found everything torn apart." The reed-thin archivist righted a chair.

John had an empty feeling. "Have you checked for the bishop's journal?"

"No. It's not valuable." He stooped to pick up loose papers. "It was just kids."

"Check it. Now!"

He returned in a minute, white-faced. "It's gone. How'd you know?"

John walked to the hall door. "I think you should report this theft to your prelate."

The archivist nodded. "Most certainly."

As John left, he dismissed the idea of confronting Trokev. He'd just include the missing church book on the list of items he intended to reclaim under the cover of dark.

* * *

LATER THAT AFTERNOON, AFTER VISITING A FRIEND AT THE city's power and light department, Father John drove the city van Isabel had arranged to Trokev's so-called bed and breakfast to plant a device and to scout the layout. The two-story Victorian home had a fresh coat of paint, and the mature landscaping had been artfully manicured. On the seat next to him were a building inspector's hardhat and blueprints.

A stone-faced woman met him in the lobby. "Can I help you?"

John pushed his hard hat back. "I'm here for your annual electrical inspection."

"An annual electrical inspection? Never heard of such a thing." She folded her arms. "You have some ID?"

He produced Savannah Electric and Power identification.

"Who's your boss?"

"Mr. Cheung."

"What's his phone number?"

He gave her the number.

She pointed to a lobby chair. "You park your butt here while I call your company."

He watched as she frowned when his visit was apparently verified. With her reluctant approval, he went to the electrical room, unfurled the electrical plan for the building, and began a close examination of the circuits. The woman grew impatient and left him alone to conduct his business unsupervised.

John wired a black box into the security alarm circuit to keep his intended nocturnal intrusions from triggering a report to the security monitoring company. He left the electrical room and began inspecting each room's electrical outlets. His heart sped when he found Buzzard's arm displayed in a room devoted to Trokev's collection. He activated an app on his smartphone to check for wireless security transmissions. Other than a standard window alarm, there didn't seem to be any additional security in Trokev's trophy room.

In Trokev's office, John noted the church's 1939 property ledger on the Russian's desk, and the make and model of the safe in the corner. The smartphone app showed no active wireless transmitters in the office either. The bishop's journal was nowhere in sight. It could be in the safe, the locked file cabinet, the desk ... anywhere. Damn. He'd only have one shot at recovery when he returned that evening.

After the intrusion, Trokev would increase security or would move the journal to parts unknown.

When John's reconnaissance was complete, he found the stern-faced woman and told her the building circuitry passed the inspection. She seemed relieved to have him leave.

He called Simon from the van. "You know those buddies of yours at Critter-Gitters who recovered that snake at the Falcons?"

"Yeah. What do you need?"

"How about a deadly snake without fangs?"

"When?"

"This afternoon." John pulled into a gas station. "If not this afternoon, then by ten this evening at the latest."

"I'll see what they can do," Simon said. "A deadly species without fangs huh? Are you planning to scare someone to death?"

"Just delivering an unmistakable retaliation message."

"Trokev?"

"Most certainly."

* * *

AFTER A COUPLE OF HOURS OF TRYING TO UNLOCK ONE dollhouse secret compartment after another, Meredith stood. "I'm sorry, Patricia. I guess I'm a puzzle klutz."

Patricia stood as well. "Puzzles are everywhere. Different puzzles for different people." She touched Meredith's shoulder. "You're exceptional with number, word and crime puzzles."

"Not so good, apparently, with physical puzzles," Meredith said.

"It's not a big deal."

"I like puzzles more than banking."

"You love discovery, Meredith."

Meredith nodded. "I should be going."

"Stay for supper?"

"I'd love to, honey, but I have a lot of office work to get through before morning."

"Thanks for the help today."

"Once I get home, I'll see if I can find a local puzzle expert for you."

Patricia hugged Meredith. "You think of everything."

After Meredith left, Patricia returned to the playroom and studied the dollhouse x-rays, trying in vain to see if any of the compartments held something at its center.

* * *

IT WAS WELL PAST MIDNIGHT WHEN FATHER JOHN, DRESSED IN black, eased from his Hummer. He grabbed the canvas bag with the snake and his tactical gear from the back seat and made his way through the yard of a home behind Trokev's bed and breakfast.

After scaling an ivy-covered brick wall, he dropped in behind the dense shrubs surrounding the unlit pool deck. There were no lights illuminated inside the main building, and only minimal external security lighting at the exits. Still, he'd avoid the illuminated exits because they were equipped with internal and external video monitors.

His entry point would be the rear-facing window in Trokev's trophy room. The interrupter he placed on the security circuit earlier assured his entry there would go undetected.

John cut a wide hole in the glass, unlatched the lock, and raised the window. Once inside, he exchanged the copperhead snake for Buzzard's arm and closed the lid on the display box. The agitated snake prowled the box, its mottled copper body sliding against the glass. John shuddered and

279

left the snake to it. He set the duffle with the arm beside the open window.

Moving on to Trokev's office, John found the 1939 property ledger still on the desk. After stowing the ledger in his backpack, John methodically searched the desk and the locked file cabinet for the bishop's journal. Finding nothing, he moved to the safe, melted a small hole though the exterior panel of the thick door with a high-powered laser, and inserted a glass fiber optical bundle into the inner door cavity. One fiber provided illumination, the other provided a clear view of whatever was illuminated. He melted a second hole exactly two inches to the right of the first and inserted an electrical probe. Using the optical bundle for guidance, he touched the electrical probe to the appropriate position on the safe's circuit board and the locking mechanism released.

John swung the door open and shined his penlight into the safe, immediately spotting the bishop's journal. People were so predictable. He replaced the stolen journal with a copy of the Ten Commandments printed on Papal letterhead. The seventh (not steal) and tenth (not covet) commandments were highlighted in yellow.

On the way home, he broke into Dr. Snake's unoccupied log cabin and left Buzzard's arm with a warning note to hide the arm better on top of a large glass case containing reptiles.

John and Connie spent what was left of the night moving their personal effects from the condo into his Hummer. He knew once Trokev discovered the intrusion, the Russian and his goons would come for him and his daughter, as well as Doctor Snake.

Once everything was out, John taped a letter-sized notice on the condo door-Psalm 51 (cleanse me of my sins) with nothing highlighted.

# CHAPTER 30

*S*eated at her desk, Patricia jotted an observation in her notebook. *The longer Trey is held captive, the more his personality seems to change.* At the end of the sentence she paused, sensing someone in the study. She settled her pen on the open page, eased her hand to the gun on her hip, and looked up.

Simon stood silhouetted in the doorway. "Got a minute?"

Relieved, she nodded.

He crossed the room and settled into the chair across from her. It wasn't like Simon to deliver messages seated. He was too busy for that. Something was up, but he didn't look tense. Just a guy in an easy chair with a mug of coffee. A picture of contentment.

"Father John and Connie are on their way over," he said.

"Why?"

"Don't know."

"Which means you know, but you're not telling."

He shrugged.

Being kept in the dark sucked. "Have you heard from Bishop Reilly?"

His brow furrowed. "About what?"

Obviously he didn't like being out of the loop either. For a moment, she savored one-upping him. "He's trying to set up a meeting with Father John, himself, and me."

"No. I haven't heard from him." He took a sip of coffee.

"Since Father John is on his way over, would you see if Bishop Reilly could join us?"

"Will do," he said, flatly. He took another swig of his drink then set the steaming mug on the glass coffee table. "How would you feel about having a guard dog in the house?"

Patricia had a collie as a child and was devastated when he died of old age. Because she couldn't stand to be shattered again, she hadn't had a pet of any kind since. But Simon wasn't proposing a pet; this was a dog with a job. It might be nice to have company. "Sure, but why now?"

"Trey's last scripted message made clear his captors are impatient." His face tensed. "I think they might try to kidnap you to put more pressure on the Coalition."

Damn. She twisted Trey's ring on her thumb. "You're here to prevent that sort of thing."

"Trokev has a lot of resources and appears willing to use them. If they send enough muscle in, I could be over-whelmed." He paused and stared over her shoulder as if contemplating his own demise. He blinked and returned his attention to her. "A guard dog and handler could hold off an assault team long enough for you to make it to your safe room."

"What about hiring a couple more bodyguards?"

"We're defensive. The dog is an offensive weapon. Once released by his handler, he'll attack no matter what the odds. Plus, if intruders managed to get in without setting off an alarm, a guard dog would immediately sense the intrusion and alert us."

Her mouth was dry, her face hot. "Someone could break

in without setting off my alarms? I thought the system had redundancies."

"It does, but any system can be breached. Trust me. Best we have a dog."

"Okay." She ran fingers through her hair, still trying to process the idea of her house erupting into a bloody firefight. "When?"

Smiling, he grabbed his cup and stood. "I can have a sentry dog and a handler here this afternoon."

A HALF HOUR LATER, FATHER JOHN, CONNIE, AND BISHOP Reilly arrived. John explained they'd run into a problem at their condo and asked if he and Connie could spend the night. As odd as the request was, of course Patricia agreed. After John and Connie left to take their bags to the bedrooms, Bishop Reilly, Simon, and Patricia sat at the kitchen table, waiting for John to join them.

"Do you want to bring Simon up to date on the rings, Patricia, or should I?" Bishop Reilly asked.

"Go ahead," she said.

Shortly after Bishop Reilly finished filling Simon in, John joined them at the table.

"Connie's all settled in?" Patricia asked.

"She's reading Dave McDonald's latest thriller."

Patricia glanced at the bishop. "I assume you briefed John earlier."

He nodded.

"Okay. Then everyone's on board. Since you last saw me, Bishop Reilly, I've located the remaining Illuminati ring."

The bishop's jaw dropped. "Where?"

"Preston Somerset has an Illuminati ring engraved with *HO 9*. It was his grandfather's. My friend, Meredith, has determined that Falcon House was the ninth home

283

constructed on the square. Since *SQ 25*, which is engraved on Trey's grandfather's ring, seems to refer to Falcon Square, the twenty-fifth square to be established in Savannah, we are left with only the *FO* clue unsolved."

"Does anyone have an idea what *FO* might signify?" Father John said.

Simon keyed his laptop. "It's the last name of a Nobel literature prize winner named Dario Fo, an Italian born in 1926. 'FO' is also the abbreviation for field-grade officer, field order, finance officer, flight officer, forward observer, and foreign office. Another source says *FO* is a printing industry abbreviation for folio. In Irish, *fo* translates to under, beneath or through. We have a lot of Irish in Savannah." He looked up from the screen and raised his eyebrows. "Could the relic be buried beneath the house?"

"The basement floor is hard packed dirt," Patricia said. "The bones are in a gold container. We can have someone with a metal detector come over, scan the floor, and dig in likely spots."

"I can arrange that." Simon pulled out his phone. "This afternoon okay?"

Patricia nodded. "Now there's another aspect to our relic search that I also discovered after the bishop left. The Falcon dollhouse is depicted in a painting of Trey's grandfather. Other than the Illuminati ring and Trey's grandfather, it's the only object depicted on the canvas."

"You think the relic could be in the dollhouse?" John asked.

"I thought it might, so I searched it, then had it x-rayed."

Simon nodded.

"There are no bones nor a large metal container in the dollhouse," she said.

"Then why is it in the portrait?" John asked.

"Forty-three secret, locked compartments are built into

the dollhouse and its furnishings. I believe a fourth clue is in one of the hidden chambers."

"So, we need to open those compartments," Simon said.

Patricia put the envelope with the x-ray films on the table. "Have at it. Both Meredith and I tried and failed."

"We'll get an expert," Simon said. He keyed his laptop, then frowned and keyed it again. "Nothing on local puzzle experts. Let me do some further research on this."

"We're running out of time." Patricia's mind flashed to an image of Trey tortured. She clenched a hand. "Trokev's guys are impatient, and that's not good for Trey. Right, Simon?"

"Yeah." Simon nodded.

"Let's get some old bones and have the Coalition offer them to Trokev."

"It's a good idea, but it's got to be much more convincing."

"Trokev knows John is looking for the relic," Patricia said.

John, his eyes fixed on hers, nodded.

"Why don't we have John tell Trokev he found the relic and will trade the bones for Trey?"

John shook his head. "Trokev knows the church won't give up the bones."

She studied him, taking in his set jaw and tense lips. Not much help there. "What about me telling Trokev I found the bones?"

The bishop looked at John. "What do you think?"

"She's got a clear motive," John said. "Trokev might believe her."

"It would be more convincing if we put the bones in a duplicate of the real reliquary." The bishop looked at Simon's raised eyebrow. "A container for relics. They're a means of protecting the bones. The reliquary associated with this relic is constructed of gold fashioned to resemble the forearm of Saint Gregory."

"You've seen it?" Simon asked.

"The Vatican provided me a grainy black and white photo taken in 1939 just before its shipment to Savannah."

"There are artisans in Rome who could fabricate a duplicate," the bishop said.

"How long?" Simon asked.

"Three or four days."

Simon closed his laptop. "That seems quick."

Patricia twisted the ring on her thumb. Not quick enough for Trey. Or herself.

"Trust me," Bishop Reilly said. "They'll get it done."

"Shipment to Savannah?" Simon asked.

The bishop smiled. "Overnight on a Papal jet."

"How long to come up with bones that would pass carbon dating?" Simon asked.

"Trokev is a collector. If he thinks Patricia has the relic, he'll worry the church will take it from her. He'll be in a hurry."

"So, we're searching for buried metal in the basement floor and bringing an expert over here to get into the dollhouse compartments." Patricia clenched her jaw. "And we've agreed to swap a replica relic for Trey."

Everyone nodded.

Patricia swallowed hard. "I'm concerned about Trey's welfare while we sort all this out. Why don't we give Trokev a reason to protect Trey?"

"What do you have in mind?" Simon asked.

She turned to him. "You said it was highly probable Trokev has my home under intense surveillance. Why don't we stage an argument on my front porch where I castigate Bishop Reilly and Father John for focusing their efforts on finding the relic rather than securing Trey's release? Then I'll call Trokev and see if he'll have dinner with me. There's no reason he'd say no.

"At dinner, I'll show him my Illuminati ring. Once I have

his attention, I'll tell him I've given up on Trey's so-called friends and have decided to search for the relic myself so I can trade it for Trey. If Trokev buys in, he'll see substantial progress, or at least the distinct possibility of progress, and have less reason to hurt Trey."

"We can stage the show right now." Simon glanced at Bishop Reilly, then at John.

John looked at the bishop. "Do you mind if I spend a couple nights at the rectory?"

"I'd love the company."

John met Patricia's eyes. "I think it best if Connie remains here."

"No problem. Anything else before we start our show?"

Everyone remained silent.

Patricia's stomach knotted as she deactivated the security alarm, grabbed the doorknob, and looked at Bishop Reilly and John. "Are you guys ready to rumble?"

John rubbed his palms together and laughed. "Let's give Trokev a show he'll never forget."

"Well?" The bishop nodded toward the entrance.

Patricia flung the steel door open so hard it rattled the frame when it struck the doorstop. The knot in her stomach tightened. "Get out of here," she shouted. "Leave me alone. You're both hypocrites. You aren't concerned about Trey or me! All you care about is finding that relic so you can send it to the Vatican. You place more value on a box of bones than my husband's life."

The bishop backed out to the porch with John right behind. John raised his hands defensively. "Calm down, Patricia. We're doing everything possible."

Stomach lurching, she stepped out, coming face-to-face with John. "Then where is my husband?"

John backed up.

She matched his step, keeping in his face. "Where? Where?"

His eyebrows furrowed. He shrugged.

"That's right. You haven't the slightest idea. You're incompetent idiots." She gestured wildly toward the street. "Get out of here."

The bishop cleared his throat and stepped forward. "Now, now, Patricia. Getting angry isn't going to bring Trey home."

"Home? I'll tell you who will bring Trey home." She tapped her chest. "I'll find that relic, and I'll bring him home. No thanks to you."

The red-faced bishop sighed.

"Just ... leave ... me ... alone. Go. Now." Scowling, she pointed an unsteady finger toward the curb.

The bishop touched her shoulder. "Patricia—"

"Leave!" she screeched. "Leave. Now. Or I'll call the cops."

John's eyes bulged as he stared at her like she had gone mad.

Perhaps she had gone mad. Her anger at them and the words to express it flowed too easily. Embarrassingly easy. Certainly they knew this was all a show put on for Trokev's benefit, but you'd never guess from John's expression.

Silence loomed as she waited for their response. Seconds passed.

"We'll talk more about this later." The bishop waved his arm dismissively, turned away from her sharply, and headed down the stairs.

John opened his mouth as if to speak, then followed Bishop Reilly.

She stormed back in the house and slammed the door for good effect. Her hand fisted. *God, I hope Trokev bought it.*

"How'd it go?" Simon asked.

"I didn't realize how much deep-seated anger I had for their selfish priorities, placing the church's acquisition of a box of bones over Trey's life." She fanned her face. "I really gave it to them. Not very ladylike. Particularly toward men of the cloth. I'm sure the neighbors got an earful, and I hope Trokev did too." She grabbed the phone and tapped Trokev's number on the recent calls screen. *Please let this work.*

# CHAPTER 31

*P*atricia paused at the entrance of the 17Hundred90 Inn and Restaurant. This was it. Whatever happened now would either bring Trey home or bring more retaliation. She opened the door to the ethereal music of Johnny Mercer's "Moon River" from the pianist at the grand piano, and the tantalizing aromas of fresh bread and charbroiled steak.

Her heart thumping, she strode into the slate and brick lobby and scanned the warmly lit interior of the dining room. *Grigory Trokev, where are you?*

"May I assist you, ma'am?" the hostess asked in a subdued tone that echoed the inn's ambiance. Her blonde hair and pale face stood in contrast to her black uniform.

"Trokev reservation," Patricia said.

"Mr. Trokev has already arrived. This way, please."

As they crossed the dining room, she spotted Grigory. His eyes found her and, like a snake, slid over her. She shivered.

He stood.

So far, so good. She gave him a polite smile.

Grigory kissed her hand. His lips were moist and clammy on her skin.

She resisted the urge to cringe, then sat across from him, placing her hands in her lap to wipe his clammy slime from her skin.

He changed chairs to sit on her immediate left. The reptile was so close she was forced to smell his overpowering sweet musk aftershave.

The waiter arrived to take their drink orders.

Grigory acknowledged the server, then turned to Patricia. "Champagne?"

*What pompousity.* She shook her head. "Water. Tap water, please."

"I'll have the same," Grigory said.

After the waiter poured her water, she lifted the glass, making sure her hand didn't shake. There was a lot riding on this performance. Thank God, her grip was steady. She took a sip and returned the glass to the table. "Thank you for agreeing to meet me on such short notice."

He gave a fleeting smile and nodded. "No problem."

"So, you want Saint Gregory's arm?" Her tone and words were intentionally direct.

He raised an eyebrow. "I do."

She sipped her drink again and, returning her glass to the table, met his gaze. "I want Trey."

He smirked. "I'm sure you do."

"Would you be willing to swap Trey for the saint's bones?"

He flinched. "You have the relic?"

"I will. Soon."

"How?"

"None of your business."

He paused then returned his hand to the table and glared. She took dark pleasure in his obvious discomfort. This oppressive jerk who was holding Trey and waging war on Savannah didn't like surprises, much less losing control.

He leaned forward, his eyes wide. "What makes you think you will succeed where we have failed?"

"The relic isn't missing. It's just extremely well hidden." Feeling ready to explode with nerves, she took another quick sip to wet her throat. "There are several clues to its current location. Each clue is meaningless without the others. I alone possess all the clues."

He gestured, palms up. "What clues are these?"

"Mr. Trokev, I'm sure you'll forgive me for not answering your question."

His jaw tensed. "Then why should I believe you?"

A wave of anticipation for the plan's second step surged through her. She couldn't wait to see his expression. Reaching into her purse, she removed the Illuminati ring and dropped it on the table. It whirled on the linen like a spinning coin.

Trokev, his cheeks suddenly flushed, straightened. He didn't pick up the ring. Since he didn't examine the band for an engraving, he obviously didn't know about the ring clues. "Where did you get that?"

"Mr. Trokev, I'm sure you're aware that by possessing this I have knowledge of the relic." Heart racing, she returned the ring to her purse. "Now. Are you interested in exchanging Trey for the relic? Simple answer. Yes or no?"

"If you find the arm before I do and give it to me, sure, you can have your husband back."

"Alive?"

"Of course."

"And unharmed?"

Trokev appeared to consider. What? Did he have someone who enjoyed hurting people? Of course he did. Patricia ground her teeth and suppressed a shudder.

"He'll be alive," Trokev said.

"I want him unharmed."

"You should have thought about that when you were slow to respond."

Not the answer she wanted, but to get Trey back she had to stay focused and on plan. She stood. "I'll contact you when I have the relic."

He rose and edged closer. Too close. Though inwardly cringing, she held her ground.

"Not so fast," he said. "Why did you contact me on this matter and not the Coalition?"

"I've stopped cooperating with the Coalition. I'm not sure I can trust them."

"And the church?"

"They've made it clear their goal is to secure the relic for themselves. Any interest in Trey's well-being is secondary to that."

"So, you're willing to betray your friends, your church, and the Coalition?"

Trey's life was on the line. She needed to sell this proposal. To do so she had to get in Trokev's face and call his bluff. The last thing she wanted was to get even closer to this jerk. The image of Trey from his last Skype call steeled her. She stepped forward and went eye-to-eye with him. "You want the relic, I want Trey. Pretty simple, Mr. Trokev."

"What about your bodyguard? He's not here tonight."

So he knew about Simon all along. "He's still my bodyguard."

"You're alone."

"Yes," Patricia said, surprised at the severity in her voice. "I thought it might make dialogue easier." She picked up her purse. "I believe we've said all that needs to be said." She gave him a faint nod. "The next time we meet, I'll expect my husband."

He reached for her hand.

She didn't offer hers. "Let's skip the pleasantries and stick to business."

His fake smile withered as he withdrew his hand. "Of course," he murmured.

She turned and strode out, thankful she'd actually pulled off the initial meeting.

\* \* \*

"Clear," the Coalition infiltrator said from the junction of two tunnels. His partner patted him on the back and the two men, rifles at the ready, inched forward in the quiet darkness, their way only illuminated by night vision goggles.

The infiltrator paused and consulted his map, something he rarely did topside. GPS had made paper maps old school, but satellite navigation didn't function underground, and old school was all they had. Another twenty-five feet of tunnel and they'd be on station beneath The Amber House. He moved forward, stepping over a dead rat floating in a puddle.

"I hate this," his partner whispered.

The infiltrator nodded, though he didn't mind it much. He'd seen worse. A chill went through him. A sixth sense that something was wrong. His vision clouded. Terribly wrong. He dropped to his knees, gasping for breath, knowing it would be his last. He reached for his external-com, but his arm wouldn't come up. He fell forward into the sludge-laden water, and then darkness came.

\* \* \*

For the next hour, all Patricia could do at home was pace and wonder if she'd done enough. She called the bishop for an update on the fake reliquary and was assured the process had begun. Just before eleven, Simon gave her the phone. Another Skype call from Trey.

Trey was hurt.

She shivered.

He was disheveled. Dirty. Multiple cuts littered his face. Swollen bruises rose everywhere.

Shaking, she gasped. Damn Trokev. He'd either lied, or gotten in one last beating. Unfortunately, she'd failed Trey ... again.

The camera zoomed in on his abused face. "I'm not going to last much longer."

The battered image brought tears. The tears welled, then streamed. "Trey—"

"Patricia. Please. Give them what they want. If you don't, I ... I can't take much more. I'm dying. They beat me and beat me—"

"I'm trying!" she shouted desperately, her voice breaking over a sob.

Saliva drooled from his mouth. "Between beatings, they keep me in a tiny box. Naked. Freezing. Music so loud I can't sleep. No food. If I could ... I'd kill myself."

"Trey—"

The screen went blank.

"Noooo!" Quivering, she closed her eyes and tried to clear her mind of the ghastly image of Trey's beaten face, but it was etched in deep groves and she couldn't focus on anything else.

Simon tried to comfort her.

She pushed him away.

Patricia slumped in the chair. The images returned. Now more vivid. Her fingers curled. She wanted to run. Run far, far away.

She pressed her feet hard against the floor. Setting her

palms on the armrest, she pushed herself up and locked her knees, but her legs wouldn't support her. There was no escape. She collapsed, arms limp, into the chair. Her skin prickled.

"Trey. Oh Trey," she whispered. She brushed her tear-stained cheek, then pried her eyes open, hoping to replace the retained image with something else. Something familiar. Reassuring.

A dark silhouette hovered, haloed by the overhead light. Who? Simon? She squinted, but still couldn't identify the shadow. Turning her head from the brightness, she saw the bookcase. The shelf of mementoes. Trey's chair. His desk. Finally something familiar to anchor her mind. But, even without Trey's battered image, she was still full of rage against his captors. Her stomach convulsed. The desk melted.

She was cooperating with Trokev. Hurting Trey was unnecessary. She sobbed. "Cruel." Blood surged. "Pure evil." She clenched her hands, digging her fingernails into her palms until she couldn't take the pain. Times like this she was glad she had a gun and knew how to use it. "Damn it," she growled. Trokev would pay.

She saw Simon standing in front of her more clearly. Armored vest over black. Tight-lipped. Expectant eyes fixed on her. Hovering.

*Simon failed Trey. The Coalition failed Trey. I failed Trey.* How could she live with that guilt? How could she face tomorrow knowing what they were doing to Trey?

And Trokev was orchestrating this travesty. She wanted him to pay, but first she wanted her husband free from the Russians. She swallowed and stood. Her gun hand twitched. Once Trey was safe, she'd finish her business with Trokev.

"I got a glimpse of the room before they zoomed in on

Trey's face," Simon said. "I'm pretty sure it's a conference room at The Amber House."

Neck hairs rose. "In Savannah?" Her breath caught. "He's so close! You had it staked out?"

"We were spread too thin. They took out our two operators who were watching the place. We just found their bodies. And—"

"Oh my God. Two more deaths. This man is insane."

Simon nodded. "And smart. His brothel is built over Savannah's extensive tunnel system."

"So what does that mean?"

"It means Trey was secreted away through the tunnels immediately after the call and is long gone by now. It means we continue to stake out the brothels built over escape tunnels."

"They're torturing Trey," she said in a ragged voice.

He shook his head. "Not much we can do about that."

Simon's words piqued her frustration with his complacency, with his and the Cotton Coalition's incompetence. Trey was being hurt, possibly at this very moment. She wanted Simon to know that, to feel that. She jerked her arm back and swung her fisted hand at his face as hard as she could.

He snatched her wrist in mid-flight.

She tried to wrench her hand away.

His grasp tightened. "Listen to me, Patricia."

She glared at him. "Leave me alone!"

"Get a hold of yourself," he said in an even voice. "Right now."

She set her jaw. "No!"

"Do ... it ... now."

She glared. She hated him for being strong. Hated him even more for being right. She spun the ring on her thumb. Going off on Simon didn't get Trey back. "Fine."

He released her.

Still smoldering with anger, she rubbed her wrist.

"Do you want to be involved in this or not?" he asked.

She nodded.

"Then you're going to have to see and hear things as they are. Ugly. Brutal. That's the only way we ... you can make the right decisions."

She stepped back.

"I'm going to share something frightening with you," Simon said, a twisted look on his face.

She shivered, unsure of how much additional bad news she could take.

"Patricia, it's important you understand what's going on."

Her stomach churned. "Yes, of course."

"I'm not sure Trokev has bought your story. The longer this stalemate lasts, the greater the probability that Trey's captors might kill him."

She straightened, her hands clenched into fists. "Obviously. I figured that out days ago. But I'll tell you what." Patricia jabbed a finger to her chest. "I, *personally*, will *not* let that happen."

# CHAPTER 32

*A* loud explosion sounded from the front of the safe house. Hayley eyed her apartment door. It was intact. No smoke. *What the hell was that explosion?* The evacuation siren kicked on, wailing, warbling, alerting her senses. *Oh no!* Panic surged.

Hayley rushed to her closet, swung the door open and punched in the escape code. Shots echoed in the hallway. *Gotta get outta here. Now. Right now.*

A steel panel in the back of the closet slowly slid to the side. Ducking beneath the clothing, she stepped into the small escape room and hit the button that closed and locked the hatch. She'd practiced the routine daily since arriving, but never with explosions and shots fired.

The thing was, other than two or three guards and her handler, she was the only resident. She was the target. Did they plan to capture her? She shivered. Or kill her? She descended the steel ladder.

* * *

"Patricia!" Simon shouted.

Patricia jerked her head up.

His taut face was crimson. His eyes, wide. She'd never seen him so agitated.

"Trouble at Hayley's safe house," he said.

Her chest constricted.

"She escaped uninjured, but until she shows up at the secondary location she's off our radar."

"What the hell happened? You said—"

"I don't know what happened, but she's safe."

"You don't know she's safe. She's off your damn radar! You think someone smart enough to find my daughter doesn't realize the safe house probably has an escape plan?" Her face heated. "You're all incompetent. I want Hayley back right now."

"Calm down, Patricia. Let's take it one step at a time."

"Don't tell me to calm down. I've tried being calm and cooperative, and you lost my daughter. I want Hayley home ... now!"

"You think she'll be safer here?"

She glared at him. "Apparently it's safer here in Savannah than in Atlanta."

"Let's find her first."

"Simon." She stabbed the air in front of his face. "Bring ... her ... home. No detours. No delays."

Simon left the room shaking his head.

* * *

Hayley, quivering with adrenaline overload, surged out of the subway utility room and boarded the next train just before it left. No one got on after her, but she still worried. At the third stop, she got off just before the train left. Hayley went to the ladies' room, washed her hands, then returned to the platform and walked slowly to the other end of the station. With her back to the wall, she scanned the platform for suspicious characters. She didn't know exactly what she was looking for. Her handler said she'd know. She'd never practiced this part of the escape plan. Her handler said it was too dangerous ... unless needed.

Seeing nothing suspicious, she went up the stairs to street level, hailed a cab, and rode to Ritz Carlton. Inside the building, she used her Platinum pass card to take the elevator to a private floor, and to enter her new safe room.

Hayley froze.

Sitting at the corner desk was her portly handler from the compromised safe house.

"Are you okay?" asked Mrs. Brown.

"No." Hayley dropped into an overstuffed chair next to her. "What happened?"

"We saw an assault team approach and quickly place explosives. I didn't have time to alert you before they breached the entrance, but knew you'd follow your training."

"Anyone hurt?"

Mrs. Brown shook her head.

"Now what?"

"We wait for instructions." Her tone was authoritative. "Chances are whoever initiated this isn't going to give up easily."

* * *

"WE HAVE HAYLEY BACK," SIMON SAID FROM THE STUDY doorway. She's—"

"Is she okay?" Patricia stopped her pacing mid-stride. She wasn't sure how well she would handle any more bad news. *Please God, let her be safe.*

"Hayley's rattled, but unharmed. She's with Mrs. Brown at a transition location. Everything went—"

Patricia crossed to Simon and went eye-to-eye with him. "Get her back here, right now."

Frowning, he shook his head.

"What's that supposed to mean?" she asked in a razor-sharp, no-nonsense tone.

"This wasn't a fireworks display. Someone tried to snatch your daughter today. These guys forced their way into an exceptionally secure safe house. They're pros. Now I'm even more concerned about anything that might compromise her safety."

"And I'm not?" She prowled the room, burning off frustration, then returned to Simon. "Look, Simon. If this house is safe enough for me, it's safe enough for her."

"Right now, Trokev has no idea where Hayley escaped to. If we bring her here, he'll know."

"Shut his surveillance down, then bring my daughter home."

"We've removed or blocked everything we've detected, but I have to assume he still has surveillance capability."

"Use the tunnel."

"That's only for escape. Using it now could reveal its existence, rendering it useless for its intended purpose."

"I don't care how you do it." She pointed to the phone. "Get my daughter home for dinner, or I'm sure Isabel will find someone who will."

Though he nodded, his eyes glared. He picked up the phone and tapped the display. "I'll speak with Isabel. Right now."

Simon walked to the other side of the room, carried on a short conversation, then returned. She couldn't read his expression.

"Well?" she said to him.

He gave her one of his rare smiles.

She was relieved he didn't appear to harbor anger at her earlier firmness with him.

"I spoke with Isabel. We're bringing Hayley back. She'll be here by supper."

She patted his arm. "Thank you, Simon."

"We think it's possible Trokev found Hayley by her online class. We thought using classified anonymous servers, the same technology the military uses for battlefield communications, would keep her location well hidden." He gave her an apologetic look. "There's also a possibility Trokev found Hayley though our purchases of *Sivadene*, her prescription burn treatment. If so, that was a colossal oversight on our part. Regardless of which discovery path Trokev used, Hayley will have to withdraw from her classes and—"

"Why not keep her registered and have her work submitted electronically from another location in Atlanta?"

Simon tilted his head.

"Trokev thinks Hayley is still in Atlanta. If he's tracking her class activities, why not help him maintain the assumption?"

Simon nodded. "Deception works for me."

"And we have plenty of Hayley's burn cream here, so there's no need to reorder yet. Plus, she and I use the same ointment. If she needs more at some point, I can order it on my prescription."

"Good. While we're at it, if Trokev has eyes on this house, he's probably aware that you're wearing a vest. Now that Hayley's in danger, he may be watching for us to order one from the same company in Hayley's size. I'll have someone in New York order a vest for Hayley, and have it sent to the same address that will be transmitting her homework."

* * *

A CLUNK SOUNDED FROM THE OTHER SIDE OF THE KITCHEN. Patricia, who had been watching a monarch feed on the lantana on the outside of the window, put her coffee cup down and looked up.

Simon's eyelids drooped over bloodshot eyes. He hadn't shaved. He crossed to the table, a phone in his hand. "I just got a text message that Trey will call in a minute."

"I don't know how many more of these I can take. But, thank God he's still alive."

Simon put his arm on her shoulder. "I don't know where you get the strength."

She extended her hand.

Just as he placed the phone in her palm, the cell rang. She accepted the call and gasped.

Trey had a swollen eye with a black welt below it. His split, puffy lower lip had an ugly scab. Dried blood coated his upper lip just below his nose. The damn gansters had beaten him again.

Horror filled her. It was her fault. She gave Trokev the idea by asking for Trey to be alive and unharmed. Now that Trokev knew the chance for the relic rested with Patricia, he was using Trey ruthlessly.

"I want to live," he said in a hoarse voice. "Tell Lucius to resolve this today. I'm not a strong man. I can't take much more of this. I want to survive. I want to be with you. Nothing else matters. Let them operate the brothel."

A terrible silence hung.

"You must obey their demands," Trey said. "Right away."

The screen went blank.

She stared, dumbfounded, at the screen, and then rage came like a tidal wave, smothering her, blinding her, taking her to dark, violent places of retribution. She gritted her teeth. Trokev and his bastards weren't going to get away with torturing Trey. Every last one would die the ugliest, most agonizing death she could invent. The room spun. She closed her eyes. Darkness came.

"Patricia," Simon said.

She wanted to look at him, but her mind was trapped in the dark place.

"Patricia!"

She exhaled slowly and opened her eyes to him.

His angular face hovered inches from hers. "Are you back?"

Her arms hung limp. Fighting nausea and dizziness, she felt his hands pushing on her shoulders. She wanted to nod, but thought she might throw up if she did.

"You fainted," he said softly.

When she blinked, the image of his face sharpened. "It's getting worse with each call."

"Unfortunately." He released her shoulders and nodded. "That's how they do it."

"Do what?"

"Break us. Make us give in."

"I have an agreement with Trokev to give him exactly what he wants." She balled her fist. "What's the logic in beating Trey?"

Simon exhaled. "He's pressuring you to wrap up your business with him as fast as you can." Simon took the phone from her. "I'll take care of this. Go lie down. Get some rest."

She pointed to the phone. "Get Trokev on the phone. I'm going to tell him I'll kill him if he touches Trey again. I won't stand for this. Not at all."

"I understand. I'll talk with Trokev."

"Do it now." Her voice was bitter and firm. "Do it right now, or I'm going to."

"I'll take care of it. Right now."

He left, only to return moments later. "Incoming," Simon said.

Patricia turned in his direction, wondering what was up. "Another call from Trey?"

"No. Hayley's in the tunnel." He conferred with the man handling the guard dog, then walked to the basement door.

Patricia, her heart thumping, followed Simon down the stairs and across the cellar to the steel hatch that opened to the ancient tunnel. Simon unbolted the door and swung it open. Musty, cool air flowed into the basement from the illuminated tunnel. Patricia went to step into the entrance, but Simon held her back. "The footing is rough in there. It's better to greet her out here in the open."

Time slowed. The tunnel from Sheila's florist shop to Falcon House was just one block long. Patricia strained to hear footfalls and, when the sounds finally came, her heart raced. Moments later, a larger, disguised Hayley emerged from the tunnel.

Patricia wrapped her arms around her padded and wigged daughter. "Thank God you're safe. Welcome home, sweetheart."

"Mom." Hayley returned the hug, clinging tightly.

Patricia stepped back, looked at her daughter's face, and brushed tears from Hayley's eyes.

"I'm so relieved to be home. How's Dad?"

"He's alive." Patricia couldn't believe how distorted Hayley's voice sounded. Did the facial prosthetics do that? She took Hayley's hand and gave it a squeeze. "Let's go upstairs and get you out of those pads."

"They're stifling."

"And the facial prosthetics." Patricia touched Hayley's built-up cheek. "They're so real."

Hayley nodded. "They did a great job on me."

Patricia knew Hayley didn't eat before flights. "I know you need to eat—"

"And shower and change."

"Yes, but do it fast because—"

"What?"

"Some new dollhouse puzzles that might help us find Daddy. Your specialty. Now go take a shower ... and hurry."

* * *

HAYLEY PUT THE SET OF X-RAY FILMS ON THE SIDE TABLE AND stood. "Wow! I wish I had these when I was a kid." She crossed the playroom and stooped in front of the dollhouse. "So many hidden compartments in there."

Patricia, seated across from Hayley, calmed herself. There was so much at stake.

"I'll start at the top and work down." She removed the roof. "Not much here in the attic. Just this cedar chest, a hat box, and that wardrobe." She removed the chest and looked it over. She pushed and probed on its sides to no avail, then examined the small chest more closely. Turning the end handles sprung the lid. Hayley, smiling smugly, tilted the box toward Patricia to show there was nothing inside. "One down," Hayley said. "Forty-two to go."

The hatbox and wardrobe yielded to Hayley's nimble hands just as quickly, but produced no clue. With Patricia's help, they lifted the attic floor from the house, exposing the bedrooms. "Master bedroom first?" Hayley asked.

Patricia nodded. It was an exquisite room filled with finely carved furniture and delicate furnishings. It was always Hayley's favorite room in the house.

Hayley removed the sheer canopy from the four-poster bed, then the bedding, pillows and mattress, and handed them to Patricia who placed them on the table. "None of those things appear as puzzles on the x-ray. I just want them out of the way to get better access to the dresser."

Hayley reached in, removed an intricately carved

mahogany dresser, and examined it. Three drawers opened when she tried them. One didn't. Frowning, Hayley stared at the dresser for a moment, then partially closed the drawers in various combinations until the locked drawer clicked opened. "Mom!" she shouted. "There's something in here."

# CHAPTER 33

*S*miling broadly, Hayley handed Patricia a folded note secured with an Illuminati embossed seal. Patricia cracked the red wax, opened the yellowed parchment paper, and read. *49-74-65*. A combination? Geographic coordinates? A numbered sequence needing additional decoding?

"What's it say?" Hayley edged closer, looking down at the note.

"Just numbers."

"For what?"

"I don't know." Patricia stared blankly at the playroom wall trying to decide what to do. She'd start with the most obvious option.

"It could be a combination," Patricia said. "The only safe in the house dating to 1939 or before is the one I discovered in the cellar a year ago. When I asked Daddy about it then, he brushed off my question. Come on, honey." She took her daughter's hand. "We're going to the basement."

"The relic is down there?"

"Might be. There's certainly an old safe down there."

Patricia took two steps at a time descending to the first floor. If she was right, each step brought her closer to Trey's return. She stumbled on the basement stairs, barely caught herself and, with Hayley huffing behind her, held the banister the rest of the way.

Once in the musty cellar, Patricia eagerly ripped off the thin wall panels concealing the old safe. "Get me a flashlight from the workbench over there."

Hayley handed her the flashlight and a rag.

The safe was bigger than she remembered. At least as tall as her. She wiped debris from the tarnished brass dial, dropped the rag, and handed Hayley the flashlight. "Keep the light on the dial."

Patricia pulled the note from her pocket. Her hand shook as she tried to turn the cold dial. It didn't move. When she tightened her grip and applied more pressure, it popped free. Heart thumping with anticipation, Patricia eased the dial to the right, passing zero before stopping on 49. So much was at stake. Trey's life. What could trump that? *Please let this be the place.*

Her hand relaxed a bit as she twisted the dial left to 74. *Please. Please. Please.* Then Patricia dialed 65. She stepped back, grasped the large brass wheel, and tugged it clockwise. It didn't move. *Did I screw this up? Damn. Hmmm.* A lock that hadn't been accessed for decades might have frozen mechanisms.

She grabbed the brass wheel again and tried to force it to the right. The wheel squeaked and moved, just a bit.

"It turned," Hayley said.

"The combination worked. Thank God." Hard-won progress was still progress. The relic had to be here. *Trey honey, it won't be long.*

"Let me help you, Mom."

With Hayley's assistance, the stiff wheel slowly started to turn.

"Push harder," Patricia said.

The wheel suddenly moved freely. When it stopped, Patricia, now sweating with exertion, pulled, but the door remained stuck. *Damn it.* She gripped harder and yanked on the wheel. The door wouldn't budge.

Hayley put her hands alongside Patricia's. Between the two of them, they pushed and pulled until they got the protesting door slightly ajar. Her heart thudding, Patricia grabbed the exposed edge and yanked the creaking door fully open.

She retrieved the flashlight and swung the beam through the open space until it caught the gleam of something shiny. Stepping closer, with Hayley on her heels, Patricia could hardly believe what she saw. A tremor ran through her.

On a tall stack of gold bricks rested a full-sized replica of a human forearm fashioned from gold. On one finger was an Illuminati ring. The relic. *Thank you, God.*

To assure everything was there, Patricia reverently opened the reliquary, revealing an interior of padded red silk. Nestled in the thick cushioning were several loose bones. She felt guilty for invading the sanctity of the reliquary and closed the lid with a prayer requesting forgiveness.

"That's ... that's the relic," Hayley. "And a huge stack of gold!"

Patricia leaned her head back and closed her eyes. The key to Trey's release. Progress. Sweet, sweet progress. She said a prayer of thanks, then opened her eyes and turned to Hayley, who was grinning broadly and jumping up and down. "Go upstairs and bring me my cell phone and today's paper."

Hayley nodded and dashed up the stairs.

Patricia picked up the heavy reliquary and examined it. The workmanship meticulously detailed a forearm from extended fingertips to the elbow. The hand was open, as if giving a blessing. Taut muscles extended from the elbow to the wrist. Truly magnificent. It would take modern metal workers days to duplicate the container. Too many days.

Hayley returned with the phone and paper.

Patricia shut the vault door, spun the dial to lock the safe, and led Hayley back into the well-lit part of the basement. She grabbed one of the wall panels she'd removed to access the vault and put the panel face-up under an overhead light. After placing the newspaper and reliquary side-by-side on the panel, she took several pictures, including a couple with the reliquary open to show the bones. Proof she possessed the complete relic.

With Hayley at her heels, she carried the relic up the two flights of stairs to her bedroom and put it in the walk-in safe.

"That's a lot of gold in the basement." Hayley's eyes lingered on hers. "My finance professor says those kind of bricks are worth a quarter of a million dollars each. There's got to be forty or fifty bricks."

"It's locked up. Right now let's stay focused on getting Daddy home."

"But what if Trokev knew the relic and the gold were hidden together?" Hayley's tone was tight. "What if he was just using the search for the relic as a way to find the treasure?"

"Oh my. Good thinking, Hayley." Whatever Trokev sought, she had it. "I guess we'll find out soon enough when we offer to exchange the relic for Daddy."

"I thought you said you were giving the relic to Bishop Reilly."

"I am." Patricia put her arm around Hayley's shoulder and

walked with her to the stairs. "I'm giving a replica reliquary with old bones to Trokev."

"You have the replica?"

"Not yet. The church is making one for me. I need to see if Bishop Reilly can speed things up."

"I know you and the bishop are old friends, Mom, but how reliable is he, and the craftspeople making the replica? If you give him the relic, what incentive does he have to cooperate with you? I mean ... like ... he's dedicated to the church, and Daddy's life is at stake."

"I believe he loves your father like a brother, and he'll do whatever he can to bring Daddy home."

"I hope you're right, Mom."

Once on the main floor, Patricia told Simon she found the relic. He gave her a surprising hug. Short. Sincere. Then he stepped back, apparently embarrassed by his show of emotion.

Patricia called the bishop and asked for him to come over for the relic. To avoid tipping Trokev to the bishop's visit, Simon arranged for Bishop Reilly to use the tunnel from Sheila's flower shop.

While she waited, Hayley's conversation echoed in Patricia's mind. Could she trust the bishop? Should she? Did she have a choice? She had no answer but faith.

A half hour later, Bishop Reilly and Father John arrived. The guard dog, Ness, alerted, but remained in place beside his handler.

"So, Patricia, you've found the relic?" the bishop asked excitedly. He gave her a big smile and clutched the gold cross hanging from his neck. "I guess your call to action was indeed heaven-sent."

"Hayley and I found a gold box shaped like a forearm." Patricia paged her phone to the photo gallery, selected one of the relic photos, and turned the screen to the bishop. "You'll have to tell me if this is actually the relic everyone is after."

The bishop nodded, then handed the phone to Father John.

John examined the photo, then a couple more. "The object in these photos certainly looks like the image I was given."

"Where did you find the relic?" Bishop Reilly asked.

Did he know about the gold? "I'd prefer not to say."

The bishop stared at her as if she had misbehaved. Did they sense what she was up to? She didn't care if they knew. Her husband was in peril.

"Where's the relic, Patricia?" Bishop Reilly said in a low, almost threateningly harsh tone.

"Hidden. It's hidden, and it will remain hidden until Trey is home."

The bishop's jaw dropped. "You asked me to come over to pick up the relic."

"I changed my mind."

"Why?"

"I want to speed things up."

"Surely you're not going to give Trokev the relic."

She nodded. "I might."

John cleared his throat. "What's really going on here?"

"I want my husband back."

"We have a well-thought-out plan to achieve that," John said, sternly. "The goldsmiths are working on a replica reliquary. I called the FBI for help with the bones. I have them in hand. So what's the problem?"

She shot the bishop a glance. "Where's the substitute box?"

"We'll have it in our hands in thirty-six to forty-eight hours," the bishop said.

Patricia thought of Trey's swollen, bloody face. "Trey could die in that time. Speed the goldsmiths up."

"I can't do that."

She set her jaw and narrowed her eyes. "If you want the relic, you'll get the substitute in my hands immediately."

Apparently startled, the bishop took out his phone. He made a call, asked a few questions in what Patricia thought might be Italian, and then put his phone away. "It can be in Savannah twenty-four hours from now."

It still wasn't good enough. Patricia stood. "Then that's when you'll have your relic."

The bishop and John remained seated. "Sit down, Patricia," the bishop said. "Let's talk this out. John has the bones. All we're waiting for is the substitute reliquary. It has occurred to me the reliquary you possess is simply a vessel to contain the bones we seek. I doubt that it's over a couple of hundred years old. Nothing more than an antique box. If you give me the saint's bones, I'll give you the original reliquary, and John will give you the substitute bones."

Could she believe him? Trusting the bishop was the only option for getting Trey back as soon as possible. "Okay." She turned to John. "Do you have the bones with you?"

"They're in my briefcase."

"I'll set up a meeting with Trokev." She grabbed her phone and tapped Trokev's name in her contact list.

Trokev picked up on the first ring. "Patricia."

"I'd like to meet with you to discuss the return of Trey."

"We've already done that." He sounded irritated.

"We haven't worked out the details."

"We'll discuss the details when you have the relic," he said.

"I have the relic."

"Really?"

"Yes."

"Are you certain it is the relic?"

"Positive."

"The bones are marked for authenticity."

"I wouldn't know about that, but I assure you the relic I have is the same relic put away in 1939."

"Then I suppose we should get together right away. Come over."

"Fifteen minutes?"

"Sure."

She disconnected and turned to Bishop Reilly. "Meeting is set for fifteen minutes from now."

"We need to make the bone transfer," Bishop Reilly said.

"I'll get the relic," Patricia said. Minutes later, she returned and handed him the reliquary.

He made the sign of the cross, genuflected, said a prayer, then examined the container. "Do you have a tablecloth I can use?"

She brought him her finest linen tablecloth. A shroud fit for Saint Gregory's bones. With great solemnity, he opened the reliquary and, using the edge of the tablecloth to avoid touching the bones, he wrapped them in linen. John placed the substitute bones in the container.

"Trokev said the real bones are marked."

"These are too."

"How do we pull off the exchange?" Patricia said.

"If Trey is still in Savannah, Trokev will want to make the exchange tonight," Simon said. "We need to be prepared for that. He'll want to see the bones before he produces Trey, so I'll wait in his parking lot with the reliquary. When it's time for the exchange, just give me a call."

"It's that easy?" she said.

"Hopefully so." Simon gave her a smile. "Just go in there and negotiate the deal. If he wants to swap tonight, we're ready. If it's going to take until tomorrow, I'll leave when you do and Trokev will have no idea how close he was to his prized bones."

SIMON DROPPED PATRICIA AT THE ENTRANCE TO THE AMBER House. Having left her gun and armored vest with Simon to avoid them being taken by the Russians, she felt vulnerable.

A uniformed greeter held the front door for her, then a woman in black escorted her through an elegant lobby into a sterile waiting room with no chairs. It was like being transported from contemporary Savannah into Victorian England, then into the airlock from *2001: A Space Odyssey*.

She paced the room. It was odd how much she anticipated negotiating with the man who was torturing her husband. She wanted to drop-kick him back to Russia. But, she'd settle for what she could get. Trey. Having the upper hand was magical. But life had taught her not to celebrate victory prematurely. Anything could happen in the next five minutes.

# CHAPTER 34

The woman in black returned and showed Patricia into a large, stark office.

Trokev, remarkably well-dressed considering the hour, stood, removed his glasses, and came around his neatly organized desk to shake her hand. His prideful stride and posture bordered on arrogant. Once the brief handshake was completed, he stepped back. He'd given up on the *lecherous* hand kissing. *Thank God.* He dismissed his assistant.

"Did you bring the relic?" His eyes glittered.

"Is my husband here?"

He smirked. "He's close enough."

"As is the relic." She gave him a wooden smile.

"Are you prepared to make the exchange right now?"

"Only if you can produce my husband immediately."

"I'll not produce Mr. Falcon until I see the relic and ascertain its authenticity." His demeaning tone was as tight as a violin string.

"You're not seeing anything until I determine my husband is released."

He inched closer, sneering. "Mrs. Falcon, you're in no position to dictate terms."

She rolled her eyes, turned, and headed for the door, listening closely for his capitulation. Thank God the office was big, giving her plenty of room for a dramatic exit. She made it to the door and, without hesitation, grabbed the doorknob.

"There's no need to leave," Trokev said in a gentle voice.

She turned to him.

His expression was sheepish.

Her eyes fixed on his. She crossed her arms. "Is that so?"

"Give me a moment." Trokev picked up his phone, briefly conversed in a foreign language, then returned the phone to his desk. "I've arranged for Mr. Falcon to be brought out. Now, can I examine the relic?"

"Not until I see Trey."

He gave her a cocky smile then laughed. "Why should I believe you have the relic?"

She offered him the phone photo of the reliquary with today's newspaper.

He put on his glasses and compared the picture with several photos he had. "It certainly looks authentic."

"I assure you, it's the real thing, recently recovered from its extraordinarily secure hiding place."

As he was returning his glasses to the desk, his phone chimed. He answered it and then looked up, a smug expression on his face. "You husband has arrived."

Her heart exploded. "I have to see him."

"Not until I examine the relic."

"Here's how it's going to happen, Mr. Trokev," Patricia said in a low voice. "You produce Trey. I assure he's okay. He and I leave in our car. I tell you where the relic is."

His face knotted. "I can't do that."

"You have no choice."

319

"Mrs. Falcon, I don't give a damn about you or your husband." His brows knitted. "You've cost me millions, and I'd just as soon kill both of you. But you have something very important to me. Mr. Falcon is at the Forsyth Park fountain. He's out in the open, but in the crosshairs of snipers. On short notice, your bodyguard wouldn't be able to neutralize more than one or two, if that. So if you try to take Mr. Falcon without delivering the relic, I'll kill him. Understand?"

She nodded.

"Once you verify Mr. Falcon is there, you tell me where the relic is." He cocked his head. "I'll let you leave Amber House as soon as I obtain possession of the relic."

"I can do that," she said. "As long as you understand you won't leave this building alive if you fail to deliver Trey to me."

He smiled. "You might be surprised—"

"By the way, there are armed men with orders to kill blocking your escape tunnel."

The smile slipped. "Impossible."

"The security cameras and the poisonous gas systems in the tunnel are presently non-functional. Check, if you wish."

"Well then." He cleared his throat. "I'd say we need to close this deal." He made a call. Moments later, he looked up at her. "Are you able to verify Mr. Falcon is at the Forsyth Fountain?"

"As long as he's visible to one of the park's security cameras."

Simon's voice in her ear mike confirmed Trey's presence at the fountain, and the dispatch of a hostage rescue team. She kissed Trey's wedding ring. "Yes. I have verification."

"Where's the relic?" Trokev said.

"Outside. I'll have someone bring it in."

His eyes widened.

Moments later, Simon entered Trokev's office, removed

the relic from his leather satchel, and handed the reliquary to Trokev.

"Why are you giving this up?" he said to Simon. "Surely the church—"

"Higher good," Simon said. "There is nothing more precious than life itself."

Trokev put on his glasses and admired the reliquary, then took the relic to his desk and compared it to his photos.

Her stomach clenched.

After a moment, he looked up and nodded. "Thank you, Mrs. Falcon. It's been a pleasure doing business with you."

"You'll understand if I do not share the sentiment."

The woman in black returned and escorted Simon and her to the lobby. They entered the limo.

"Trey?" she asked.

He accelerated from the driveway into a gap in the traffic, then crossed the centerline to pass a logjam of slow-moving vehicles. "Trey's safe," he said.

At Simon's words, delivered with such certainty, relief poured through Patricia. The tight bindings of worry, days and sleepless nights, slowly began unraveling, leaving her feeling weak and disoriented. Only seeing Trey with her own eyes-Trey, her anchor-would calm this torrent of emotion. She twisted his ring on her finger. Only when seeing him alive and holding him in her arms would she accept the euphoria this long awaited moment promised.

At the first intersection, Simon jammed on the brakes, turned left with the wheels locked up, and sped down the empty side street toward Forsyth Park.

The manic ride to Forsyth seemed to take forever. Any minute now. Finally the limo pulled to the curb on the edge of the park.

She forced the door open and bounded from the back-seat. Her eyes slowly adjusted to the dark as she dashed blindly across the grass toward the illuminated fountain a hundred yards away. A gaggle of people dressed in black milled at the distant fountain. The hostage rescue team?

No sign of Trey. Her throat tightened. She pushed her legs harder. Simon had verified he was there fifteen minutes ago. Where was he? Apprehension gripped her. Was something wrong?

Closer now, she saw the heavily-armed, black-clad security team lit up by the overhead lights. So many people, but no Trey. A wave of nausea hit. Was Trey okay?

Her heart hammering, lungs wheezing, she pushed through the tightly-packed wall of people. She wanted to see Trey. His face. His eyes.

Finally she spotted him, standing in the center of the security team. Joy surged.

He saw her, smiled and moved toward her, arms wide.

Her thighs burning from exertion, she leapt into his fit arms, nearly knocking him over.

He wrapped his arms around her and drew her in close. He smelled foreign. Spicy. Not the familiar pine scent.

With tears streaming down her cheeks, she shivered in the comfort of his arms, and stroked his battered face. She cupped his cheeks and kissed him. He moaned. She slid her hands behind his head, closed her eyes, and deepened the kiss. His arms crushed her into his solid chest. Her body tingled. Another second of this and she'd be ripping his clothes off right in the middle of Forsyth Park. Oh my.

Still clinging to him, she leaned away a bit, opened her eyes, and took in his face. Her man. Home. Safe. Thank you, Lord.

Trey looked around. "Where's Simon?"

"He's over there." She nodded at the edge of the park. "With the limo."

His arm around her shoulder, he guided her toward the parked car.

The security personnel fanned out, covering their flanks.

"How's Hayley handling this?"

"Hayley's been incredible. She's very proud of being instrumental in securing your release."

He paused. "How?"

"It's complicated." She gave him a squeeze and urged him on toward the limo. "We'll go over all the details later. Right now, I have other plans for you." She removed the ring from her thumb and slid it on his finger.

# CHAPTER 35

*D*octor Snake, now shorn of his dreadlocks and traveling as Father Cardoza, legate of the Armenian Apostolic Church, let out a sigh as he stepped aboard Flight Seven-Fifteen for Lebanon. Inside the diplomatic pouch cuffed to his wrist was the relic he was sworn to protect with his life.

Eustis, also shorn of dreadlocks and wearing the same type clerical cassock as Father Cardoza, trailed behind.

Father Cardoza scrutinized the disinterested faces of his fellow first-class passengers, then took his seat and buckled up.

Eustis settled next to him, creating a formidable barrier to intrusion.

They'd not always been so careful with their treasure. For decades, they'd protected the saint's relic by hiding it in plain sight. Recently, a thief challenged the wisdom of that strategy. Mercifully, an anonymous benefactor had returned the stolen bones. Once advised of events, the mother church ordered the relic returned.

As the jet taxied to the runway, Father Cardoza fingered the Illuminati cross hanging from his neck. Lebanon was a troubled country of zealots, and he worried for the safety of the precious relic.

## THE END

Continue for a preview of
Savannah Justice

Book Three of the Vigilantes for Justice series

**Due out October 2018**

# SAVANNAH
## *Justice*

VIGILANTES
FOR
JUSTICE
BOOK 3

# ALAN CHAPUT

# CHAPTER 1

*P*atricia Falcon so enjoyed her visits to Meredith Stanwick's bank. Behind the ordinary double doors on an ordinary street was one of Savannah's most successful private banks. Access through the locked security doors was by appointment only.

The middle-aged receptionist opened the door and greeted Patricia by name. The interior of the facility was more like a plush legal office than a commercial bank. Business was conducted with client managers in private, oak-paneled offices.

Patricia wasn't there for banking. She was there to discuss a personnel matter with her close friend, Meredith. Patricia smiled to herself as the elegant receptionist led her to the conference room, a place Patricia had visited often. Meredith was already there. Patricia glanced at the wall clock. Still five minutes before their meeting. She loved how Meredith always seemed ahead of the game.

After greeting Meredith, Patricia poured a cup of coffee from the carafe, sat at the conference room table across from Meredith, and powered up her laptop. Reforming the rescue team was long overdue. "Are you sure you want to do this, Meredith?"

Meredith, dressed in a gray tweed business suit, smiled. "Somebody has to transport the abused women to the shelter, and it's way too dangerous for only the two of us." Meredith's eyes went distant for a moment.

Patricia sensed she was remembering how much trust they'd had in the other members of their team. One who'd died and, well, the other who had been responsible. Judy. Patricia immediately straightened and shook off a chill.

Meredith blinked. "Doctor Caldfield is a great addition, but we need at least one more person."

Patricia glanced at the resume on her screen. "Kira Chanel is outstanding on paper, and she aced the Skype interview. Did anything stand out in the background check you did?"

"Apart from her father being convicted of domestic abuse?"

"That was decades ago, and Kira's own record is clear. It's important family history, but Kira's record speaks for itself."

Meredith nodded. "I agree, but she's a former Special Ops, and I'm concerned about her temperament. We don't need her over-reacting during pickups."

"She survived Special Ops, so she should do well under pressure." Patricia's eyes met Meredith's. "Besides, Simon recommended her."

Meredith shrugged. "He's former military too. I wonder if he can objectively judge military temperament. Maybe Doctor Caldfield should interview her before we make a decision."

"I don't think we should involve Summer Caldfield until we're sure about Kira and get a confidentiality agreement from her." Patricia studied Meredith for any reaction, but Meredith remained unreadable. "Each new person we speak with has the potential to undermine our safety. For our protection, we have to keep our membership confidential. Often those husbands want revenge, and we're obvious targets."

"Okay," Meredith said. "But, let's at least address temperament in Kira's interview today. Press her a bit. See how she handles it."

"Agreed. Any other concerns?"

Meredith closed her laptop. "No. As I said, she's my top candidate from a totally outstanding field." Meredith stood and headed for the door. "I'll bring her in."

While Meredith was gone, Patricia reviewed Kira's resume one more time, then shut down her laptop.

Moments later, Meredith returned with Kira.

Patricia stood, studied the middle-aged African-American woman, looking closely for any sign of discomfort, and offered her hand.

Kira Chanel, dressed in a black business suit and her gray-streaked hair neatly braided and tied at her nape, shook Patricia's hand with a firm but polite grip.

"Thank you for coming in today," Patricia said. "We just have a few more questions." Patricia gestured to the chair at the head of the table. Once Kira had settled, Patricia asked, "Would you care for some coffee?"

"No thank you."

Patricia sat. "You would think that we would jump at the opportunity to have you on the team, but there are some issues here. Not only are the lives of the victims on the line, but our lives are at risk as well."

Kira, her face dead-serious and her back ramrod straight, nodded.

Patricia smiled trying to ease the formality. "I understand you joined the military right after high school?"

"Yes." Kira's posture relaxed a bit.

"Thank you for your service."

"You're welcome."

"Military service during active combat is dangerous." Patricia leaned forward. "Would you mind telling us what attracted you to the military?"

"I was recruited."

"No interest in college?"

Kira straightened. "No."

"How'd you get into the Medical Corp?"

"I applied and passed training."

"Why the Medical Corps?" Patricia pressed, watching Kira for any sign of stress.

Kira's composure remained in place. "I like helping people, people in trouble, people who are hurting."

Patricia settled back in her chair. "I understand you served in Special Ops?"

"Yes."

"What specialty?"

"I'm not at liberty to discuss that subject," Kira said in an even tone through tight lips.

"I need to know," Patricia prodded.

Kira remained as poised and polished as Patricia's family silver. "I can assure you my Special Ops specialty has nothing to do with rescuing abused women."

"So," Meredith said, "why do you think you would be of value to our team?"

Kira's eyebrows rose as she turned toward Meredith. "In order to help the women your organization serves, I assume you must gain their confidence, which is something I'm very good at."

"You do make an excellent first impression," Patricia said, picking up the stick pen in front of her. "Any other special skills?"

"Other than Special Ops skills and medical skills, I speak

333

several languages, I'm adept with leading-edge electronics, and, as a team leader, I've planned and lead many missions."

"Those are extremely impressive skills." Patricia made a written note of Kira's answer. "But getting close enough to an abuse victim for them to trust us so we can get them to safety is very delicate work."

"I've often worked undercover with civilians. And I've never once had a problem gaining their trust."

"Okay. But I have to admit your former line of work gives me concern." Patricia paused to let that sink in.

Kira showed no sign of stress.

Patricia returned the pen to the tablet in front of her. "You served twenty-four years. Why'd you retire?"

"I recently married a wonderful, supportive man and was ready to settle down."

"Why do you want to join our group?" Meredith asked.

"Let's say joining the military right out of high school had more to do with escaping a terrible home life, something my mother was never able to do. And that's all I'll say about that."

Patricia looked at Meredith, who nodded.

"Since this is a volunteer group without pay," Patricia said, "you'd think we'd accept any and all volunteers. But this work is potentially dangerous, dangerous for the abused women, and for my crew. Plus, we walk a fine line with the law. And we all have reputations to protect. And we are very private about what we do, very private. So with that said, why don't we see how you do in our training program?"

Kira sat back. "Training?"

"Our procedures. Role playing."

"How long?"

"Until you get everything right. Or we decide there's no fit."

"When do I start training?"

"Tomorrow if you're available."

"I'm available."

"Do you have a weapon?"

Kira placed her hand on her purse and nodded.

"Permit?"

"Of course."

"We'll need a copy of it. Do you own a ballistic vest?"

Kira shook her head.

"Get one by tomorrow, if possible. Bring your weapon and vest to this address tomorrow morning at nine."

Patricia gave Kira a business card with the address of a Pooler gun club.

Kira held up the card. "I shoot here all the time."

"So do we." Meredith slid the confidentiality agreement and a pen to Kira. "This is a standard non-disclosure agreement. You can sign it now, or take it home and bring it with you tomorrow."

Kira signed the agreement and returned it. "Anything else?"

"That's it." Patricia stood and gave Kira a wide smile.

Patricia and Meredith walked Kira to the front lobby of Meredith's bank. After Kira left, Meredith turned to Patricia. "She a keeper. Definitely cool under pressure."

"I agree," Patricia said. "I hope she works out. She has a great background and she's interested. But like a landing gear, we've got to be sure she'll function right the first time and every time thereafter."

End of preview of *Savannah Justice*
Coming October 2018

Sign up for my New Release Newsletter at
www.alanchaput.com for an email note when *Savannah Justice* is available

Or

Text CHAPUT to 31996 to receive a text notice when *Savannah Justice* releases

# ACKNOWLEDGMENTS

I am grateful to you for reading *Savannah Secrets* and hope you enjoyed it. You are the reason I write. I appreciate your comments and support in email, in person and on social media. Your comments keep me focused.

Thank you to the reviewers and bloggers who've so generously spread the word about *Savannah Secrets* and who've taken the time to give readers an opinion about it.

Thank you to my wonderful wife who has been by my side at each stage of bringing *Savannah Secrets* to you. I'm so fortunate to have her support and unconditional love.

Thank you to my critique partners, Natasha Boyd and Dave McDonald. Without their relentless advice, you would have been reading a vastly inferior book.

Thank you to my editor, Elizabeth White, who further improved my writing, pacing, grammar, and punctuation. And who also meticulously fact-checked all things Savannah.

Thank you to my cover designer, Fayette Terlouw, who brought Patricia Falcon so vividly to life on the cover of *Savannah Secrets*.

And, finally, thank you to my beta readers (Amy Coury, Nancy Huntington, Ellie Merola and Patsy Sams) who each did one final edit so you'd have the best possible read.

As you can see, it takes a team to produce a book, and I'm very grateful to be on this particular team.

Discussion questions for *Savannah Secrets*

1. What was your initial impression of *Savannah Secrets*?
2. How realistic was the depiction of Savannah? Did it add to the story? How?
3. Was the story plot-driven or character-driven?
4. How original is *Savannah Secrets*?
5. Did the characters seem believable?
6. Who was your favorite character? Why?
7. How did the characters change through the story?
8. What was your favorite quote/scene?
9. How do you feel about the ending?
10. Overall, what did you like best about *Savannah Secrets*?
11. Would you recommend this series to a friend? Why?

Contact Al at al@alchaput.com for information on inviting him to Skype or FaceTime with your book club.

# ABOUT THE AUTHOR

Alan Chaput writes Southern mysteries. His novels have finaled in the Daphne and the Claymore. Al lives with his wife in Coastal South Carolina. When not writing, Al can be found Shag dancing, pursuing genealogy, or interacting on social media.

BOOKS BY ALAN CHAPUT

The Vigilantes for Justice Series:

1. *Savannah Sleuth* (published December 2017)
2. *Savannah Secrets* (published April 2018)
3. *Savannah Justice* (coming October 2018)
4. *Savannah Passion* (coming 2019)

## End Note

Thank you for reading *Savannah Secrets*. Please consider leaving a review for this book at Goodreads and your favorite book retailer. Your comments will help other readers decide if they want to read *Savannah Secrets*. It's a fact —reviews make a difference.

Please stay in touch. I love reading your messages and enjoy hearing what you want in future books.

Warmest regards and happy reading,
Al

If you want to keep in touch with me between books, you can find me on social media at these profiles:

https://www.instagram.com/alan_chaput

https://www.goodreads.com/user/show/22658428-alan

http://www.facebook.com/alchaput

http://www.pinterest.com/alanchaput

https://twitter.com/alanchaput

And you can find me on the web at:

www.alanchaput.com

CPSIA information can be obtained
at www.ICGtesting.com
Printed in the USA
LVOW10s1021050418
572418LV00011B/167/P